VOID

Library of
Davidson College

NIKOLAI GOGOL

Hanz Kuechelgarten, Leaving the Theater & Other Works

EDITED BY
RONALD MEYER

Ardis, Ann Arbor

Copyright © 1990 by Ardis Publishers

All rights reserved under International and Pan American
Copyright Conventions

Printed in the United States of America

Ardis Publishers
2901 Heatheway
Ann Arbor, Michigan 48104

Library of Congress Cataloging-in-Publication Data

Gogol', Nikolai Vasil'evich, 1809-1852
Hanz Kuechelgarten, Leaving the theater, & other
works.

Translated from Russian.
1. Gogol, Nikolai Vasil'evich, 1809-1852—Translations,
English. I. Meyer, Ronald. II. Title.
PG3333.A6 1989   891.78'309   88-35008
ISBN 0-88233-822-6 (alk. paper)

Contents

Introduction 9

HANZ KUECHELGARTEN 17

LEAVING THE THEATER AFTER THE PRESENTATION
OF A NEW COMEDY 61

ESSAYS
Woman 95
Boris Godunov 99
On Kozlov's Poetry 103
The Trend of Journal Literature 105

BOOK REVIEWS 121

LETTERS 141

Notes 185

ILLUSTRATIONS

Cover — N. Gogols's sketch of a cathedral (1830s)

Frontispiece — Portrait of N. Gogol by Karolina Pavlova (1840s)

Page 94 — Portrait of a woman by N. Gogol (1820s?)

Page 122 — Sketches of Alexander Pushkin by N. Gogol (1838?)

Acknowledgments

All translations are based on the Russian text as published in Gogol's *Polnoe sobranie sochinenii* (Moscow, 1937-52). The commentary to this edition provided the basis for much of the explanatory material in the Notes.

I would like to thank Isabel Heaman, Irene Kiedrowski and Paul D. Putz for their patience and contributions to this long-aborning volume. Helena Goscilo read earlier versions of some of the translations and suggested marvelous solutions to difficult problems. Bart Casad, David Lowe, Ellendea Proffer and Moscow friends on Krasnoarmeiskaya helped in ways that are difficult to describe. This anthology was conceived by the late Carl R. Proffer and would not have appeared without his encouragement and contributions.

R.M.

Introduction

Nikolai Gogol is one of the geniuses of Russian prose and Russia's greatest comic writer. This salmagundi of Nikolai Gogol's juvenilia and previously uncollected writings spans the years from his disastrous debut in 1829 to 1842, the year of the publication of his masterpiece, *Dead Souls*. The Gogol presented in this volume appears in several unfamiliar guises (poet, essayist, critic and book reviewer), rounding out our appreciation of this thoroughly enigmatic writer.

Hanz Kuechelgarten, Gogol's verse idyll, was published pseudonymously and at the author's expense in St. Petersburg in 1829. The work endured indifference until the appearance of two negative reviews, the first of which appeared in *The Moscow Telegraph*:

> The publisher of this book writes that Mr. Alov's [Gogol's pseudonym] composition was not intended for publication, but that reasons of importance only to the author caused him to change his intention. We believe that he had even greater reasons for not publishing his idyll. The merit of the following lines points to one of these reasons....[1]

After Gogol read in *The Northern Bee* that "the world would not be any poorer if this young talent's first attempt had never seen the light of day,"[2] he and his servant collected all the unsold copies (the bulk of the edition) from the Petersburg booksellers, burned them, and then suddenly left for Europe. Gogol's authorship of this great bibliographical rarity was only established posthumously.

Gogol abandoned poetry, but not literature, and turned to prose, leaving *Hanz Kuechelgarten* behind as a curiosity, a work that only vaguely hints at his genius, but which does reveal the degree to which romanticism, particularly of the German variety, influenced him in his youth. The plot of Gogol's idyll is simple: the hero, Hanz, who enjoys a happy, tranquil life with his beloved Luisa, is overcome by the malaise of wanderlust ("But soon a secret sadness took/Possession of him—in the distance/He often stares with cloudy look"). And so, Hanz sets out from his native Germany for foreign lands, only to return home to his Luisa in the end.

Hanz Kuechelgarten is a child of its literary era. Echoes and snatches from Voss's idyll *Luise*, Chateaubriand's *René*, Byron's *Childe Harold*, the sentimental journeys of Sterne and Karamzin and the works of Zhukovsky and Pushkin all make their presence felt.[3] In hindsight, we can discern glimmers of the mature Gogol—there are a number of startling images that are of the same stuff as Gogol's prose. Vladimir Nabokov has singled out the graveyard scene in which a skeleton "With self-important nod/Dusts his bones off—what a guy," remarking that the "jarring ejaculation" shows the "young Gogol's Ukrainian spirits getting the better of German romanticism."[4] The portrayal of the serene, domestic life, which is indebted to the depiction of the Larins in Pushkin's *Eugene Onegin* as well as Voss's work, will be transplanted to native soil in Gogol's "Old-World Landowners." Finally, the semi-autobiographical rendering of the dreamer-poet-artist, whose individualism is at odds with his surroundings and aspirations, will be developed later in such works as "Nevsky Prospect" and "The Portrait."

Gogol relinquished all aspirations to becoming a poet. The next important step in his career as a writer was the publication two years later of *Evenings on a Farm near Dikanka*, of which Alexander Pushkin was an early admirer: "I have just read *Evenings by the Dikanka*. It astonished me. Here is real gaiety, which is sincere, unforced, without affectation, without pomposity. And in places what poetry!"[5] The poetry and sensitivity Pushkin finds in *Evenings* are precisely what *Hanz Kuechelgarten* lacks. Gogol's evocation of the rural German village and its Romantic hero, though written in verse, is not poetic. The recreation of the Ukraine in *Evenings* is poetry. Gogol's desire to become a poet will be fully realized in *Dead Souls*, which he subtitled a "poem."

Of his contemporaries, Gogol is the only Russian dramatist to achieve and retain an international reputation. Pushkin's dramatic works are known in the West primarily as the bases for opera libretti and Gogol's contemporaries—the Kukolniks—have been deservedly forgotten even in Russia.

Tsar Nikolai I attended the premiere of *The Inspector General* on April 19, 1836. Gogol had high expectations for his play, but disappointed by both the performance and the reviews, he left Russia as he had done after the failure of *Hanz Kuechelgarten*.

Gogol's reaction to the reception of *The Inspector General* is puzzling. As is often the case with any major new work, the critical response was both negative and positive, not the resounding indifference and sneers which had greeted *Hanz*. According to all reports, the Tsar liked the play, but the Petersburg bureaucrats were incensed that such a caricature had been allowed to be staged. Nestor Kukolnik, a popular playwright of the time, declared *The Inspector General* to be a farce, not art. But Gogol had as many admirers as detractors. The critic V. V. Stasov recalls in his memoirs how "all the young people were ecstatic over *The Inspector General*. We recited entire scenes and lengthy dialogues to each other."[6] A number of contemporary accounts attest to the play's success and significance, but Gogol nevertheless concluded that "the contemporary writer, the comic writer, the writer of morals and manners should be farther away from his fatherland. The prophet finds no glory in his homeland."[7]

Leaving the Theater after the Performance of a New Comedy, a hybrid that couples the genres of drama and criticism, is in part Gogol's response to *The Inspector General*'s reception. The first draft was most likely written in 1836, soon after the negative reviews that appeared in *The Northern Bee* and *The Library for Reading*, traces of which made their way into the play. Gogol viewed the play, which was first published in a much reworked form as the final piece in his *Collected Works* (1842), as a summation and justification of his work as a comic writer.[8]

Gogol's closet drama about the mission of the writer of comedies is set in a theater lobby, where the Author gathers the theater-goers' appreciations and criticisms.[9] The play is judged farcical, amusing, entertaining, both a reflection and a distortion of reality. The complaint that the play is a caricature and a vulgar work echoes the reviews by Senkovsky and Bulgarin. One character in *Leaving the Theater* remarks: "but that is all nonsense, it's just his friends, the ones praising it are his friends! I've already heard that they are practically making him out to be a Fonvizin." As Gogol scholars have shown, this comment echoes Bulgarin's critique of Pushkin's review of *Taras Bulba*, in which he writes that "[Pushkin] speaks about Gogol, his colleague, compares him to Fonvizin and shamelessly states that *Taras Bulba* is a work worthy of Walter Scott."[10]

The dramatis personae in *Leaving the Theater* are identified by uniquely Gogolian tags, no character is dignified with a name or surname (for example, Mr. A., First and Second Overcoats). The Very Modestly Dressed Man, newly arrived from the provinces and a proponent of social criticism, offers the distinction that the real-life Petersburg bureaucrats failed to make: "Let them distinguish the government from the bad exponents of government." As he rejects a lucrative job offer from Mr. A., we realize that his modest appearance mirrors his true modesty and character.

Leaving the Theater concludes with the Author's monologue. Critics have latched onto it as a formulation of Gogol's artistic credo. The Author gratefully accepts the lesson provided by his eavesdropping, but is saddened that nobody has recognized the "honest character in my play. Yes, there was one honest, noble character taking part throughout. This honest, noble character is *laughter*." That is Gogol's ultimate rebuttal to the Francophile Overcoats, who deplore the absence of *société*, and the Society Lady who complains: "Well, why don't we have authors who write like the French, like Dumas and the others, for example? I don't demand models of virtue; show me a woman who might go astray, who might even deceive her husband, abandoning herself, let us suppose, to a most immoral and illicit love; but present it appealingly so that she arouses my sympathy, so that I grow to love her..." Gogol, however, was not the person to write *Anna Karenina*.

Gogol's essays and reviews have received relatively little attention either in Russia or the West. For decades the reconciliation of the purely aesthetic criteria Gogol proposes and the stereotype of Gogol as the spokesman for the "little man" largely rendered his criticism irrelevant in the Soviet Union. A complete English translation of *Arabesques* (1835), which collects Gogol's short fiction and essays on literature, art and history did not appear until 1982.[11] True, one would hardly turn to "On the Middle Ages" for information about the Middle Ages—the essay reveals much more about Gogol's aesthetics than his presumed subject matter. The majority of the essays and reviews translated in this collection are every bit as idiosyncratic. In Gogol's rapturous lyric on *Boris Godunov*, the Pushkin work fulfills the function of a springboard for a rhetorical disquisition on aesthetics and reader reception, but Gogol is not really interested in the play itself.

The essay "Woman," the first work published under Gogol's name (*Literary Gazette*, 1831), imitates the form of a Platonic dialogue. Telecles, Plato's pupil, accuses his teacher of an over-idealization of woman. The cause of Telecles' outburst is easily found: Telecles believes that the beautiful Alcinoe has betrayed him. The philosopher responds with a lengthy discourse on love and woman. At the conclusion of his tribute to the superiority of woman over man, teacher and pupil become aware that Alcinoe has entered the room unnoticed to reclaim Telecles: "In awe and wonder the youth threw himself at the proud beauty's feet, and a hot tear from the demi-goddess bending over him fell on his burning cheek."

The twentieth-century Russian critic V. V. Gippius has drawn the parallel between "Woman" and *das ewig Weibliche* (the Eternal Feminine) of the German Romantics, noting that the "Romantic idea of the feminine was perceived by Gogol as an aesthetic idea."[12] Woman is "the language of the gods," "poetry" and "the Idea." Plato contrasts man and woman by the formula that a painting in the artist's imagination is woman, but that once it is realized it is man. Ultimately, Telecles must acknowledge the gifts that only Alcinoe can bestow: "...From that time when you read eternity in the divine features of Alcinoe, how many secrets, how many revelations have you perceived and discovered with your eternal soul, and how much closer have you moved toward the supreme good?" The language and imagery render Woman an aesthetic ideal, a measure of beauty, a goddess, but not flesh and blood, ideas which are given a very different treatment in "Nevsky Prospect."[13]

Gogol penned "*Boris Godunov*. A Narrative Poem by Alexander Pushkin," in the early months of 1831, before he was introduced to Pushkin by Pyotr Pletnyov, the essay's dedicatee. The essay, one of Gogol's earliest attempts at criticism and his first piece on Pushkin, was not published until 1881.[14] Gogol's admiration for Pushkin was conceived while he was still at school, where he handed in as his own compositions Pushkin's poems, which were then duly corrected by the instructor.

"Boris Godunov" has been characterized as an extended lyric on literary creation. The publication of Pushkin's drama provided the inspiration for Gogol's essay, but there is no critique of the work—the essay could as easily be titled "*Eugene Onegin.*" The essay opens in a St. Petersburg bookshop, where the new Pushkin work has just gone on sale. Using the same strategy of eavesdropping as in *Leaving the Theater*, we overhear opinions of *Boris Godunov*, which range from grudging condescension to rapt enthusiasm. Two friends, Elladius and Pollior, leave the shop together, whereupon Elladius asks his companion, who has kept his silence, for his opinion of the new drama. Pollior unleashes such an excessively rhetorical effusion that the reader is apt to forget that *Boris Godunov* is the subject of this verbal torrent and that Pollior had ever been mute. The substance of Pollior's metaphor-laden speech is that art is supreme, which renders superfluous and heretical the ranking of true works of art. He concludes that one should instead search for a kindred soul with whom one can experience and communicate spiritually the poet's creation.

This is Gogol in his arch-Romantic, art-for-art's sake guise: the supremacy of art, the classic misunderstanding of the poet by the marketplace and the rabble, the non-verbal communication between two souls—all awash in "spiritual seas" and "floods of grateful tears." In the better-known "A Few Words about Pushkin" from *Arabesques*, Gogol again registers his admiration for the poet. The second essay, which is more firmly grounded in Pushkin's works, begins with the statement that "the name Pushkin immediately calls to mind Russia's national poet," but concludes with the paradox that "the more a poet becomes a poet, the more noticeably his entourage diminishes, until it finally becomes so small that he can count on his fingers the number of people who appreciate the true value of his works."[15]

Pushkin reappears in Gogol's essay "On Kozlov's Poetry" as the ultimate poet: Gogol writes that we cannot expect from Kozlov "that which we can rightly demand only from Pushkin." It is impossible to fault Gogol's judgment here. Ivan Kozlov achieved his popularity through *The Monk* (1825), a diluted Byronic narrative poem, which was followed by *The Mad Girl* (1830).[16] Today Kozlov is remembered, if at all, for his translation of Thomas Moore's *Evening Bells*. Though Gogol describes Kozlov's powerlessness before Byron's "gigantic, dark soul," he does not belittle the poet's talent. Instead, he concludes that "Kozlov stands in relation to Pushkin as a part to the whole.... And who would not find this glorious, who would not envy this fate: to be a part of the boundless Pushkin!!"

The inaugural issue of Alexander Pushkin's journal *The Contemporary* was published in 1836. Gogol appears in the journal as fiction writer ("The Carriage"), dramatist (*The Morning of a Government Official*), literary critic ("On the Trend of Journal Literature in 1834 and 1835") and book reviewer. In addition, his *Evenings on a Farm Near Dikanka* is reviewed by Pushkin himself, though the review is unsigned.[17] However, Gogol's hopes for a popular forum and a close collaboration with Pushkin were dashed and he again left for abroad, never to see Pushkin again. The exact nature of their disagreement is not known, but in his letter to Zhukovsky, Gogol writes: "I did not even have time to say good-bye to Pushkin, and I could not; however, he is to blame for that."[18]

Pushkin entrusted to Gogol the writing of a survey of the major journals in Moscow and St. Petersburg. "On the Trend of Journal Literature" shows a radically different side of Gogol the essayist. In this polemical diagnosis of the state of literary journals, Gogol writes as practically and concretely as he did lyrically and abstractly in the three essays discussed above. Gogol considers the journal's format, circulation, the punctuality of the issues, the editorial board, the journal's program and contents. In essence, Gogol's survey, which was received as *The Contemporary*'s program, not only outlines a journal's obligations, but in a broader sense what constitutes contemporary literary culture.

Gogol aims his critical guns at Osip Senkovsky and his hugely successful *Library for Reading*. Senkovsky, who also published his own prose fiction under the pseudonym Baron Brambeus, is characterized as unscrupulous, dictatorial and as a person without taste ("in his reviews there is no positive or negative taste—there is no taste at all"). Gogol is kinder to the majority of the opposition journals, but in general is appalled by the blandness, petty squabbles, the absence of editorial direction and "the literary faithlessness and literary ignorance." Pushkin, who had tempered some of Gogol's barbs, still found the tone too abrasive and published a "Letter to the Publisher," signed A.B. but of his own composition, in the third issue of *The Contemporary*.[19] Pushkin adds a note to this "Letter," which reads: "The essay 'On the Trend of Journal Literature' was printed in my journal, but it does not follow from this that all the opinions expressed in it with such youthful liveliness and straightforwardness are completely in accord with my own. In any case, it is not and could not be the program of *The Contemporary*."[20]

The Book Review section of *The Contemporary* printed twelve reviews—all unsigned. Two belong to Pushkin, while another eight have been identified as Gogol's. Drafts of another eighteen reviews, obviously intended for the same issue, were found in Gogol's papers, but were never published during Gogol's lifetime.²¹ The pieces run from one-sentence annotations and quips to full-length reviews on a bewildering range of subjects. Gogol comments on books about agriculture, ship-building, cooking, history and travel. Of the purely literary works, Kantemir, Karamzin and Zagoskin are the only authors represented with any reputation today. Nevertheless, Gogol's division of literature into fifteen-, eight- and five-ruble novels in his review of *He and She* and his burlesque of the pseudo-historical novel in his analysis of *The Founding of Moscow*, not only highlights another facet of Gogol's critical acumen, but also delineates the background of what we have come to think of as Russia's Golden Age.

The sixty-three letters translated here by Carl R. Proffer complement his edition of *Letters of Nikolai Gogol* (Ann Arbor: University of Michigan Press, 1967).²² Only a small portion of the five volumes of more than 1300 letters are available in English translation, yet they yield a unique insight into Gogol's life and work. The correspondence collected here begins in 1827, when Gogol was still in Nezhin, and ends in 1850, just two years before his death. Gogol appears as son, anxious playwright, European traveler, author of *Dead Souls* and moral instructor. As is the case with the other works in this volume, one is struck not so much by the differences between the young and mature Gogol, as by the connecting thread.

Ronald Meyer
Ann Arbor, July 1990

Hanz Kuechelgarten
An Idyll in Scenes

V. Alov

TRANSLATOR'S NOTE

Nikolai Gogol composed *Hanz Kuechelgarten* in 1827, while still a high school student at Nezhin in the Ukraine. He brought it with him to St. Petersburg the following year and in 1829, encouraged by the publication of his short poem "Italy" (published anonymously in *Son of the Fatherland*, March 1829), undertook to publish *Hanz Kuechelgarten* at his own expense. It was printed in book form in May 1829, under the pseudonym V. Alov with an introduction by a fictitious editor, and distributed by Gogol to various Petersburg booksellers. His high hopes for literary discovery fell flat, however, when neither the public nor the critical press took any notice of the work. Eventually two short and rather sneering reviews did appear (*The Northern Bee*, June 1829; *The Moscow Telegraph*, June 1829),[1] causing Gogol to buy up all remaining copies of the work and burn them. He thereupon booked passage on a steamer to Luebeck (early August and not far from the setting of *Hanz*) and spent the next month traveling on what Vladimir Nabokov termed a "freak trip through Northern Germany,"[2] returning to Petersburg in September. *Hanz Kuechelgarten* (literally, *Gants Kiukhel'garten*–it is uncertain if Gogol intended Hanz or Heinz as his protagonist's name) has acquired a rather infamous reputation among Gogol critics for its bad versification, silly sentimental characters and plot, which are based in part on a longer verse idyll, *Luise* by J. H. Voss. The following criticisms have been leveled at *Hanz Kuechelgarten* and they are all true: uneven, unscanning lines, overuse of fill words, slant rhyme, tampering with syntax and word forms for the sake of meter, open and ineffectual copying of style and images from much greater poets—in particular Pushkin and Zhukovsky. The list goes on. The story itself is stock romanticism à la Chateaubriand, well worn out by the time of the poem's composition, and perhaps its only interesting aspect is the odd parallels between it and the later peregrinations of Gogol's life. In spite of all these faults, there is something to be said for the poem: there are glimpses in it here and there—when Gogol either forgets to put on the studied poet's mask or gets so sweaty under it that he tears it off—of the Gogol who was later to appear in full force in the stories, plays and *Dead Souls*. There is in it that eye for uncanny detail, the excessive rapture over food, the unmistakable beginnings of the delight and fascination with the extended rhetorical description, and more than one flash of the sardonic and at times grotesque sense of humor, all of which were to become trademarks of the mature Gogol. For these reasons anyone interested in Gogol should find *Hanz* a necessary part of the oeuvre, and for this reason the translation was made.

Rhyme and meter, with the exception of masculine and feminine endings, I have tried to preserve (or break) throughout as they are in the original. Notes to the translation are my own.

P.D.P.

Notes

1. A more favorable review was written the following year by O.M. Somov in *Northern Flowers* (1830).

2. Vladimir Nabokov, *Nikolai Gogol* (NY: New Directions, 1944), p. 156.

The work presented here would never have seen the light had not circumstances, important only to the author, forced him to do so. It is the work of an eighteen-year-old youth. Not taking it upon ourselves to judge either its merits or its shortcomings, but leaving that to an enlightened public, we will only say that, unfortunately, many scenes from this idyll have not survived. Most likely they would have served to better connect the presently disjointed fragments and to more fully round out the portrayal of the main character. We can at least take pride in the fact that, insofar as possible, we have helped acquaint the world with the creation of a young talent.

Scene I

It lightens. Here a village has appeared,
Some houses, gardens, all in view and bright.
The belfry of the church gleams all in gold,
And on an aging fence a sunray glistens.
All things are turned enchantedly around,
Reversed, head first, within the silver water:
The fence and house and garden—all repeated,
All making movements in the silver water:
A vault of blue and flowing waves of clouds,
And woods that stir but only without sound.

Upon a shore extending far to sea,
By lindens shaded, stands the pastor's cottage,
Quite cozy; there the old man's lived for years.
It's starting to decay, the aging rooftop
Is all poked through with holes; a blackened chimney.
A flow'ring moss still clings from long ago
Onto the walls; the windows are askew;
Yet somehow it's a pleasant place, and nothing
Would make the old man give it up. That linden
'Neath which he likes to rest is likewise shaky,
Although the lawn around it, like a counter,
Lies flat and green. The hollows of the tree
Are filled with nesting birds, whose happy song
Resounds throughout the aging house and garden.
The pastor, having spent a sleepless night,
Had gone at dawn outside to sleep,
And in an old chair dozes 'neath the linden,
And, freshening his face, a breezelet stirs
And, like a fan, it lifts his whitened hair.

But who's this beauty towards him hastens,
Refreshing as the morning, bright,
As she her gaze upon him fastens,
Then stops and stands, a charming sight?
Just watch how sweetly she awakes him
With hand that's lily white and fair,

Caressing him with gentle care—
And back into our world it takes him.
And, eyes half opened, he takes stock
And, half awake, begins to talk:

"What wondrous, wondrous creature is it
That comes to pay my place a visit?
Now why's my soul pierced sudden through
With sadness, secret and prolonging?
Why does your wondrous image, too,
This old and graying head imbue
With feelings of strange, distant longing?
Just look at me: I'm sick, I'm old,
Towards living things I've long grown cold,
Myself now in myself lies buried;
Each day I wait now to be carried
Unto that peace which seems ordained,
And talk of which now strikes me vain.
What is it makes you so attractive,
Young guest, to one as dead as I?
Could it be heaven makes you active
On my behalf, to fortify
My hope, to call me up on high?
Oh, I'm prepared, though lacking worth:
The sins I've done are grave and great.
An evil knight upon this earth
Was I, who made meek shepherds quake.
To me cruel things are nothing novel;
But I've renounced the devil's ways,
And the remainder of my days
Is my small payment for the days
When I in wickedness groveled..."

Dejection, then complete confusion.
"His words," she thought, "are all delusion.
He's rambling God knows what about...
And gone delirious, no doubt."

But once again sleep wraps him round
And by oblivion he's bound.

She leans above him, breathing sparely.
How he slumbers! How he sleeps!
A sigh inflates his chest, just barely;
A guardian angel o'er him keeps
His watch with airy, unseen sweep;
From lips a heav'nly smile flowing,
And overhead a halo glowing.

Then, looking up, he met her eyes:
"Luisa? Strange... I dreamed about...
You scamp, you're early up and out;
The morning dew has still not dried.
Another foggy day, no doubt."

"No, grandfather, the skies are clean
And bright the sun the grove adorning;
The branches there are still and green,
And it is hot, though barely morning.
And do you know why I have come?
Today a holiday's in store.
The fiddler's here, old Lodelham
And Joker-Fritz, what's more.
We're going sailing if it's calm...
If Hanz..." The pastor, kind, good-hearted,
Waits with a crafty smile the end
Towards which these carefree accents wend,
Which have so frolicsomely started.

"You, grandfather, alone it's you who might
Give help in this strange misery.
My Hanz is deathly ill: all night
And day he paces by the sea
So gloomily and serious.
And to himself he often mumbles.
He's not himself. He's bored with us.
And if you ask a question, grumbles
Some unrelated thing. His pride
Is puffed up with despair. He's dying—
Yet one thought makes me horrified:
That with me he's dissatisfied,

That when he speaks of love he's lying.
It stabs me like a knife inside.
I beg you, angel..." Her voice breaking,
She bent above his shoulder, shaking,
And breathing strainedly and low,
Her face flushed red, confused and fearful—
Oh, my beauty, oh, my soul!—
Her eyes began to glisten, tearful...
Oh, how Luisa's goodness shows!

Then spake her spiritual father:
"Don't cry, calm down. You know, dear friend,
That crying shames us in the end;
God gives us strength and patience rather.
Now if your prayers are true, sincere,
The Lord will grant you all that's due you.
Believe that Hanz still holds you dear;
Believe, and He will prove it to you.
Why, then, allow your mind's caprice
Disturb your inner spirit's peace?"

Thus did the old man comfort his Luisa,
While clasping her unto his shaky breast.
Then came old Gertrude, setting out the coffee,
Hot and, just like amber, full of light.
The old man liked outside to drink his coffee,
While holding in his mouth a cherry pipe,
From which the smoke puffed out and fell in ringlets.
Luisa, waxing thoughtful, with some bread
Fed from her hands a cat beneath her feet
That purred and slinked and sniffed the sweet aromas.
The old man stood up from his flowered armchair,
And to his granddaughter stretched out his hand;
Then he his fancy dressing gown put on,
All silvery brocade, and glint, and shining,
The festive cap, as well, he'd never worn—
Brought from the town not long ago by Hanz,
Presented to our pastor as a gift—
And leaning on Luisa's lily shoulder,
Our old man hobbled out into the field.

Oh what a day! The happy, twisting larks
Meandered by and sang; a golden zephyr
Sent rippling waves across the wheaten fields;
Above them groves of trees stood thick and heavy,
Fruit ripening upon them in the sunlight
Translucently; green waters in the distance,
Showed dark and through an iridescent haze,
There wafted fragrant oceans of perfume;
From waving blooms the humble worker bee
Was gathering its honey; dragonflies,
Those whirling mischief-makers, crackled by.
From far away a song—the daring oarsmen's—
Rebounded rakishly; the forest thins,
A valley shows, within it playful flocks
Are bawling; further still a rooftop shows:
Luisa's house, with rows of reddish tiles
Along whose edges brightly slips a sunbeam.

Scene II

By thoughts disturbed, obscure and groundless,
Our Hanz looked round with mind distrait,
Upon a world immense and boundless,
Upon his enigmatic fate.
Until this time he'd played serenely,
Sedately, happily through life;
His young soul growing tender, greenly,
With eyes still closed to grief and strife.
A carefree youth, unhesitative,
His childish breast did nothing know
Of noxious earthly passions, though
He of this earthly realm was native.
And happiness his soul did fill.
Amongst the children, animated,
He'd sweetly play; believed no ill;
And life, a wonder, floreated.
His playmate from those childhood days,
Luisa, angel, child of light,

Shone with her charming turns of phrase;
Through rings of light-brown hair her gaze
Burned playfully, yet plainly, bright.
And if she were to dance or sing
In her green jumper, she would bring
A soul that spoke with eloquence
Of lively, childish innocence;
A rose kerchief around her neck,
Upon her breast just slightly flapping;
White shoes that gleam without a speck,
Her shapely little feet enwrapping.
If in the woods they play and push
Or race together, she outruns him,
And, passing him, hides in a bush
And with a wicked scream she stuns him.
Or if by chance he is asleep,
She paints all over on his face,
And, as her ringing laughter seeps
Into his dreams, he wakes and leaps
Upon the prankster—they embrace.

Thus spring succeeded spring. The ring
Of childish games became less cheery,
And life no more a gleesome thing:
The fire within his eyes turned weary,
And sorrow did her shy heart sting.
First signs of love is what you'd guess—
Of course! Can there be any doubt?
Oh, for the moment, sweet distress!
Days redolent with joy throughout!
Luisa can't be happier:
He's with her evenings, with her days;
What wondrous power draws him to her;
A shadow he that never strays.
Their artless elders them admired,
Filled with a heartful lovingness,
And never got their fill nor tired
Of gazing on their happiness.
Far off seemed days of doubt, dejection:
A peaceful Genius spread protection.

But soon a secret sadness took
Possession of him—in the distance
He often stares with cloudy look,
Estranged and with disturbed persistence.
His mind seeks something boldly out,
His soul a melancholy bout
Withstands of brooding agitation.
He sits as if he were enchained,
By storming sea his gaze detained.
Amidst the hum of ancient waters,
As in a dream, he hears a voice.

* * * * * *

Or lost in thought he walks the valleys,
Eyes glistening exultantly,
Whene'er the noisy wind makes sallies
And thunders argue heatedly;
Then will the fire a moment pierce
The clouds, and rainsource clamor fierce,
Then loudly split, inflammably.
At midnight when thoughts, dreaming, roam,
He'll sit behind some ancient tome,
And, leafing through it, he is stirred
By letters mute upon the pages,
Through which intone the gray-haired ages,
And through which thunder glorious words.
Engrossed an hour in meditation,
He'll not remove from it his glance.
Whoever might look in on Hanz,
He'd boldly make this observation:
The past his life holds in a trance.
He often goes on summer days,
Allured by some fantastic thought,
Beneath an oak, a shady spot
And gloomy—there a phantom strays:
A person's shadow, never caught,
Although he stretches out his arms,
Embracing it, lost in its charms.

    But, simple-souled and quite alone,
Luisa-angel, what of her?
Her heart no longer is her own,
And sleep to her remains unknown.
The same caresses she confers
Upon him, twining arms around
And innocently kissing him.
He, happy for the interim,
Then joins again the singing round.

    Most beautiful these moments are
When crowds of lucent visions throng
About him sweetly from afar,
And with them take the youth along.
But if this peaceful mood should stray
And he forget this cozy nook,
He will indifference display,
And on the plain folk downward look.
For can they youthful dreams fulfill,
Or joy within his heart instill?

    Until this time his varied dreams
Have seemed a riddle, but now we
Shall listen to them stealthily,
Whilst worldly cares about us teem.

Scene III

O land of classical, of marvelous creations
    And fabled deeds, O land of liberty!
O Athens, in the heat of wondrous trepidation
    Of soul I bind myself to thee!
Here from the very tripods[1] unto Piraeus seethes,
Ferments the people of a grand, triumphant nation;
Where flows the thundrous, flaring speech of Aeschines,
    Headstrong and without hesitation,

Like waters of Ilissus, loud and crystalline.
This marble Parthenon: how mighty, yet so fair!
Its rows of Doric columns thrust into the air;
With chisel Phidias did move Minerva there,
And brush of Parhasius, Zeuxis shines.
An old sage to the portico steps down,
Declaiming words most high into the vale below:
On whom, for valor, immortality bestow,
   On whom disgrace, on whom a crown.
Accordant fountains rush, discordant songs are shouted;
Within the amphitheater crowds, since dawn, recline
And mill about; a Persian *kandis*,[2] mottled, shines,
   And tunics by the wind are pouted.
The lines of Sophocles impetuously sound;
And crowns of laurel leaf are festively tossed round;
From lips of Epicurus, favored counselor,
Sweet-sounding, archons, warriors, servants of Amor
Do hasten to imbibe the rules of wisdom's craft:
How life is lived and how enjoyment quaffed.
But here's Aspasia! Oh, trembling youth don't stir,
Don't dare to even breathe when dark her eyes invite;
How burning are those lips! Her words throw fire and light!
And somehow, blacker than the night, her curls
   Shake free upon her breast, unfurled,
   Upon her shoulders, marble-white.
But what this crash of timbrels? What this savage cry?
To Bacchus consecrated, maidens, ivy-crowned,
Run in a rout with wild, disordered cadence down
Into the sacred wood and vanish... why?...

   You're gone and I'm alone, I fear.
Again despair and agony.
If only could a faun appear
Or, in the shade of this bleak tree,
A Dryad show herself to me.
How magic was the world wherein
You dwelt, O Greeks, as in a dream!
Oh, how you charmed it, made it gleam!
And ours: it's pallid, bare and thin,
And squared off by a mileage scheme.

And once again dreams new and fair
Come laughing to his side, embrace him;
And, lifting airily, they raise him
From out this sea of worldly care.

Scene IV

In lands where the rivulets, shimmering, flow,
Where magical sunrays resplendently glow;
Where breathing of love and the rose of the night
Envelope luxuriously heaven's blue light;
Where cloudlets of incense smoke upwards and hang,
And burns the gold fruit of far-off Mangustan[3];
The meadows of Kandahar[4] carpets invent
That shimmer, above which sky spreads her bold tent;
Bright rain upon flowers luxuriously lies—
Then butterflies flutter and, sparkling, arise;
The Peri I see there, though she does not see,
Nor anything heed: in oblivion she,
And dreaming, her eyes like two suns shining bright,
Like Hemasagara's,[5] her curls throwing light;
Her breath is the silvery lilies' sweet scent
When over the languishing garden it's spent
By deep-breathing breezes that now and then blow;
Her voice is the sound that the Sirens bestow
At night, or like silvery wings' rustling sound
When Israzil[6] playfully frisks them around,
Or splashing of mystical streams as they race
Through Khindara;[7] and of her smile? Her embrace?
But see how she turns now and airily flies,
And hastens back home to her region of skies.
Oh stop! Turn around! Oh, but nothing she hears,
And into a rainbow she sinks, disappears.
Yet ever her memory earth will retain,
And, twined with the air, will her fragrance remain.

* * * * * *

The yearnings of the ardent youth
Were permeated through with dreams.
There came to him at times, it seems,
The traits of heaven and of truth
Borne by a soul of beauty. What,
Lost in the haze of unclear thought
And quake of heart, did he pursue?
What did he wish for, what desire?
Where did he fly, soul all afire
And passionate and greedy, too,
As if he would the world engulf—
He did not even know himself.
It seemed to him so stifling, dusty,
This backwoods province of his birth;
And strongly beat his heart, robustly,
For far-off corners of the earth.
Oh, only then, if you could view
How wild his breast would flare and heave,
And how he glances proudly threw,
How thirstily his heart did cleave
Unto this dream so vaguely dreamed.
What splendid ardor in him teemed;
What hot tears from within did rise
To fill his animated eyes.

Scene VI

About two miles from Wismar was the village
Which formed the limits of our heroes' world.
I do not know the township's name at present,
But Luenensdorf is how they called it then—
A cheery name. And from afar there gleams
The modest house of farmer Wilhelm Bauch,
Who long ago had wed the pastor's daughter
And built the place himself. A cheery farmhouse!
It's painted with a lively green, the roof
Is handsomely, of ringing tiles, constructed;
Around the house there stand old chestnut trees

With branches hanging over as if wishing
To poke through all the house's windowpanes;
Behind them, wrapped with splendid vines, is glimpsed
A trellis, work of craftsmanship and beauty,
And Wilhelm's very hands; upon it hops
Hang down and twist like snakes; a pole is stretched
From out a window, on it linen dries
White-gleaming in the sun. Some fluffy pigeons
Are crowded in a gap within the attic;
Unhurried turkeys cluck and, with a flap
Of wings, the roosters cry to greet the morning
And strut around the yard with grave importance
And, midst the dappled hens, scratch heaps of grain.
Here also stroll two goats that frisk and nibble
The perfumed grass. Long has the chimney now
From out its stacks of white poured curls of smoke
And, ringing up, they multiply the clouds.
On one side, where the paint is chipped and flaking
And gray bricks are protuding from the wall,
Where ancient chestnut trees have spread their shadows
Which sunlight penetrates from time to time,
Whene'er the playful breeze their topmost branches heaves—
In shadow of these ever-pleasant chestnuts
Since morning stood a table, oaken, spotless,
Laid with a tablecloth and sets of dishes
All heaped with fragrant food: some yellow cheese,
Quite tasty, radishes, and butter in
A server made of porcelain, beer, wine,
And bishop sweet, and sugar, and brown wafers;
And in a basket fruits, all glistening and ripe:
And fragrant raspberries, translucent grapes,
And pears that glow deep yellow, just like amber,
And dark-blue plums, and peaches, light and brilliant,
All stacked up in an intricate arrangement.
Today was lively Wilhelm celebrating
The birthday of his dear beloved spouse;
The pastor, too, was there, and precious daughters:
The elder one, Luisa, younger Fanny.
But Fanny is not there: some time ago
She'd gone to fetch back Hanz, and as of yet

Has not returned. Of course, there is no question:
He's wandering about somewhere again,
Engrossed in thought. Still sweet Luisa looks
Attentively upon the darkened pane
Of neighbor Hanz's window. Not two paces
Was Hanz's house from theirs, yet my Luisa
Would not go over, thinking he might see
That wearisome depression in her look,
Or read the keen reproach within her glance.
Then up speaks Wilhelm to his eldest daughter:
"Make certain Hanz is scolded good and proper:
Why does he have to make us wait so long?
It's you, you know, who's spoiled the fellow rotten."
Luisa then her father answered thus:
"I am afraid to scold my good, dear Hanz:
Besides, you know, he's sick and pale and thin..."
"A splendid sickness," mother said,
The lively Bertha. "He's not sick, just sad...
And brings it on himself for no good reason.
Just let him marry. He'll be feeling fine.
Just like a tender shoot, all dry and thirsty:
A spray of rain and instantly it blooms.
And what's a wife if not her husband's joy?"
"Well-spoken words," pronounced the gray-haired pastor.
"If God desires something, it will be.
In all things is His holy will made patent."
Already had he twice knocked ashes from his pipe
And launched upon an argument with Wilhelm
About the current stories in the news:
About the ruined crops, about the Greeks and Turks,
And Missolonghi and the war affairs,
The fabled rebel chief Kolokotroni,
And Canning and the British Parliament,
The troubles in Madrid and the rebellion,[8]
When suddenly Luisa gave a cry,
And catching sight of Hanz she flew upon him.
Embracing then her light and supple figure,
The youth with strong emotion gave the girl a kiss.
But then the pastor started, turning towards him:
"Ech, shame, Hanz, shame, to have forgot your friend.

Now if you're so forgetful of Luisa,
Then do you ever think of us, her elders?"
"Quit scolding him now, Papa—that's enough,"
Said Bertha. "Better that we all sat down
To table now, before the food gets cold:
The porridge made with rice and fragrant wine,
The sugared peas, the plate of piping chicken
With raisins fried in butter sauce." They all
Then calmly sat down at the table.
And in a trice the wine their spirits quickened
And poured its laughter, bright, into each soul.
Together then, in honor of the mistress,
The ancient fiddler, Fritz, on ringing flute,
Burst fourth into a surging, whirling waltz.
Our ruddy Wilhelm, spirits raised, arose
And danced off with his wife as with a peahen;
And like a whirlwind, Hanz with his Luisa
Went rushing in the fervid waltz headlong;
Around them spun in wondrous, loud disorder
The world, and sweet Luisa could not breathe,
Nor even look, all lost was she
Completely in the sway. The happy pastor,
Admiring them, could not resist exclaiming;
"Oh, what a splendid, loving pair they make!
My dear Luisa, child so sweet and cheerful,
Intelligent and modest, handsome Hanz;
In truth they were created for each other,
And happy will their journey be through life.
Lord, great and merciful, my thanks to Thee I offer!
For having my decrepit strengths prolonged
And having filled my waning years with pleasure—
So that I might behold such splendid offspring
And say, when I depart this worn out body:
'Such splendid things I saw upon the earth.'"

Scene VII

With coolness falls the peaceful, silent evening,
And here and there the dusky sea is kissed

By sunbeams taking leave; sparks golden, lively,
Touch branches of the trees; far in the distance,
Through ocean's fog, gleam rocks of many colors.
And all is calm, all absolutely peaceful.
There only sounds that lone, dejected voice
Of shepherds' horns blown on some happy shores,
Quite far away from here. The quiet sound
Of splashing fish just barely cuts the silence,
And on the placid water ripples rise.
A swallow skims a wave-crest with its pinion,
Then circles in the sky, then glides, is gone.
Glinting from afar, a point of light
A dory—who within that dory sits?
The pastor sits, our old and graying pastor,
Along with Wilhelm and his darling wife;
And Fanny, that forever playful prankster,
A fish rod in her hands, hung o'er the rail
And, laughing, stirred up wavelets with her hand;
Along the stern, Luisa and her Hanz
Stared longly in each other's eyes in silence.
Then rippled in the wake behind the stern
A wide wave broken by the shifting oar
That flashed and tossed off fiery, trembling sparks.
And as the distance cleared on the horizon,
All colored rose, the south wind started breathing.
And then the pastor, filled with tender feeling,
Pronounced: "How sweet this blessed evening is!
So beautiful and quiet, like the life
Led by a sinless soul: it ends its journey
In just such peaceful style, as lovely tears
Are sprinkled, tenderly, on its remains.
The time for me has come: the date is set,
And soon, oh very soon, I'll not be yours.
But is there not thus beauty in my passing?..."
All shed a tear. And Hanz, engaged in playing
Some soft, sweet melody upon his oboe,
Lapsed into thought and let the oboe drop;
And once again a dream of some sort cast
A shadow on his brow; and far away
His thoughts rushed to and fro, then something fine

Accumulated in his soul. Luisa
Spoke thus to him: "Hanz, if you love me still,
Please tell me how I might rouse in your soul
At least a spark of sympathy, of pity.
You mustn't keep tormenting me: please say,
Why do you always sit alone at night
Behind a book? (I see all that you do,
Our windows being right across each other.)
Why shun all other people? Why be sad?
Oh, how the sorrow in your face disturbs me!
Oh, how I'm saddened by that look of sadness!"
And touched within, with clouded look,
Hanz squeezed her to his breast in mute dejection,
And from his eye a tear, unwilling, fell.
"Oh, please don't ask, don't ask me, my Luisa,
And do not agitate yourself with sorrow.
Believe me, dear: when I seem plunged in thought,
It's only you that occupies my musings.
I'm only thinking how I might defend
You from these thoughts of anxious, sad dejection,
How I might fill your heart with joyful feeling,
And how preserve the peace that's in your soul,
Protect your innocent and childlike dreams;
So that you'll never be approached by evil,
Nor touched by e'en a shadow of despair,
So that your happiness will ever bloom."
She dropped her little head upon his breast
And in a flood of grateful, heartfelt feeling,
Fell silent and she not a word could utter.
The boat flew swift and smooth along the shoreline
And suddenly it docked. Within a trice
They all had disembarked. "Take care now, children,"
Said Wilhelm. "It is damp here with the dew.
Take care now you don't catch some dreadful cough."
Our dear Hanz wonders: "What would be the outcome,
Were she to hear what is not necessary
For her to hear?" And looks he on Luisa,
Experiencing within his heart self-censure:
As if he had some evil just committed,
Or in God's presence played the hypocrite.

Scene VIII

The tower strikes the midnight chime,
The chime that signals thought's set time,
When Hanz alone now always sits!
A lighted lamp before him flits
And palely luminates the gloom,
As if it doubt spread through the room.
And all's asleep. No straying gaze
Meets with another in the night;
The waves a distant discourse phrase,
As sea sounds, moon above it bright.
All's quiet, but for night's soft breath.
And Hanz, lost now in thoughts profound,
Is not disturbed by outer sound;
The silence hangs as still as death.

    And what of her? She straightway rises,
And by the window sits, surmises:
"He will not look, I'll keep from sight,
And with my eyes his form caress.
Unsleeping for my happiness!...
O, Lord above, his spirit bless!"

    The sea sounds, moon above it bright.
And wafts upon her, slowly, sleep.
Her head unwillingly inclines.
But Hanz his thoughts still intertwines,
Submerged within them, far and deep.

    1
    It's all decided. Really, now,
My soul: Is it to perish here?
No other end is it to know?
No better course for it to steer?
Myself to sacrifice, to doom
My life to this inglorious tomb?

2
Now is my soul, in love with glory,
Its love on paltry things to waste?
Now is my soul, still gustatory,
Of life's emotions not to taste?
Meet nothing beautiful in it?
Its own existence not admit?

3
What power puts me in your sway,
O lavish lands beyond the sea?
Like trilling birds, both night and day,
I hear your voices summon me.
Both night and day by dreams enchained,
By you, by you am I entrained.

4
I'm yours! I'm yours! These wastes I'll quit
And enter into paradise;
As pilgrims to their shrines will flit,
....
The ship will launch, the waves will break,
And joyful feelings make their wake.

5
This cloudy veil shall be pierced through,
'Neath which, known but by dreams, you hide,
And, rich in pleasures always new,
Its wondrous gates thrown open wide,
A world of beauty, world of truth
Shall be prepared to greet the youth.

6
Creators of superb sensations!
I see your chisel and your brush,

And with your fiery creations
My soul is filled, must onward rush.
Sound on, my ocean wide, sound on!
And bear my lonely ship along!

    7

Forgive me now, my narrow room,
And forest, meadow, field—forgive!
God grant you longer time to bloom,
And heaven rains more often give!
It seems my soul keeps watch on you,
And thirsts for one last rendezvous.

    8

Forgive me too, my angel quiet!
Nor tears allow to cloud your glance!
Don't fall into a sad disquiet,
And please forgive your troubled Hanz!
Oh, do not cry, I'll come to get you;
I'll soon return—could I forget you?

Scene IX

Who is this comes before the dawn
And quietly his way does pick?
A knapsack to his back strapped on
And in his belt a walking stick.
A cottage there upon his right,
And to his left the open road,
Along which he would make his flight:
He begs God make him firm and bold.
But in him secret torments fight,
And, turning feet round in their track,
He to that cottage hastens back.

There but one window open shows;
Within it, lost in sweet repose,
The maiden slumbers, head on arms:
A feath'ry breeze around her blows
And wafts on her sleep's wondrous charms;
And, head replete with pleasant dreaming,
She smiles, her face composed and beaming.
With quaking soul he towards her hastens...
With heart contracted, trembling tear...
His eyes, now glistening, he fastens
Upon this beauty sleeping here.
Towards her he bends, his passions flaring,
Then kisses her, then moans, despairing.

   Then starting up, he rushes out
Again unto the open road;
His look is gloomy, filled with doubt,
And heavy is his soul's dark load.
And, turning round, he backwards tries
To look, but fogs obscure the view,
The achings in his breast renew,
And with a glance he says good-bye.
Then as the early wind awakes,
The oak grove, stern and green, it shakes.
All disappears into the distance.
Through dreams, at times, with vague persistence,
It seemed the porter Gottlieb heard
That someone through the gate had stirred,
And that the faithful hound's loud bark,
As if reproachful, filled the dark.

Scene X

The bright king's long kept from his reign.
A morning foul: unto the clearings
A grayish, twisting fog adhering;
And on the roofs rings frequent rain.
The beauty's been awake since dawn
And wonders how it is she might

Have, at the window, passed the night.
Her hair she straightens, smiles anon,
But in her eyes, alive and clear,
Against her will there gleams a tear.
"What's keeping him?" the thought distresses.
"He said he'd come at light's first glance.
Oh, what a day! How it oppresses—
A thick fog on the fields presses,
And shrieks the wind; but where is Hanz?"

And now her anxious look she's keeping
Fixed on his cherished windowpane.
But it is closed—and does remain.
Her Hanz, undoubtedly, is sleeping,
Sees divers things in dreams appear.
But day has broken now. Rain soaks
And rends the valleys; tops of oaks
Shake loud; yet Hanz is still not here.

It's noon now. Imperceptibly
The fog dissolves; the woods fall still;
Yet thunders still the distance fill
And rumble meditatively;
A rainbow's seven hues burn clear
Across the sky; the old oak throngs
With flashes. From it ringing songs
Resound; yet Hanz is still not here.

What could this signify?... Old Nick
Finds ways to make things troublesome;
The ear is wearied by the tick
Of passing hours... Does someone come?
Yes, through the door... It's him... Not him...
In pink and cozy dressing gown,
And apron bright with trim around,
Her mother, with a worried frown,
Walks in. "My angel, say what whim
Disturbs you. All night as you slept
You tossed and turned. You look so pale
And tired. Was it the rain that kept

You up? Or roaring waves? The wail
Of rooster as he brawled and leapt
About all night? Or unclean spirit
That did your maiden's sleep dispirit
And with black woe your soul imbue?
Please say, my whole heart pities you."

"No, it was not the rain that kept
Me up, nor roaring waves, nor wail
Of rooster as he brawled and leapt
About all night. They do not ail
My young breast; not those cares or woes
And not those dreams that blight my soul;
By them my spirit's not made sad,
But by a wondrous dream I had.

"I dreamed I was in backwoods dark,
Around me barrens and a fog,
And not a dry spot one could mark
Upon this plain that was but bog.
A heavy smell, yet delicate
And viscid. I'm afraid to stray;
You take a step, the ground gives way;
My panic then I can't relate,
My panic—oh, I can't explain...
Then suddenly my Hanz appeared,
So strange and wild, with wounds blood-smeared—
And over me he sobs in pain;
Yet down his face no teardrops streak:
Some cloudy water runs instead...
I woke up: on my breast, my cheek,
The light-brown tresses of my head,
The rain ran down in vexing streams;
A premonition in me teems,
My heart's uncomfortable and numb...
And I have yet to wring my hair,
And have all morning felt despair;
What's wrong? Where is he? Won't he come?"

Her mother stood up, then did shake
Her head before her, sensibly:
"Well, daughter, what of this to make
I know, poor one, as much as thee.
Let's go to him. Then we'll find out,
God willing, what it's all about."

Then both of them went to his room;
But it was empty. In the gloom
Some ancient tomes with dust are thick:
Here Aristophanes and Tieck,
Here Plato, headstrong Schiller and
Petrarch, forgotten Winckelmann.[9]
And here some paper—torn up scraps,
And on a shelf some fresh-cut flowers.
And here the pen with which he maps
His dreams, filled with courageous powers.
Here something glimmered on the desk:
A note!... Luisa reached for it
With trembling hand. To whom addressed?
From whom?... And what upon it writ?
Her tongue with foam then strangely bubbles,
And to her knees she sudden doubles;
An anguish presses on her, glows;
A gravelike cold within her flows.

Scene XI

O brutal tyrant, look upon
The breast of this pour soul you've killed!
How fades this flower, lonely, wan,
Left in these barrens, foggy, chilled.
Here, take a look at your creation:
You've robbed her of all happiness
And changed her joy of life to stress,
Despair and Hell's excruciation,
Into a devastated press
Of graves. Oh, how she loved you so!
With what exalted breadth of feeling

Did she her artless words bestow!
See how you heeded their appealing!
How flaming, yet how innocent,
Within her eyes that flashing ray!
How dully did the hours weigh
Upon her longly when she spent
That day despairing, prey to fear
And doubts, when you did not appear.
And was it you, *you* her forsook?
And you who turned your back on all?
The path to foreign lands you took
To follow—whose? what's?—distant call.
But, brutal tyrant, look again:
Just as before she waits and sits
Beneath the window, deep within
A dark despair which no light splits.
The day expires; the evening glows;
On all is thrown a wondrous flashing;
A cool wind through the heavens flows;
Far off sound waves just barely splashing,
As night its shadows starts to spread;
Yet in the west it still glows red;
A reed-pipe barely strains, while she
Sits at the window fixedly.

Night Visions

The evening dims, its beauty pining,
While earth to sleep's sweet rapture yields;
And clearly now above the fields
A self-important moon is shining.
And all glows bright, translucently;
The sea, like glass, glints flashingly.

   Twisting up and then untwisting,
Wondrous shadows skyward flee
Up sky's staircase wondrously,
Rush back down, then up, persisting.
Bright it grows: two candles glow:

Shaggy knights, a pair, come pacing;
Double swordblades, saw-toothed, show,
And cuirasses, worked with chasing;
Seek they something, stand in line,
For some reason break their queueing,
Start to fight and, moving, shine,
Do not find what they're pursuing...
All then darkly slips away;
Moonbeams on the water play.

   Tsar Nightingale's resplendent song goes winging
Throughout the grove. The clear notes softly spread.
Night barely breathes; with dreamy head,
The sleepy earth harks to the singing.
The forest does not stir; all sleeps;
His song the only vigil keeps.

   Flowing out of air the palace
Of a splendid fairy gleams;
Through the open window streams
An inspired singer's sallies.
On a carpet silvery,
Wove of clouds, a spirit hovers
In a flame, incredibly.
North and south with wings he covers.
Glances in: the fairy sleeps,
Locked within a cage of coral;
Crystal is the tear he weeps,
Breaking down the walls of pearl.
They embrace... slip dark away.
Moonbeams on the water play.

   Through steamy mists just barely glimmers
The near surroundings; what a mound
Of cryptic thoughts the sea's strange sound
Brings on! A whale's immense back shimmers;
A fisherman curls up and sleeps;
And sea its moaning vigil keeps.

Then from out the sea come swimming
Maidens in first youth, divine;
White the waves around them skimming,
                    Fiery, bright blue they shine.
Falling into thoughts, the water
Sways a breast that's lily-white,
And the beauty's breath draws tauter...
With one lavish leg she smites
The water, rippling in double rows...
Smiles invitingly, then laughs,
Beckons ardently, calls out,
Then lost in thought, she swims about—
Is it yes or no? Perhaps—
Then starts singing, lost in thought,
Of herself, a Siren youthful,
Of sly treachery, untruthful...
From a sky blue as the day
Moonbeams on the water play.

  A graveyard to the side, forsaken:
A shaky fence encircles round,
Some crosses, gravestones... all moss-bound:
The homes of those whom death has taken.
And naught but flight and cries of owls
Disturbs the sleep of empty palls.

  Slowly rises up a body,
Whitely shrouded but still spry.
With a self-important nod he
Dusts his bones off—what a guy!
From his brow a chill is blowing,
Sallow flames eyesockets breed,
Under him a mighty steed,
Boundless, all in whiteness glowing,
Rapidly increasing size,
'Til it overwhelms the skies;
With a calm provoking horror,
Corpses in a crowd stretch forward.
Earth splits open—pitwards slam
All the shades together... Wham!

The window, without hesitating,
She banged shut, trembling now and scared,
Her heart in turmoil palpitating,
The flow within it alternating
'Twixt chill and fever. She despaired,
And off into the distance stared.
When if Fate's hand unmercifully
A chilly stone rolls over dully
Upon some wretched heart—whose wit,
Pray tell, is guaranteed judicious?
Whose soul to ashes won't submit?
Whose self-possession infinite?
Ill luck makes whom not superstitious?
Whose steadfast soul will not turn white
Before a dream destroyed outright?

    With hidden grief, with dread-filled grimness,
She throws herself into her bed;
In vain she waits for sleep to spread.
Should some chance noise disturb the dimness,
A scrabbling mouse perhaps run by—
From eyelids fickle sleep will fly.

Scene XIII

Oh, Athens' sad antiquities.
The rows of rotting statues, columns
Stand midst a plain of wild debris.
Sad traces of the ages solemn:
A graceful monument stands wrecked,
Its broken granite's power checked,
And only fragments to be found.
Remaining stately to this day,
An architrave shows black decay,
And capitals are ivy-bound;
Into a trench long overgrown,
A cornice, broken loose, has tumbled.
Still shines this frieze of wondrous stone,

As does this metope, uncrumbled;
And still unto this day there grieves
This intricate Corinthian order—
A swarm of lizards from it reaves—
Which coldly with contempt receives
The world; though pressed in time's dim quarter,
Its splendidness it yet preserves,
And nothing its attention swerves.

   Oh, Athens' sad antiquities.
Dim scenes of bygone days are these.
Upon cold marble, head in hands,
At last the pilgrim understands:
It's all in vain; with all his soul
He'd tried to raise the past; the scroll
Of deeds long done he'd tried unwinding,
With feeble anguish little finding;
His troubled gaze reads everyplace
Both devastation and disgrace.
A turban midst the columns flashes,
A Muslim moves about the walls,
These stones, these ditches, ruined halls;
Upon his steed he fiercely dashes,
And, with a cry, the relics smashes.
A sadness inexpressible
Engulfs the pilgrim for a moment.
There murmur in his soul grave omens;
He feels both pitying, sorrowful.
Why did he here his path direct?
Not, surely, for these graves of dust
Did he his placid home reject,
Betray his chamber's quiet trust.
Oh, let one's thoughts be permeated
By airy, insubstantial dreams!
Oh, let a heart be agitated
By beauty pure, which mirror-like gleams!
How murderously now, how coldly
The world you from its balance tore;
How cruel, how heartlessly you boldly
Slammed shut upon this soul the door,

You sons of such importance paltry,
A quiet dream-world's door, and hotly!—
The pilgrim quits then grievously
The ruins, footsteps slowly falling;
His soul, he swears, of them is free,
Yet all the same he keeps recalling
The victims of blind frailty.

Scene XVI

Two years passed by. In peaceful Luenensdorf,
Just as before, all's beautiful, in bloom.
The very same concerns, the same amusements
Continue to disturb the folks' calm hearts.
But all is not the same with Wilhelm's clan.
The pastor long ago has left this world.
His hard and heavy path he has completed
And sleeps a sleep now different than ours.
The populace saw off his saintly relics
And paid their last respects with tearful eyes,
Remembering his actions and his deeds:
Was it not he for our salvation worked,
And shared with us the host of his own spirit,
Instructing us, with ringing words, in goodness?
Not he who was the comfort of the mourning,
Of orphans and of widows the firm shield?
On holidays how meekly he'd ascend
The pulpit stairway! And with touched emotion
He'd speak to us of martyrs, pure and sinless,
And of the weighty sufferings of Christ,
And, deeply moved, we'd harken his oration
And, marveling, weep tears of exultation.

From Wismar, if a person keeps the road,
Upon the left-hand side he will encounter
A cemetery: there old crosses lean,
Bent over, on them mosses grow,
And time's stern chisel they have come to know.
But in their midst a white urn glistens sharply,

Upon a stone of black, and o'er it humbly
Two greening sycamores sway rustlingly,
Embracing with their shadows cold the distance.
Here lie the mortal relics of the pastor.
Good peasants volunteered on his behalf
To set up here above his grave, this marker,
In memory of his being on this earth.
On all four sides inscribed, the testament
Resounds, of how he lived, how many years
He passed in peace amongst his flock, and when,
His long path quit, he gave his soul to God.

   And at that hour of day when east untangles
With modesty her russet locks of hair,
A fresh wind rises up across the fields,
And diamonds are cast round upon the roses.
The happy robin sings out from its bushes,
The half-sun, rising o'er the earth, shines bright—
In its direction wend young peasant maids,
With roses and carnations in their arms.
Upon the stone they drape the fragrant flowers
And with a greening garland twine it round.
Then once again they tread the wonted path.
Yet one among them, young, remains behind
And, leaning on a hand of lily white,
She sits above the grave and longly ponders,
As if she tried to grasp what can't be known.
Who in this meditative, grieving maid
Would not well recognize the sad Luisa?
So long now since joy's shimmered in her eyes,
Or since that smile's appeared, so wry yet harmless,
Upon her face; no happy feelings flit
Across it now, unless it is by error;
How sweet she is, though, in her languid sadness!
Oh, how ennoblèd that glance of innocence!
'Tis thus that angels bright despair
When pondering the baneful fall of mankind.
Luisa was quite dear to me when happy,
Yet somehow in unhappiness she's dearer.
But eighteen years had barely passed her by

When left this life the perspicacious pastor.
With all her childlike soul she'd loved this man,
This elder who tried e'er God's ways to follow;
And thinks she at the bottom of her heart:
"No, all the ardent hopes you had are vanished.
Oh, how you wished, dear father, kind and good,
To marry us before the holy altar,
Our union to forever consecrate.
Oh, how you loved my Hanz, that wistful dreamer!
While he..."

    Let's take a look in Wilhelm's cabin.
Already autumn. Cold. At home he was,
And on his lathe with clever art was turning
Some mugs of hard and layered beechwood,
And carving on them complicated patterns;
Beneath his feet, curled snugly up, there lay
His cherished friend and faithful comrade Hector.
And Bertha, too, is here, sound-witted mistress:
Since morning bustling briskly with her chores
About the house. Beneath the window, too,
There crowds a gang of long-necked geese, and also
Some restless chickens cackling in the yard;
And bands of sparrows impudently chirp,
All day upon the dung-heap swarming;
They've seen the handsome bullfinch is about;
A long time now the fields have smelled of autumn,
A long time since green leaves have turned to gold,
A long time now since swallows have flown southwards,
Beyond the seas, magnificent and far.
Then mistress of the house, sound-witted Bertha,
Cries out: "When will this end for our Luisa?
It's getting dark now; not at all like summer:
Already damp and wet out, fogs are thick
And penetrating everything with cold.
Why roam about? She'll be the death of me;
She'll never rid herself of Hanz's image.
While God knows if he's living or he's dead."
But Fanny, in a corner with her lace-frame,
Was contemplating nothing of the sort.

Just sixteen years of age and full of sadness
And secret thoughts of her ideal friend,
With absent mind she indistinctly spoke:
"I, too, could be like that, I could have loved him."

Scene XVII

The days of autumn often pine;
Today's day is, however, splendid:
In heaven waves of silver shine,
And sun, bright glowing, has ascended.
Along the post road, all alone,
Upon his back a knapsack thrown,
A pilgrim from strange lands is straining.
Tormented, sad and wild is he,
With back bent over crookedly:
Not even half a Hanz remaining.
With roaming, half-dim eyes he views
The fertile hillocks, cornfields tawny,
A mountain chain of many hues.
It seems a dream descends upon him,
As in a sweet oblivion;
But just as soon the feeling's gone:
He falls deep into rumination;
His soul needs quiet's restoration.

 He's trod, it's plain, a long, hard road,
Breast suffering a heavy load;
His soul, too, suffers, sorely aching,
But still no chance of respite taking.

 What can his ruminations be?
He marvels at life's vanity:
How thoughts of fate his soul tormented;
With evil leering, malcontented,
Laughs at himself, that with his dreams
A world so hateful and weak-minded
He could esteem; that empty gleams
Could make his foolish soul so blinded;

And how, unshaking, boldly he
The human race, with open feelings,
Embraced, then spellbound, drunkenly,
Saw only evil in their dealings.
How cold these people, as the grave;
What wretches they, low, mean, disgusting;
Naught close or precious to them save
Prestige, self-glory, money-lusting.
They but defame gifts marvelous,
And trample down all inspiration,
Despise all candid revelation;
Their ardor's cold, erroneous,
Their waking wreaks but devastation.
Oh, who untremblingly would breach
The wall of their lethargic speech?
Oh, how their breath blows poisonously!
And how their hearts beat spuriously!
Their heads with treachery abound!
Their words with emptiness resound!

   And many are the truths that, sadly,
He's come to know and recognize;
But is he happier otherwise,
Within this soul disgraced so badly?
A bright star's distant radiance
Enticed him, glory pulled him thither;
Its heady fumes, though, proved pretense,
The gleaming poison tasted bitter.

   The day unto the west inclines,
The evening shadows stretch their lines.
Much brighter is that crimson section
Of sky than clouds that whitely gleam:
On leaves of yellowed, dark complection,
There's glimmering a golden stream.
Then suddenly the sorry rover
Caught sight of native meadows dear.
His pallid gaze then covered over
A moment with a hot, bright tear.

A swarm of those naive diversions,
Those childish pranks, those old discursions,
Weighed all at once upon his breast
And would not give him space to rest.
He wonders what it signifies...
And, like a weakened child, he cries.

A Thought

That wondrous moment is most blest
When at a time of full self-seeing,
When one's strong forces reach their crest,
One, chose by heaven, gains his quest,
Attains his lofty goal of being;
When neither glory, tawdry, bright,
Nor empty shadows of vain dreaming,
Ferment within him day and night,
To worlds attract him, loud and teeming;
When he to but one thought gives worth,
Both firm and cheerful: the desire
For righteousness and good on earth;
Then towards great work he will aspire,
For which his life he will not spare.
In vain the mob may madly swear:
He's firm amidst these wrecks still living,
And of one sound alone aware:
Posterity its blessing giving.

But when dreams treacherous excite
With craving for a fate of brilliance,
Yet in the soul no steeled resilience,
Nor strength against the whirl to fight—
Not better, then, in quiet leisure,
Across life's field to proceed,
From modest family gain pleasure,
And pay the noisy world no heed?

Scene XVIII

The stars come out, a chorus flowing,
About them glances meek bestowing
Upon a world entranced by sleep;
Maintaining watch on man's quiet dreaming;
With peace do they the good ones keep,
But grant the wicked poison teeming
With foul reproach. You stars, then why
Will you not calm send to the grieving?
Why to a wretched mind deny
Delight? And, calmly you perceiving
With his repining, grief-filled look,
Within his soul by passion shook,
He'll hark a dialogue and call you,
Find firm belief in you to value.
As torments still her strengths exhaust,
Luisa's yet her bonds to sunder;
She cannot sleep; in dreams she's lost
And views the autumn night with wonder.
Her thoughts the self-same theme begin...
Then fills her soul with sudden raptures:
A song's sweet harmony she captures,
As sounds the joyous clavecin.

 The sound of falling leaves attending,
Among the trees where shows the fence
Beyond the latticed walls extending,
In sweet oblivion is standing,
Wrapped up and near the garden, Hanz.
What happened to him then on hearing
The notes of that familiar song—
That voice which, since his disappearing,
He had not heard for, oh, so long;
Those words, too, which with burning passion,
In love, when wondrous strengths arose
Within his soul in bright elation,
Harmoniously he did compose?
They ring across the garden, soaring,
Then flow, their quiet rapture pouring:

I call your name! I call your name!
Bewitched, I'm in your smile's possession.
An hour, no, two, I will remain,
Eyes fixed upon you just the same.
Nor shall I tire of my obsession.

* * *

If you should sing—and if your voice,
Mysterious, innocently ringing,
Across the empty air go winging—
Then flows a nightingale's singing,
And thundrous silver streams rejoice.

* * *

Come hold me tight, with all your might,
In heat of splendid excitation.
In silence does my heart ignite;
They burn, they flame with fiery light,
Your movements of cool moderation.

* * *

I waste without you in dismay,
And to forget you have not power.
In evening or at break of day,
Incessantly for you I pray,
For you, my angel, every hour.

* * *

Then suddenly to her it seemed
That someone's eyes beside her gleamed,
Their wondrous glow intensifying,

And then a sound of someone sighing,
And fear and trembling on her press...
And looking round her...
    "Hanz!..."
                Oh, who could guess
The rapture of that joyous meeting!
The fire of eyes in ardent greeting!
The heartfelt weight of happiness!
Oh, who so ardently discerning
As to describe the wave that swept
Her soul, that fired her breast with yearning
And rent her heart unto its depths;
You shake, you tremble, thrill all over,
Nor thought nor word for it discover
When, rapturous, midst torments sweet,
With ringing harmony you meet!

   Then coming to himself, tears streaming,
Hanz looks into his sweetheart's eyes;
And thinks: "Enough, I'm only dreaming;
But may I never wake and rise.
Her love for me is still aglow,
Her childlike soul is just the same!
But deeply sorrowed is her brow,
Her rosy looks have faded now:
Her perished youth she can't reclaim;
Yet I, head filled with contradictions,
Went flying after new afflictions!"
Then from his soul the sleep was torn
Of heavy suffering; calm, ardent,
Anew our hero was reborn.
A storm revolts, and on the morn
Thus shines our world again concordant;
Thus, tempered in the fire, a blade
A hundred times more bright is made.

   The cups and glasses round them clatter,
As at the feast the guests regale;
Our old folks sit about and chatter
And young ones into dances sail.

All day, like drawn-out, booming thunder,
There sounds bright music's harmony;
The house a joyous spell is under,
The rooftop gleams hospitably.
A band of peasant maids proposes
To give a gift unto the pair:
They bring them violets, sky-blue posies,
They bring bouquets of fiery roses,
Together heap them, then declare:
"Just like these violets, field posies,
We hope your youth's bloom never closes!
And may your hearts forever share
Love burning like these fiery roses!"

    With rapture then, with ecstasy,
The youth shakes in anticipation—
His bright eyes gleam with exultation;
Unfeigned and with sincerity,
As chains restraining him now break,
His heart of pleasure can partake.
And you, perfidious, false dreams—
He gives up idolizing you,
And earthly beauty now esteems.
But yet there's something clouds his view:
(Oh, will the man be understood?)
On parting with those dreams for good,
It seems old faithful friends he's leaving,
And for them, lost in thought, is grieving.
So will a restless schoolboy wait
For his confinement's final date.
As studies fly to their conclusion,
Thoughts fill his head in rapt profusion,
And airy dreams he will create:
He's independent, been released,
And with himself, the world, quite pleased.
But parting with this family
Of friends with whom he ardently
Shared pranks, work, quiet company—

He moans and falls into reflection,
And sheds a tear unwillingly,
With inexpressible dejection.

Epilogue

In backwoods wastes uncultivated,
In solitude which no man sees,
Within my sanctum consecrated,
Unknown, henceforth shall be created
My quiet soul's calm reveries.
Could sounds that are akin to clamor
Be wafted here, disturb someone?
A maiden's ardent breast enamor,
Cause keen thoughts through a youth to run?
Involuntarily, with passion,
My quiet song will from me spring,
And, with unguessed determination,
Of my own Germany I'll sing.
A country after high thoughts racing,
Where airy specters rendezvous,
Oh, how my soul is filled with you!
Just like some Genius, you embracing,
Great Goethe keeps you in his sight,
And, with the grand, harmonious spacing
Of hymns, a cloud of cares shines bright.

Translated by Paul D. Putz

Leaving the Theater After the Presentation of a New Comedy

Leaving the Theater After the Presentation of a New Comedy

Lobby of the theater. On one side there are staircases leading to the boxes and gallery, in the middle is the entrance to the stalls and circle, and on the other side is the exit. The distant rumble of applause can be heard.

AUTHOR OF THE PLAY* *(entering):* I never thought I'd free myself from that quicksand. At last cheers and clapping! The whole theater is thundering!... Fame is at hand! Lord, how my heart would have pounded seven or eight years ago! How every part of me would have throbbed! But that was a long time ago. I was young then, with the venturesome thoughts of youth. Providence was kind in withholding the taste of early rapture and acclaim from me! Now... But the cold reason of passing years brings wisdom to everyone, no matter whom. Ultimately one comes to realize that applause signifies, in fact, very little and is handed out as a reward to all and sundry. If an actor fathoms the human soul and heart in all its mystery, if a dancer makes skillful patterns with his feet, even a juggler's tricks—all are greeted by the same tumultuous applause! It is the same whether the head is thinking, the heart is feeling, or the soul speaking from its depths, whether feet are being kicked or hands juggling tumblers, they all reap the same applause. No, applause is not what I would wish for now, I should like to be transported to the boxes, the circle, the stalls, the gallery, to penetrate everywhere, to hear everyone's impressions and opinions while they are still virginal and fresh, before they have been subjected to the interpretations and views of connoisseurs and journalists, while each person is still guided by his own judgment. I need this, I am a humorist. All other works and genres are subject to the judgment of a select few; only the humorist must submit to the judgment of all. Every spectator has a right over him; no matter what a man's calling, this man becomes his judge. Oh, how I would like everyone to show me my faults and defects! Even though they make fun of me, and hostility, prejudice, indignation, hatred—anything you like—moves their lips, still, these opinions should be voiced. It is not possible for a word to be uttered for no reason, and the spark of truth may fall anywhere. Someone who has taken it upon himself to show life's comic aspects to others must take it in good part when his own feeble and comic side is pointed out to him. I shall try and stay here in the lobby the whole time the theater is emptying. It is impossible that the new play won't be discussed; a man becomes animated when overcome by a first impression and he hastens to share it with others.

(Steps aside.)

---

* *It is self-evident that the author of the play is an idealized figure; he represents the situation of the humorist in society—a humorist who finds his subject in ridiculing the abuses that occur in different levels of society and branches of officialdom.*

64 Leaving the Theater After the Presentation of a New Comedy

Several well-dressed people appear.

ONE *(turning to another, says)*: It's best to leave now. Some trivial sketch is about to start. *(Both exeunt.)*

Two thick-set, impeccably attired men come down the stairs.

FIRST IMPECCABLY-TURNED-OUT MAN: It will be a good thing if the police haven't moved my carriage away. Do you know the name of that young actress?

SECOND IMPECCABLY-TURNED-OUT MAN: No, but she's not at all bad looking.

FIRST MAN: No, not bad at all, but she still lacks a little something. Now, let me recommend a new restaurant to you. Yesterday they served us fresh green peas *(kisses the tips of his fingers)* exquisite! *(Both exeunt.)*

An officer runs in while another tries to restrain him by the arm.

FIRST OFFICER: Come on, let's stay.

SECOND OFFICER: No, my friend, wild horses couldn't drag me to a vaudeville sketch. We all know what these plays put on as curtain-raisers are like—instead of actors you get lackeys, and the women—what a collection of frights. *(Exeunt.)*

FASHIONABLY-DRESSED SOCIETY MAN *(going downstairs)*: That rogue of a tailor made my trousers too tight, I was terrified of sitting awkwardly the entire time. Just for that I shall keep him dangling and will put off paying my debts for another couple of years. *(Exit.)*

A SECOND, MORE HEAVILY-BUILT SOCIETY MAN *(speaking to a third, with animation)*: I assure you, he will never, ever sit down to cards with you. He never plays for less than 150 rubles a rubber. I know all about it because Pafnutiev, my brother-in-law, plays cards with him every day.

AUTHOR OF THE PLAY *(to himself)*: And no one has said one word about the comedy so far!

MIDDLE-AGED CIVIL SERVANT *(walking out with outspread hands)*: Well, really, heaven only knows what that was!... It's a!... It's a!... It's like nothing on earth! *(Exit.)*

GENTLEMAN NOT OVERLY CONCERNED WITH LITERATURE *(turning to another)*: Anyway, I suppose it's a translation?

SECOND: I ask you, how can it be a translation! The action takes place in Russia, it makes reference to our customs and even to our ranks and titles.

GENTLEMAN NOT OVERLY CONCERNED WITH LITERATURE:

Yes, but I seem to remember something of the sort in French, though not quite like this. *(Both exeunt.)*

ONE OF TWO SPECTATORS *(also leaving)*: You can't tell anything just yet. Wait and see what the papers say, then you'll know.

TWO WINTER OVERCOATS *(one to the other)*: Well, what do you think? I should like to hear your opinion of the comedy.

SECOND OVERCOAT *(making significant movements with his lips)*: Well, yes, of course, one can't deny that there was any... in its way... Well, of course, if you are against this, so that there shouldn't be any more, and... where this is, so to say... while, moreover... *(Pressing his lips together in confirmation.)* Yes, yes! *(Exeunt.)*

AUTHOR *(to himself)*: Well, so far these people haven't said much. However, there will be talk; I see people ahead gesticulating furiously.

Two officers enter.

FIRST: I have never laughed so much in my life.

SECOND: I think it's an excellent comedy.

FIRST: Well, no, let's wait and see what the newspapers say, one must bow to the view of the critic... Look, look! *(Nudges him.)*

SECOND: What?

FIRST *(pointing at one of two men coming down the stairs)*: There's a literary man!

SECOND *(hastily)*: Which one?

FIRST: That one there. Shh! Let's listen to what they say.

SECOND: And who is the other man with him?

FIRST: I don't know; some nobody or other. *(Both officers step aside and make way for them.)*

UNCERTAIN SOMEONE: I am no judge of literary merit, but it seems to me to make some witty comments. Pointed, very pointed.

LITERARY MAN: I ask you, what was witty about it? What of the low class of people portrayed, what of the tone? The jokes were the feeblest imaginable; it was unvarnished, even crude!

UNCERTAIN SOMEONE: Ah, that's another matter. As I was saying, I am no judge of literary quality. I only remarked that the play was funny and I enjoyed it.

LITERARY MAN: But, it's not even funny. I ask you, what was so funny about it, where was the enjoyment? It has a totally improbable subject. It's a string of absurdities, there is no plot, no action and no argument of any kind.

UNCERTAIN SOMEONE: Well now, I am not denying that. In a literary sense that is so, in a literary sense it isn't even funny; but in one sense, so to speak, from one aspect there is...

LITERARY MAN: What is there? Come now, there isn't even that! And what about the colloquial language? Who talks like that in high society? Well, tell me then, well, do you and I talk like that?

UNCERTAIN SOMEONE: That's true. You have made a very telling point there. Indeed, that is just what I thought myself: there is no distinction in the dialogue. It's as though none of the characters can conceal his coarser nature—that's true.

LITERARY MAN: Well, and are you still singing its praises?

UNCERTAIN SOMEONE: Who is singing its praises? Not me. I see now that the play is rubbish. But, you know, you can't always grasp that right away. I am no judge of literary matters.

Both exeunt.

ANOTHER LITERARY MAN *(enters accompanied by an audience whom he is addressing, while gesticulating)*: Believe me, I know what I'm talking about. It's a dreadful play. Disgusting, an absolutely disgusting play! There isn't one authentic character, they're all caricatures! You won't find anything like it in real life, believe me. No, I know more about this than anyone: I am a literary man myself. There's talk about vitality and observation... but that's all nonsense, it's his friends and connections that are responsible, they are the ones who rave on about him, it's all because of his friends! I've already heard that they are practically making him out to be a Fonvizin, but the play can't even be dignified by the name of comedy. It's a farce, nothing but a farce, and a complete flop at that. The latest mindless little skit by Kotzebue is, in comparison, like Mont Blanc beside Pulkovo Hill. I shall prove it to them all, prove it mathematically like twice times two. It's simply that his pals and cronies have acclaimed him beyond all measure and by now he must be convinced he is a second Shakespeare. In our country you can always count on your friends for plaudits. Look at Pushkin, for example. Why is the whole of Russia talking about him? It's all because of his connections. They ranted and raved on about him until al of Russia followed suit and joined in the chorus. *(Exit, accompanied by audience.)*

The two officers move forward and resume their places.

FIRST: That's right, that's absolutely right. It really is a farce, as I remarked earlier: it's a stupid farce, promoted by his friends. I must say, much of it was positively repugnant to watch.

SECOND: But I thought you said that you had never ever laughed so much.

FIRST: But that's something else entirely. You don't understand, I shall have to explain it to you. What does this play have to offer? First of all, there is no plot, neither is there any action, there is a total absence of any argument, it's full of absurdities and then again, all the characters are caricatures.

Two other officers appear behind.

FIRST *(to the other)*: Who is that holding forth? He's from your regiment, isn't he?

The other looks sideways at the face of the speaker, then waves his hand.

What, he's a fool?
SECOND: No, not exactly... He has a mind, as soon as the journal appears, that is, but if it is held up at the printer, then his mind is a blank. Come on, let's go. *(Exeunt.)*

Two lovers of art.

FIRST: I am not one of those who rely on words like filthy, disgusting, in bad taste and the like. It is pretty much accepted that these words are mostly employed by those who come from a very dubious background themselves and who pontificate about the drawing room, while they are never admitted any further than the anteroom. That is not the issue here. I merely wish to make the point that the play has no plot.
SECOND: Well, yes, if by plot you understand what it is usually taken to mean, that is, a love story, then, you are correct, there isn't one. But surely, the time has come to stop relying on that everlasting plot. It is worthwhile taking a good look around. Everything has long since changed in the world. The urge to find a good job, to outshine the next fellow at any cost, and to pay back any neglect and ridicule that has been suffered nowadays is the stuff for a good drama. Isn't there more electricity generated nowadays by rank, financial gain and an advantageous marriage than by love?
FIRST: That's all very well, but all the same I don't see any plot in the play in that sense either.
SECOND: I am not going to argue right now about whether the play has a plot or not. I shall only remark that people on the whole look for a personal theme and don't wish to see a general one. People in their simpleminded way have grown accustomed to those eternal lovers and the play can't come to an end unless they get married. Certainly that's a plot, but what kind? It's like a neat little knot in the corner of a handkerchief. No, comedy must gather all the

threads together in a dense, interwoven mass to form a single big, comprehensive knot. The plot must embroil all the characters and not just one or two, it must touch on something that affects all the participants to some degree. Here everyone is a hero: the flow and direction of the play transmit a tremor that is felt throughout the entire vehicle; not one wheel can be left out as rusty and not pulling its weight.

FIRST: But they can't all be heroes; one or two must drive the others?

SECOND: Not drive them, though perhaps dominate them. Even in a carriage some wheels move more noticeably and vigorously than others—they can be called the chief ones; but it is the concept, the idea that drives a play. Without that it can have no unity. And anything can work to pull it together: real terror, the fear of impending events, the threat of the law hovering in the distance...

FIRST: But the result of all this is to give comedy a more universal meaning.

SECOND: Well, isn't that its true, primary meaning? Comedy was originally created from social and national elements. At least, that is the form its father, Aristophanes, gave it. Afterwards it fell into the narrow crack of individual concerns and introduced the course of true love as the one and only inevitable plot. And yet, how shallow is this device even in the work of the best writers of comedy! How trite are these theatrical lovers with their cardboard love!

THIRD (*approaching and tapping him on the shoulder*): You are wrong. Love, just like other feelings, may also have a place in comedy.

SECOND: I am not saying that it doesn't have a place. But love and, similarly, all the other, higher emotions only produce a lofty effect when they are treated in depth. If they are dealt with, then everything else must necessarily be sacrificed to them. Everything that properly makes up the comedic element will pale and, inevitably, the social significance of comedy will disappear.

THIRD: It follows, then, that comedy has no choice but to deal with low subjects? Comedy turns out to be a low form of entertainment?

SECOND: That is indeed the case if one looks at the words without paying heed to their meaning. But may not the positive and negative serve the same end? May not comedy and tragedy express the same lofty idea? Is it not the case that every slight turn and twist in the soul of a dishonest rascal draws the picture of an honest man? Is it not the case that this entire catalog of shame and blots on law and justice clarify exactly what is demanded of us by law, duty and justice? In the hands of a skillful physician both cold and hot water can cure the same illness with equal success. In talented hands, anything can serve as an instrument of the beautiful, if it is guided by the exalted thought of serving the beautiful.

FOURTH (*approaching*): What can serve the beautiful? What are you discussing?

FIRST: We got into an argument about comedy. We have been talking about comedy in general and so far nobody has said anything about the new comedy. Do you have anything to say?

FOURTH: I should like to say this. There is obvious talent, observation of life, and much that is funny and true to life; but taken as a whole, there is something lacking in the play. Somehow you get neither an exposition nor a conclusion. It is odd that our writers of comedy can't get along without the government. If it weren't for the government, not a single Russian comedy would be resolved.

THIRD: That's true. But, on the other hand, it is very natural. We all belong to the government, we are almost all in some form of government service; the interests of all of us are more or less bound up with those of the government. So it is hardly to be wondered at if that is reflected in the works of our writers.

FOURTH: True. Well then, let this connection be felt. But the amusing thing is that a play cannot come to an end without the government. It steps in without fail, as inevitable as doom in the tragedies of the ancients.

SECOND: You see, it's quite involuntary on the part of our humorists. It even gives a distinctive quality to our comedy. A kind of secret faith in the government is locked in our breasts. What of it? There's nothing wrong with that: God grant that the government always and everywhere perceive its calling to be the representative of Providence on earth and that we believe in it as the ancients believed in the doom that overtook transgressions.

FIFTH: Greetings, gentlemen! I keep hearing the word "government." The comedy has roused shouting and discussion.

SECOND: It would be better to talk about all the shouting and discussions at my house rather than in the theater lobby. *(Exeunt.)*

Several distinguished and well-dressed people appear, one after another.

NUMBER 1: Yes, yes, I see; it's true that such things go on here and in some places it's even worse. But what is the point? What is it all leading to—that's the question. What are these performances for? What good are they? Tell me that! Why do I need to know that there are rogues in such-and-such a place? I simply... I don't understand the need to put on this sort of thing. *(Exit.)*

NUMBER 2: No, what they are doing here is not making fun of wrongdoing; this is an obscene gibe at Russia itself—that's what it is. It means that the government itself is put in a bad light, because if you expose corrupt officials and abuses that exist in certain areas, it means you are exposing the government itself. Quite simply, performances like this should not even be allowed. *(Exit.)*

70 *Leaving the Theater After the Presentation of a New Comedy*

Enter Mr. A. and Mr. B., men of humble rank.

MR. A.: That's not the point I'm trying to make: on the contrary, we need to be confronted by abuses; we need to see our faults and I don't in the least share the opinions of many overheated patriots; only I feel, is there not perhaps something a little too sad about it...

MR. B.: I wish you would have heard the comment of one very modestly dressed man who was sitting near me in the stalls... Ah, there he is!

MR. A.: Who?

MR. B.: This very modestly dressed man here. *(Turns to him.)* We didn't finish our conversation that started in such an interesting way.

VERY MODESTLY DRESSED MAN: I must admit I, too, am very glad to continue it. Only a minute ago I heard people saying that it's all untrue, that the government and our customs are being held up to ridicule and that such performances should be banned. This led me to recall and ponder the entire play in my mind, and I confess that it now seems to me to be even more significant as an expression of comedy. As I see it, what laughter strikes at more forcefully and incisively than anything else is hypocrisy—the mask of respectability that covers up meanness and trickery, the swindler who puts on a virtuous face. I admit I was overjoyed at seeing how comical fine words are on the lips of a scoundrel and how the entire audience from the stalls to the gallery was convulsed by laughter at the false front he assumed. And then there are some people who say that this sort of thing shouldn't be staged! I heard one remark made by someone who looked quite a decent sort: "What will the common people say when they see abuses like that going on among us?"

MR. A.: You must excuse me, but, I confess, the same question occurred to me involuntarily: what will the common people say when they see all this?

VERY MODESTLY DRESSED MAN: What will the common people say? *(Moves aside.)*

Two men in peasant coats walk by.

BLUE COAT *(to a gray one)*: Heaven knows, the brass were slippery customers, but they all turned pale when the Tsar's reckoning came!

They both walk away.

VERY MODESTLY DRESSED MAN: Did you hear that? That's what the people will say.

MR. A: What?

Leaving the Theater After the Presentation of a New Comedy

VERY MODESTLY DRESSED MAN: They will say: "Heaven knows, the brass were slippery customers, but they all turned pale when the Tsar's reckoning came!" Do you sense how truthful a man's natural instinct and feeling are? How keen is the simplest eye if it has not been clouded by theories and ideas extracted from books, but if these are drawn instead from man's own nature! Surely, it is patently obvious that after a performance like this the people will develop an even greater faith in the government? Yes, they need performances like this. Let them make the distinction between the government and its corrupt exponents. Let them see that abuses stem not from the government but from those who have no understanding of what government demands and who refuse to face up to their responsibilities to the government. Let them see that the government is noble, that its unsleeping eye watches equally over everyone, that sooner or later it will catch up with those who betray law, honor and the sacred duty of man, and that those men who have a guilty conscience turn pale before it. Yes, they must see these performances; believe me, if they have personally had occasion to experience oppression and injustice, they will leave these performances feeling comforted with a firm belief in an unslumbering higher law. There's another remark I like: "The people will get a bad opinion of their officials." That is, they imagine that the people are seeing their officials here in the theater for the first time; so that if at home some thieving foreman is squeezing them dry, they will never notice, but, if they go to the theater, then they will notice. It is true that they consider our people thicker than a block of wood—so dense that they cannot tell a meat pie from a buckwheat pie. No, I now find it is even advantageous that not a single honest man is shown on stage. Men are smug: show them one good attribute in a multitude of bad ones, and that's enough for them to walk proudly out of the theater. No, it is advantageous that only exceptions and vices are presented and in such a glaring light that no one would choose them for fellow countrymen, and are ashamed even to admit that they may be so.

MR. A.: But surely, people who are exactly like that in every particular don't actually exist in our country.

VERY MODESTLY DRESSED MAN: May I say the following on this subject: I don't know why, but I always feel sad when I hear a question like that. I can talk to you frankly: something in your features predisposes me to frankness. People always ask straightaway: "Surely people like that don't really exist?" But has anyone ever asked himself: "Am I myself completely free of all these taints?" Never, never! But there is this to consider—I shall speak to you without holding back. I have a good heart and there is a lot of love in my heart, but if you knew the spiritual struggles and upheavals it has cost me so as not to fall into the many vicious proclivities which, willy-nilly, assail one when living in the world! And how can I assert that I don't at this very minute harbor these self-same tendencies that we were laughing at ten minutes ago and which I laughed at too.

MR. A.: *(after some silence):* I confess, your words give one pause for thought. And when I remember, when I think how proud our European education has made us, how it has, for the most part, hidden us from ourselves, how we have looked down with condescension and scorn on those who do not boast an external polish like our own, how every one of us practically makes himself out to be a saint and speaks about evil constantly in the third person—then, I admit, one can't help becoming sad at heart. But, forgive my forwardness—you, by the way, are guilty of the same error—allow me to know with whom I have the pleasure of conversing?

VERY MODESTLY DRESSED MAN: I am no more nor less than one of those officials from whose ranks the comic characters were derived, and I only arrived from my small town the day before yesterday.

MR. B.: I would never have thought it. Won't you find it offensive, after this, to live and work among such people?

VERY MODESTLY DRESSED MAN: Offensive? This is how I will reply to that: I admit that I have often lost my patience. Not all the officials in our little town display integrity and getting something worthwhile done is often as difficult as scaling a wall. On more than one occasion I have thought of leaving the civil service; but now, precisely because of this performance, I feel refreshed, ready to return to my post with renewed vigor. I now take consolation in the thought that wrongdoing will not remain hidden or condoned in our country, but will be lampooned in the full view of good people, that there is a pen out there that will not shun exposing our discreditable actions and that, even though it may not flatter our national pride, a noble government will permit all concerned to witness this—this alone gives me the zeal to continue my useful service.

MR. A.: Let me make you an offer. I hold a fairly responsible government position. I need staff who are high-principled and honest. I can offer you a position where you will have a wide scope of duties, one that will be very much to your advantage and where you will be noticed.

VERY MODESTLY DRESSED MAN: Allow me to thank you for your offer with all my heart and soul and at the same time to decline it. If I feel that I am useful where I am, is it admirable of me to give it up? And how can I leave, if I cannot be entirely certain that I shall not be succeeded by some young hopeful who will not hesitate to accept bribes? If you made me this offer as a reward, let me add that I applauded the author of this play along with everyone else, but I didn't call for him to take a bow. What should be his reward? The play was well received—so it should be given its due, but as for him, he was doing no more nor less than his duty. Truly, we have now reached a point in this country that a person considers himself to be a philanthropist and becomes irate if he

Leaving the Theater After the Presentation of a New Comedy

isn't noticed and rewarded, not because he has done something outstanding, but simply because he has not defiled anyone's life or work. "Please," he says, "I have led an honest life, hardly ever made any mischief—so why haven't I been promoted or rewarded?" No, in my opinion, if somebody cannot do the right thing without an incentive, then I do not believe in his nobility: his mouse-like nobility is not worth a kopeck.

MR. A.: At least do not deny me your acquaintance. Forgive me my persistence; you see for yourself that it is a consequence of my sincere regard. Give me your address.

VERY MODESTLY DRESSED MAN: Here is my address; but you can be sure that I shall not allow you to avail yourself of it and I shall come and call on you tomorrow morning. Excuse me, I was not raised in the fashionable world and am not adept at speaking... But to meet with such generous attention in a government official, such aspiration towards good... God grant that every ruler be surrounded by such people! *(Exit hurriedly.)*

MR. A. *(turning the card over in his hand)*: I look at this card and at this name I don't know and somehow my heart is overflowing. My first melancholy impression has dispersed on its own. May God preserve you, our Russia, whom we know so little! In the wilds, in a forgotten corner of you there is hidden a pearl like this, and in all likelihood, he is not alone. These people are scattered among its coarse, dark granites like gleaming sparks of golden ore. Seeing him brings deep solace and my soul is as radiant after a meeting with this official as his was after the performance of the comedy. Good-bye! Thank you for arranging this meeting for me. *(Exit.)*

MR. C. *(approaching Mr. B.)*: Who was that with you? He's a state minister, if I'm not mistaken?...

MR. P.: *(approaching from the other side)*: I ask you, my friend, what is all this, how can they do this?...

MR. B.: What?

MR. P.: Well, put on something like this?

MR. B.: Why not?

MR. P.: Well now, just think, well really, how can they? It's just one form of vice after another. Well, what kind of a model does that offer the spectators?

MR. B.: Well, are these vices being praised? Surely, they are being showered with ridicule.

MR. P.: Well, yes, but all the same, whatever you say: respect... You know, it's this sort of thing that destroys any respect for officials and their duties.

MR. B.: Respect is not destroyed either for officials or their duties, but, rather more to the point, for those individuals who perform their duties atrociously.

MR. C.: Allow me to remark, however, that this is, to some degree, an insult that casts its shadow over almost everyone.

MR. P.: Exactly. That's what I wanted to say myself. It is an insult that casts its shadow. Today, for example, they are taking aim at a titular councillor, next it will even be... uh... an actual state councillor.

MR. B.: Well, what of it? Only individuals must be inviolate; but if I were to invent a character and endow him with various blemishes such as occur among us and I gave him any rank I chose, even that of a state councillor, and I said that this state councillor was not all he should be: well, what of it? Does it not happen that an ass crops up even among state councillors?

MR. P.: No, my friend, that's too much. How can a state councillor be an ass? Well, maybe a titular councillor... No, you're going too far.

MR. C.: Why make a show of what is bad, why not show something that is good and worthy of emulation?

MR. B.: Why? That's a strange question: "Why?" You can ask a lot of these "why's." Why is it that one father, wishing to snatch his son from a disorderly life, did not waste words and sermons but took him to a hospital where he was confronted by all the hideous consequences of a dissolute life? Why did he do that?

MR. C.: But may I say that these are, to some extent, our social wounds that should be hidden and not exposed.

MR. P.: That is true. I am in complete agreement. We should hide the bad things and not expose them.

MR. B.: If these words had been spoken by anyone but you, I would have said that they sprang from hypocrisy and not true love of our native land. According to you, all that is needed is to close these social wounds, as you call them, and somehow patch them up on the surface, so they can't be seen for the time being; meanwhile, let the disease rage inside—that is not what is needed. What is not needed is to have it break out exhibiting symptoms in such an advanced state that it is too late for any cure. That's not what is needed. You choose to ignore the fact that without heartfelt confession, the Christian acknowledgment of our sins, examined truthfully and without exaggeration, we cannot rise above them and let our soul fly over the shameful aspects of life. You prefer not to know that. Let a man remain deaf, let him sleep away his life, neither shuddering nor weeping in his innermost heart, let his soul be so stupefied that nothing makes it tremble! No... forgive me. It is a cold egotism moving the lips that pronounces these speeches, not a pure and holy love of humanity. *(Exit.)*

MR. P. *(after some silence)*: Why are you silent? What did you think of him? Wasn't he full of himself, huh?

Mr. C. *remains silent.*

(Continues.) He can say anything he likes but all the same these are our wounds, so to speak.

MR. C. *(aside)*: These wounds have really taken his fancy! He will harp on about them to everyone he meets!

MR. P.: Let's face it, I could carry on like that, too, but what's the point?... Ah, there's Prince N. Listen, Prince, don't go away!

PRINCE N.: Well, what is it?

MR. P: Stop and let's have a talk! Well, what did you think of the play?

PRINCE N.: It was funny.

MR. P.: But tell me, then, how can they put on something like this? What are things coming to?...

PRINCE N: Why shouldn't it be put on?

MR. P.: Well now, just think, well, how can you have this sort of thing: right away there's this rogue on stage—well, these are our wounds.

PRINCE N.: What wounds?

MR. P.: Yes, these are our wounds, so to speak, our social wounds.

PRINCE N. *(with irritation)*: You can have them! They may be your wounds, but they aren't mine! Why are you trying to foist them off on me? It's time for me to go home. *(Exit.)*

MR. P *(continuing)*: And then, again, what rot he was spouting just now! He says a state councillor can be an ass. Well all right, a titular councillor, perhaps, that could happen...

MR. C.: However, let's go, we have said enough; I think all the passersby already know that you are a state councillor. *(Aside.)* There are people who have the knack of trivializing everything. They only have to repeat your own thought for it to sound so pointless that you blush. You say something stupid that might otherwise slip by unnoticed—but no, along comes a friend and admirer who puts it into circulation and makes it even more fatuous than it already is. It's really and truly exasperating, like being dumped in the mud.

Exeunt. A military man and a civilian come out together.

CIVILIAN: You military men are all alike! You say, "This should be on the stage" and you're ready to laugh your heads off over some civilian bureaucrat; but if the military is touched on in any way, and without even mentioning depraved tendencies, if there is even a suggestion that there are officers in such-and-such a regiment who have vulgar taste and offensive manners—that's enough for you to run to the Imperial Cabinet to lodge a complaint.

MILITARY MAN: Listen now, what do you take me for? Of course, there are Don Quixotes like that among us; but believe me, there are also many truly discriminating people who will always take pleasure in seeing someone who is a disgrace to his profession made a fool of in public. Where is the insult in that? Go on, bring it on! We are ready for it any day.

CIVILIAN *(aside)*: People always say: "Go on, bring it on!" but when you do, they get angry.

Exeunt. Two winter overcoats.

FIRST OVERCOAT: The French do it too, for example, and they carry it off in the most delightful way. Well, do you remember that vaudeville sketch yesterday: he gets undressed, lies down in bed, then takes a salad bowl from the table and puts it under the bed. Of course, it's indelicate, but delightful. You can watch it without taking offense. My wife and children go to the theater all the time. And here, well really, what do you get? A scoundrel, a peasant, whom I wouldn't let into the house, sprawling around in boots, yawning or picking his teeth—well, really what is all this? What on earth do they think they are doing?

SECOND OVERCOAT: The French do things differently. There they have *société, mon cher.* Here it is out of the question. After all, our writers are virtually uneducated: most of them were trained in seminaries. A writer is nothing but riffraff, really, with a weakness for the bottle. There was one once who used to pay visits to my footman: wherever would he get any notion of decent society from?

(Exeunt.)

SOCIETY LADY *(accompanied by two men, one in a frock coat, the other in a uniform)*: Really, the types of people, the characters portrayed! If only there were one attractive person... Well, why don't we have writers like the French, Dumas, for example, and the others? I am not asking for paragons of virtue; show me a woman who goes astray, who may deceive her husband even, and surrender to the most sinful and illicit love; but present it so that it is beguiling, so that I feel sympathy for her and come to love her... But as for all these characters here—each is more nauseating than the last.

MAN IN UNIFORM: Yes, it's trivial, quite trivial.

SOCIETY LADY: Tell me, why is everything here in Russia still always so trivial?

MAN IN FROCK COAT: My sweet, I'll explain later why it's trivial: they are calling for our carriage.

Exeunt. Three men come in together.

Leaving the Theater After the Presentation of a New Comedy

FIRST: Why shouldn't you laugh? Well, you can laugh, but what kind of target of ridicule is that—abuses and immorality? What is so funny about that?

SECOND: So, what should you laugh at then? Surely not at virtues and people's good qualities.

FIRST: No, but this is not a fit subject for a comedy, my dear man. After all, in a way it affects the government. As though there were no other topics to write about.

SECOND: What other topics are there?

FIRST: Well, is there any shortage of funny happenings in daily life? Well, let's say, for example, I set out for a drive to Apothecary Island and my coachman suddenly takes me to Vyborg Street or the Smolny Convent. Is there any shortage of funny incidents?

SECOND: So, you want to strip comedy of any serious meaning. But why lay down a hard and fast law? There are already plenty of comedies in exactly the vein that appeals to you. Why not allow the existence of two or three such as the one performed here just now? If you like the sort of thing you were speaking of, just go to the theater and on any given day you will see a play in which one person hides under a chair while another drags him out by the legs.

THIRD: Well, no, listen, that is not what I'm trying to say. Everything has its limits. There are some things which should not be laughed at, you know, that should be considered sacred.

SECOND *(to himself, with bitter amusement)*: That's always the way of the world: if you laugh at something genuinely noble, at what constitutes the soul's precious treasure, nobody will step in to defend it; if you laugh at what is corrupt, deceitful and vile, everyone shouts: "He is making fun of what is sacred."

FIRST: There you are, you see, you have now been convinced, I see: not another word. Believe me, you can't help being convinced: that's the simple truth. I myself am devoid of prejudice and I am not saying it because... but this is simply not an author's prerogative, this is not a fit subject for comedy. *(Exit.)*

SECOND *(to himself)*: I admit I shouldn't wish to be in the author's shoes for anything. You are supposed to please! If you take humdrum, everyday incidents, people say: "He's writing drivel that lacks any deep moral purpose"; but if you pick a subject that has the slightest bearing on any serious moral issue, they say: "That's not his business, let him write trifles." *(Exit.)*

A young lady from the fashionable world enters, accompanied by her husband.

HUSBAND: Our carriage cannot be far away, we can go soon.

MR. N. *(approaching the lady)*: What do I see! You came to see a Russian play!

YOUNG LADY: What of it? Don't I have any patriotic feelings?

MR. N.: Well, if that's the case, you didn't find much food for your patriotism. No doubt you find fault with the play?

YOUNG LADY: Not at all. I find that there is a good deal of truth in it—I laughed heartily.

MR. N.: Why did you laugh? Because you enjoy laughing at anything Russian?

YOUNG LADY: Simply because it was amusing. Because it exposed mean and vicious behavior which, however it is decked out, and even if it were not in a provincial town but here around us, would still be just as mean and vicious—that is why I laughed.

MR. N.: A minute ago a very clever lady told me that she laughed too, but that, all the same, the play left her feeling melancholy.

YOUNG LADY: I am not interested in what your clever lady felt; my nerves are not as sensitive and I am always ready to laugh at something intrinsically funny. I know that certain people among us are ready to laugh at a person's crooked nose, but lack the spirit to laugh at his crooked soul.

In the distance another young lady appears with her husband.

MR. N.: Now, here comes your friend. I should like to know her opinion of the comedy.

Both ladies shake hands.

FIRST LADY: I watched you laughing from a distance.
SECOND LADY: Well, who didn't laugh? Everyone was laughing.
MR. N.: And you didn't feel any trace of sadness?
SECOND LADY: I confess, I did indeed feel sad. I know that it is all true to life; I myself have witnessed many things like this, but all the same I felt heavy hearted.
MR. N: So, you didn't like the comedy then?
SECOND LADY: Now, listen. Who said that? I already told you that I laughed with all my heart, perhaps even more than anyone else; I think they took me for a madwoman... But I was sad because I wanted to find respite in at least one good character. There was more than enough sordidness, too much even...
MR. N.: Do go on!
SECOND LADY: Listen, advise the author to introduce at least one honest person. Tell him that people are clamoring for this, that it is right and proper.
HUSBAND OF THE FIRST LADY: And that is exactly what you must

advise him against doing. The ladies are determined to have a knight whose every word would affirm his noble sentiments even in the most shopworn platitudes.

SECOND LADY: Not at all! How little you know us! It's you who have the monopoly in such matters. You are the ones who are fond of fine words and speeches about nobility, just as long as it stops there. I heard your group's opinion: a fat man was screaming so loudly, attracting everyone's attention, that it was slander and that no one in this country would ever stoop to such miserable, shabby tricks. And who was saying this? The shabbiest and most miserable of wretches who wouldn't hesitate to sell his soul, his conscience and anything else you might want. Only I am reluctant to name him.

MR. N.: Well, tell us, who was it?

SECOND LADY: Why do you need to know? And he is not the only one; I kept hearing them calling out on all sides: "This is an obscene gibe at Russia, a gibe at the government! How can it be allowed? What will the people say?" And why were they making this fuss? Because this is what they really thought and felt? I think not! They did it to create a commotion and have the play banned, because they recognized perhaps something of themselves in it. There are your real-life knights for you, not the theatrical ones.

HUSBAND OF THE FIRST LADY: Oh, a little vexation is starting to flare up in you.

SECOND LADY: Vexation, yes, indeed. I am vexed, really extremely vexed. How can one escape vexation when one sees deceit masquerading behind all kinds of false fronts?

HUSBAND OF THE FIRST LADY: Well then, you would like a knight to jump out right now, leap across a precipice, breaking his neck in the process...

SECOND LADY: Not at all.

HUSBAND OF THE FIRST LADY: Naturally, what do women need? They have a burning desire for life to be like a novel.

SECOND LADY: No, no, no! I am ready to say no two hundred times. That's a threadbare, old idea that you perpetually try to foist on us. Women have more true generosity than men. Women are not capable of, simply cannot bring themselves to do, all the wicked and degrading things that you do. Women cannot play the hypocrite as you do, and turn a blind eye to the disreputable dealings that you manage to overlook. They are upright enough to speak out on all these matters without looking sideways to see whether their words find favor or not, for the simple reason that they need to be said. What is wrong is wrong, however you try to cover it up or make it look. It is wrong, wrong, wrong!

HUSBAND OF THE FIRST LADY: I see you are out of temper with all sorts of things.

SECOND LADY: Because I am candid and cannot stand listening to lies.

HUSBAND OF THE FIRST LADY: Well, don't be angry, give me your hand! I was joking.

SECOND LADY: Here's my hand, I am not angry. *(Turning to N.)* Listen, advise the author to introduce a noble, honest person into the comedy.

MR. N.: But how can he do that? What if he brings in an honest man and this honest man turns into a theatrical knight?

SECOND LADY: No, if he feels strongly and deeply, then his hero will not be a theatrical knight.

MR. N.: Yes, but I don't think it's quite as easy as that.

SECOND LADY: Simply say, rather, that your author doesn't experience deep, strong feelings.

MR. N.: How so?

SECOND LADY: Well, someone who laughs constantly and continuously cannot experience too many of the higher emotions; he cannot be privy to what only a tender heart can feel.

MR. N.: A fine thing! According to you, then, the author cannot possibly be a noble person.

SECOND LADY: Look, you are now misinterpreting me in another way. I never said a word about the humorist lacking nobility or a strict conception of honor in the full sense of the word. I merely said that he could not... drop a heartfelt tear nor love anything ardently from the bottom of his heart.

HUSBAND OF THE SECOND LADY: But how can you make such a definite statement?

SECOND LADY: I can do so because I know. The scoffers and jesters of this world are all given to self-satisfaction and almost all of them are egotists; high-minded egotists, of course, but egotists all the same.

MR. N.: Then you have a definite preference for those works in which only the higher human emotions are engaged?

SECOND LADY: Of course! I would always rate them more highly, and, I admit, I place a greater spiritual trust in that kind of author.

HUSBAND OF THE FIRST LADY *(turning to Mr. N.)*: Well, don't you see, it turns out to be the same thing in the end. That is women's taste. For them the most lackluster tragedy is valued more highly than the finest comedy, by the mere fact of it being a tragedy...

SECOND LADY: Be quiet, I am losing my temper again. *(Turning to N.)* Well, tell me, did I not speak the truth: a humorist must have a cold heart?

HUSBAND OF THE SECOND LADY: Or a fiery one, because an irritable temperament also gives rise to mockery and satire.

SECOND LADY: Well, or an irritable one. But what does that mean? It means that the source of all these works is bile, bitterness, discontent, perhaps

Leaving the Theater After the Presentation of a New Comedy 81

justified in all cases. But there is no evidence that they were born of an intense love of humanity... in a word, of love. Isn't that so?

MR. N.: That's true.

SECOND LADY: Tell me, does the author resemble this portrait?

MR. N.: What can I say? I don't know him so intimately that I can pass judgment on his soul. But taking into consideration everything that I have heard about him, he must indeed be either an egotist or a very irritable man.

SECOND LADY: There, you see, I knew it.

FIRST LADY: I don't know why, but I shouldn't like him to be an egotist.

HUSBAND OF THE FIRST LADY: Ah, there's our footman, our carriage must be ready. Good-bye. *(Shaking the hand of the second lady.)* You are coming over to our house for tea, aren't you?

FIRST LADY *(leaving)*: Please do!

SECOND LADY: Of course.

HUSBAND OF THE SECOND LADY: Our carriage seems to be ready, too.

They go out after them. Two spectators come out.

FIRST: Explain something to me: why is it that, when you take every action, personage and character separately, they all look authentic, lively and true-to-life, but put them together and they somehow seem overblown, exaggerated caricatures, so that when you come out of the theater you can't help asking whether people like that actually exist? Yet at the same time, they are not exactly evil.

SECOND: No, not at all evil. As the saying goes, "He's not an evil sort, simply a thief, in short."

FIRST: And there's another thing: this massive accumulation, this excess—isn't that a failing in comedy? Tell me, where is the society that consists entirely of such people without having, if not half, at least some decent people? If comedy is to be the picture and mirror of our social life, then it must reflect it accurately.

SECOND: First, in my opinion, this comedy is not a picture but more of a frontispiece. You see, neither the setting nor the location are ideal. Otherwise the author would not have made obvious mistakes and anachronisms, and put speeches into the mouths of characters for whom they are inappropriate by virtue of their nature and position in society. Only an initial rancor led to something that was not even the shadow of an individual personality being taken for one, while it is, by and large, part of the personality of all people. This place is a watershed. To it flow from all parts, from all the different regions of Russia, misrepresentations of the truth, blunders and abuses, in the interests of serving one idea—of producing in the spectator a violent and worthy revulsion from anything tinged with dishonor. The effect is all the more powerful because none of the characters introduced has lost his human form: humanity is everywhere felt. The heart is stricken more painfully as a result. And, laughing, the spectator turns around in spite of himself as though feeling that what he is laughing at is close at hand and must continually be guarded against so that it doesn't creep into his own heart. I most particularly enjoy hearing the charge against the author: "Why are your characters and heroes not attractive," when he has done everything in his power to make them repellent. Yes, if the comedy had had even one honest man, and, what's more, one with all his shining qualities intact, then everyone without exception would have been on his side and forgotten all about the people who had given them such a fright earlier. Then, perhaps, these images would not have come back to haunt them persistently, like living beings, at the end of the performance; then, too, the spectator would not have carried away a melancholy mood and said: "Surely, people like this don't exist?"

FIRST: Yes. But that is not something that will be immediately understood.

SECOND: That is only natural. It always takes time to work out the inner meaning. And the more colorful and vivid the images that are employed to flesh it out and diffuse it, the longer the general attention lingers on those images. Only when they are all assembled do you arrive at a total, complete meaning of the work. But to decipher letters quickly and put them together—to read quickly the surface clues—is not something that everyone can do. And until they manage it, they see only the letters for a long time. And you will see, I am warning you in advance: every provincial town in Russia will immediately become incensed and protest that it is a wicked satire, a tasteless and disgraceful travesty, aimed directly at itself.

Exeunt.

AN OFFICIAL: It's a tasteless and disgraceful travesty, it's satire, it's slander.

SECOND OFFICIAL: What it means is that there is nothing left now. There is no need for laws, there is no need for the civil service. This uniform I am wearing—what it means is that it should be thrown away: it's just a worthless rag.

Two young men run in.

FIRST: Well, everyone got mad. I heard so much talk that, looking round, I can guess what everyone thinks about the play.

SECOND: Well, what is that man thinking?

FIRST: The one putting on his overcoat?
SECOND: Yes.
FIRST: He's thinking: "They should send you to Siberia for a comedy like this!..." However, it looks like the upper rows are on the move; the vaudeville sketch must have finished. The rabble will be pouring out. Let's go.

Exeunt. The noise swells; there is the sound of people running down the staircases. Peasants' coats, sheepskin coats, ladies' bonnets, merchants in long German tunics, three-cornered hats and plumes, all sorts of overcoats—fringed ones, military ones, shabby ones and stylish ones with beaver collars—run past. The crowd jostles a gentleman putting on an overcoat; the gentleman moves to one side and continues putting it on. Gentlemen and officials of all shapes and sizes are seen in the crowd. Liveried footmen clear the way for their masters. Women's shouts are heard: "You there, I'm being pushed and shoved on all sides."

YOUNG CIVIL SERVANT WITH AN EVASIVE DISPOSITION *(approaching the gentleman putting on his overcoat)*: Your Excellency, allow me, I'll hold it for you!
GENTLEMAN IN THE OVERCOAT: Oh, hello! So you're here? You came to see it?
YOUNG CIVIL SERVANT: Yes, Your Excellency, there are some amusing observations.
GENTLEMAN IN OVERCOAT: Rubbish! There's nothing amusing about it!
YOUNG CIVIL SERVANT: That's true, Your Excellency, nothing at all.
GENTLEMAN IN OVERCOAT: He should be flogged for this kind of thing, not praised.
YOUNG CIVIL SERVANT: That's true, Your Excellency.
GENTLEMAN IN OVERCOAT: There they go, letting young people into the theater. Much good will come of that! Take you now, well I expect you'll come to the office and start hurling abuse directly.
YOUNG CIVIL SERVANT: How can that be, Your Excellency!... Allow me, I will clear a path for you! *(To the crowd, pushing people aside.)* Hey, you, get out of the way, a general is coming! *(Approaches two stylishly dressed men with uncommon courtesy.)* Gentlemen, be so kind as to make way for the general!

The well-dressed men move aside and make way.

FIRST: Do you know who that general is? He must be somebody well known?
SECOND: I don't know, I never saw him before.

CIVIL SERVANT WITH A GARRULOUS DISPOSITION *(catching up from behind)*: He's only an administrator on the fourth grade of the civil service scale. How successful is he? After fifteen years in the civil service he's been decorated with the orders of Vladimir, Anna and Stanislav, he has a salary of 3,000 rubles, an expense account of 2,000, and there is more coming in from the Council, the Commission and even the Department.

WELL-DRESSED GENTLEMEN *(to each other)*: Let's go.

Exeunt.

CIVIL SERVANT WITH A GARRULOUS DISPOSITION: They must be mama's boys. They probably work in the diplomatic service. I don't like comedies; tragedies are more to my taste. *(Exit.)*

VOICE FROM THE CROWD: Ugh, what a crush!

OFFICER *(making his way through with a lady on his arm)*: Hey, you with the beard, what are you pushing for? Can't you see there's a lady here?

MERCHANT *(with a lady on his arm)*: Look, sir, I got a lady too.

VOICE FROM THE CROWD: There, she's turned around. Do you see, do you see her? She's not as good looking now, but three years ago...

DIFFERENT VOICES: But listen, he took thirty kopecks change from him. It's a miserable, rotten play! It's an amusing little play. Why are you jumping down my throat?

VOICE AT ONE END OF THE CROWD: It's all rubbish. Where could that sort of thing happen? It could only happen at the back of the beyond.

VOICE AT THE OTHER END: Well now, exactly the very same thing happened in our town. I suspect that if the author wasn't there himself, he must have heard about it.

VOICE OF A MERCHANT: It is, if you care to look at it that way, it is more, so to speak, from the moralistic point of view. Of course, it takes all sorts, as they say, sir. But you know, judge for yourself, there are times when even an honest man has to... And, as for all that moralism, that's something the gentry go in for.

VOICE OF GENTLEMAN OF AN ENCOURAGING DISPOSITION: That rogue of an author, he must be a cunning devil; he's found out everything, he knows everything!

VOICE OF AN ANGRY, BUT OBVIOUSLY EXPERIENCED, CIVIL SERVANT: What does he know? Not a damn thing. And he is lying, lying; everything he wrote, it's all a pack of lies. That's not even the way you take bribes, if you get right down to it...

VOICE OF ANOTHER CIVIL SERVANT FROM THE CROWD: You keep saying: "It's funny, it's funny!" Do you know why it's funny? It's all based

Leaving the Theater After the Presentation of a New Comedy 85

on real people, you know. He's put all his own aunties and grannies into it, you know. That's why it's so funny.

UNKNOWN VOICE: Stop, someone stole my scarf!

Two officers recognize each other and converse across the crowd.

FIRST: Michel, you're going there?
SECOND: Yes.
FIRST: And I'm here.
CIVIL SERVANT WITH AN IMPOSING APPEARANCE: I would ban everything. There's no need to print anything. Make use of your education, read, but don't write. Plenty of books have been written already, there's no need for any more.

VOICE IN THE CROWD: So what, a rogue is a rogue. If you don't act like a rogue, they won't laugh at you.

A HANDSOME, PORTLY GENTLEMAN *(speaking heatedly to a small, unprepossessing individual)*: Moral standards, moral standards, that's the main thing!

SMALL, UNPREPOSSESSING GENTLEMAN WITH A VENOMOUS DISPOSITION: Yes, but you see, moral standards are a relative matter.

HANDSOME, PORTLY GENTLEMAN: What do you mean by the term "relative"?

UNPREPOSSESSING GENTLEMAN WITH VENOMOUS DISPOSITION: I mean that everyone measures moral standards relative to himself. One person considers having a hat raised to him on the street a question of morality; for another morality consists of no one taking any notice of his thieving; another calls it morality when his mistress is shown consideration. After all, how does each of us generally address his subordinates? Looking down on them, he says: "My dear sir, try to do your duty to God, the Monarch and your native land," meanwhile, work it out for yourself, what is that relative to? Anyway, that sort of thing only goes on in the provinces, you won't find it in the capitals, right? So, if someone acquires two houses in three years, what of it? It's all honestly come by, isn't that so?

HANDSOME, PORTLY GENTLEMAN *(aside)*: He's as ugly as the devil and has a tongue like a serpent.

UNPREPOSSESSING GENTLEMAN WITH VENOMOUS DISPOSITION *(touches the arm of a complete stranger next to him and says to him, pointing to the handsome gentleman)*: Four houses in one street; they all sprang up next to each other in six years. That is how honesty affects the faculty of growth, right?

STRANGER *(moving away hastily)*: Sorry, I didn't quite catch that.

UNPREPOSSESSING GENTLEMAN WITH VENOMOUS DISPOSI-

TION *(touches the arm of a nearby stranger)*: There's a lot of deafness around the city nowadays, eh? That's what comes of having a damp, unhealthy climate.

NEARBY STRANGER: Yes, and then there's the flu as well. All my children have come down with it.

UNPREPOSSESSING GENTLEMAN WITH VENOMOUS DISPOSITION: Yes, both flu and deafness, and mumps attacking the throat as well. *(He disappears in the crowd.)*

Conversation in a group to one side.

FIRST: They say that the same sort of thing happened to the author himself; he was put in jail for his debts in some little town.

GENTLEMAN ON THE OTHER SIDE OF THE GROUP *(taking up the conversation)*: No, he wasn't in jail, he was in a tower. People who traveled through there saw him. They say it was the most extraordinary thing. Imagine: a poet in an immensely high tower, with mountains all around in an enchanting setting, and there he was reading his poetry. Don't you think that this reveals a quite exceptional quality in the writer?

GENTLEMAN WITH A POSITIVE DISPOSITION: The author must be a clever man.

GENTLEMAN WITH A NEGATIVE DISPOSITION: He's not clever in the least. I know, he was in the civil service and he very nearly lost his job, because he didn't know how to write a petition.

OUTRIGHT LIAR: He's a shrewd one, all right. For a long time they wouldn't give him a post, so what do you think he did? He upped and wrote a letter to the minister. And, you know, the way it was written. In the style of Quintilius himself. Even the very way he began: "Dear Sir!" And it went on and on and on... he spun it out to a full eight pages. As soon as the minister read it, he says: "Well, I'm much obliged. I see you have many enemies. You should be the head of the department!" And he jumped straight from being a clerk to being the head of the department.

GENTLEMAN WITH A BENEVOLENT DISPOSITION *(turning to a man with a temperate disposition)*: The devil alone knows whom to believe! He was thrown in jail, he climbed a tower! He was dismissed from the civil service, and given a promotion!

GENTLEMAN WITH A TEMPERATE DISPOSITION: Well, you see, all this is said on the spur of the moment.

GENTLEMAN WITH A BENEVOLENT DISPOSITION: What do you mean, on the spur of the moment?

GENTLEMAN WITH A TEMPERATE DISPOSITION: Just that. You see, they themselves don't know two minutes beforehand what they are going to hear themselves say. Their tongues suddenly blurt out an item of news without the owners' foreknowledge, and the owner is happy—he goes home feeling as though he enjoyed a good meal. And the next day he has already forgotten that he made it up himself. He thinks he heard it from someone else and goes around, passing it on to everyone in town.

BENEVOLENT GENTLEMAN: But that is unconscionable—to tell a lie and not even realize it yourself.

TEMPERATE GENTLEMAN: Well, there are sensitive people, too. There are some who realize that they are lying, but consider it necessary for the sake of conversation, as a field is made beautiful by rye, so is speech by a lie.

MIDDLE-CLASS LADY: But what a spiteful, mocking person this author must be! I confess, I shouldn't care to come to his notice for anything. He would immediately find something in me to laugh at.

AUTHORITATIVE GENTLEMAN: I don't know what kind of man he is. He's, he's, he's... Nothing is sacred for a man like that. Today he says a certain senior official is no good and tomorrow he'll say there is no God. You know, it's only one step away.

SECOND GENTLEMAN: To be made a laughing stock! After all, laughter is no joking matter. It means all respect is destroyed—that's what it means. And the end result of all this, I suppose, is that anyone can knock me down in the street and say: "There, you see, you're the one they are poking fun at; your rank is fair game, so take this punch." That's what it means!

THIRD GENTLEMAN: And that's not all. This is a matter of grave concern! They say: "It's a bagatelle, balderdash, a theatrical entertainment." No, what we're dealing with here are not mere bagatelles, they call for strict attention. People have been sent to Siberia for such things. And if I had any say in the matter, you wouldn't hear another squeak out of the author. I would lock him up in a place where he would never lay eyes on the blessed light of day.

A group of people enter, Heaven alone knows what their disposition is, but they appear to be well bred and are decently dressed.

FIRST: Let's stand here for a bit until the crowd disperses. Well, really, what is going on! All that noise and clapping, Heaven alone knows what for! It's a bagatelle, an inane theatrical entertainment, and they make no end of fuss about it, shout, call for the author—well, what is going on!

SECOND: But the play was amusing, it was fun.

FIRST: Yes, it was amusing as that sort of nonsense usually is. But why does it provoke so much shouting and discussion? They are talking about it as though it were something important, they applaud... Well, what's going on here! I could understand it if it were some singer or dancer—that I understand:

there you are amazed by the artistry, the versatility, the agility, the innate talent. But what do you have here? They shout: "Author, author, writer!" But what does it mean to be a writer? Someone who occasionally lets fall a witty remark or copies something from nature... But what sort of labor is that? Is there anything like that here? This is all sheer fantasy—nothing more.

SECOND: Well, of course, it's quite an insignificant piece.

FIRST: Just think for a minute: well, a dancer, for example—there you are talking about artistry, there's no way you are going to do what he does. Well, say I wanted to, for example, I simply couldn't get my legs up there. Well, say I were to attempt an entrechat, I couldn't do it, not for anything. But writing is something you can do without having to learn how. I don't know who this author is, but I've been told that he's a complete ignoramus and doesn't know a thing. Apparently he was drummed out of somewhere or other.

SECOND: But still, he must know something—otherwise he wouldn't be able to write.

FIRST: Come now, I ask you, what does he know? You yourself know what these literary gentleman are like: they're complete nitwits. The whole world knows that—they're no good for anything. They tried once giving them something useful to do but abandoned the attempt. Well, judge for yourself, just what is it that they write? It's all balderdash, fairy tales! If I wanted to, I could rattle one off in a minute, and so could you, and so could he, and so could anyone.

SECOND: Well, of course, why not? All it takes is a drop of wit in one's head.

FIRST: Come now, it doesn't even take any wit. What do you need wit for? These are only fairy tales, you know. It's not as though it were a learned science, let's say, some subject or other that you haven't mastered yet. But after all, what do you have here? It's something every peasant knows, after all. It's something you can see every day on the street. All you need to do is sit down at the window and describe everything that is going on—and there you have the whole thing?

THIRD: That's true. Really, when you think about it, what drivel they waste their time on!

FIRST: That's it exactly, a waste of time—and nothing more. Fairy tales, balderdash! There should be a law against letting pen and ink fall into their hands. However, the common people are coming out, let's go. Making a fuss, shouting, cheering it on! It's all utter rubbish! Fairy tales, balderdash, fairy tales.

Exeunt. The crowd thins out, a few of those left run by.

BENEVOLENT CIVIL SERVANT: It's all very well, but if only there were one honest man on stage! It's just one rogue after another.

ONE OF THE PEOPLE: Wait for me at the crossroad, you hear. I'll run and fetch my gloves.

ONE OF THE GENTRY *(looking at his watch)*: However, it's nearly one o'clock. I've never been so late leaving the theater. *(Exit.)*

RETIRED CIVIL SERVANT: What a waste of time! No, I'll never go to the theater again! *(Exit.)*

The lobby is empty.

AUTHOR OF THE PLAY *(coming forward)*: I heard more than I expected. What a motley assortment of interpretations! Happy is the humorist who is born among a nation where society has not yet fused into a single, immobile mass, where it is not yet coated by a single crust of ancient prejudice, constraining everyone's thoughts into one and the same shape and size, where for each person there's an opinion, where each is himself the architect of his own character. What a diversity of opinions, and how the firm, clear Russian mind shone through everywhere: both in the noble exertions of the statesman and the exalted self-denial of the obscure provincial bureaucrat! In the tender beauty of the generous feminine soul! And the esthetic feeling of the critics! And in the simple, true instinct of the common people! How much there was, even in the unfavorable opinions, that the humorist needs to know! What a vital lesson! Yes, I am satisfied. But why does my heart begin to feel heavy! It's strange. I feel sorry that nobody noticed the honest character in my play. Yes, there was one honest, noble character on stage throughout: This honest, noble character was—*laughter.* It was noble because it ventured to appear despite the low value placed on it in the world. It was noble because it ventured to appear, though it caused the humorist to be vilified as a cold egotist and even cast doubts on his claim to any of the finer feelings. No one stood up to defend this laughter. I am a humorist, I have served it honorably and therefore must be its champion. No, laughter is more important and profound than they think. Not that laughter that is born of a momentary exasperation, a sick and bilious disposition; nor that easy laughter that caters to people's shallow enjoyment and pleasure—but that laughter which surges out of man's sunny nature, which surges out because a spring hidden inside it bubbles eternally at its base, and it so enlarges its object that what would otherwise have slipped past is thrown into sharp relief; without its penetrating power life's triviality and emptiness would not strike such terror into men. The degrading and the mediocre, examples of which he walks past with unruffled composure every day would not swell up before him into such a terrible, almost grotesque force that he cries out with a shudder: "Are there really such people?" even as his own experience tells him that there are even worse people. No, those who claim that laughter is disturbing are unjust. It only disturbs what is murky, but laughter itself is luminous. There is much that men would find disturbing if it were revealed in all its nakedness; but illumined by the power of laughter, the soul finds reconciliation. And someone who is set on vengeance against an evildoer will rather be inclined to make peace with him after seeing the derision aroused by his squalid subterfuges. Those who say that laughter doesn't work on the butt of the joke and that a villain is the first one to laugh at the stage villain are wrong: his sons will laugh, but today's villain will not be in any condition to laugh! He realizes that an indelible image has been created in everyone's mind and that it would take only one false move on his part for this image to become irrevocably attached to his name; and mockery is feared even by someone who fears nothing else on earth. No, breaking into good, cheerful laughter is something only a deeply virtuous person is capable of. But they are unaware of the potency of that laughter: "What is funny is coarse" says the world; only something pronounced in a harsh, strained voice is considered to be on the higher plane. But, Lord! How many people pass by every day for whom there is nothing in the world on a higher plane! For them anything that inspiration has created is balderdash and fairy tales; for them the works of Shakespeare are fairy tales; for them the sacred stirrings of the soul are fairy tales. No, it is not the offended petty pride of a writer that makes me say this, it is not because my feeble, immature creations were labelled fairy tales just now—no, I see my shortcomings and see that I merit reproach; but my spirit refuses to accept without demur the most perfect of creations being labelled balderdash and fairy tales and all the stars and luminaries of the world being designated merely the creators of balderdash and fairy tales! My soul ached at seeing how many unresponsive, dead inhabitants abound here in the very midst of life, terrifying by the impassive coldness of their souls and the barren wasteland of their hearts: my soul ached when their blank faces did not betray the slightest flicker at something that brings tears to a deeply loving soul, and their tongues did not stick at uttering the eternal word "fairy tales"! Fairy tales!... Meanwhile, centuries have passed, cities and nations have been swept away and vanished from the face of the earth, and everything that existed has been carried away like smoke—and yet fairy tales live on and are still repeated today, and they are listened to by wise rulers, thoughtful statesmen, the venerable old man and the high-minded youth. Fairy tales!... And meanwhile the balconies and galleries of the theaters sigh: from top to bottom everyone is palpitating, merged in one feeling, one moment, one being, and all the people have come together, like brothers, in one spiritual movement, and friendly applause thunders out in a grateful hymn to a person who has not lived on earth for five hundred years. Do his bones, decaying in the grave, feel this? Does his soul, which endured the fierce grief of life, respond? Fairy tales!... Meanwhile, over there, among those rows of the shaken multitude, someone has come who is weighed down by grief and the unbearable burden of life, one who is ready to raise his hand against himself in desperation—and, suddenly, refreshing tears splash from his eyes and he leaves, having made his peace with life and asking heaven for grief and suffering anew, if only he can live and shed tears anew over such fairy tales. Fairy tales!... But the world would doze off without such fairy tales, life would run aground and men's souls would be overgrown with mold and slime. Fairy tales!... Oh, let posterity forever cherish them, the names of those who listen with favor to such fairy tales: the miraculous hand of Providence presided unwaveringly over the heads of their creators. Even in moments of misfortune and persecution, all that was noblest in the kingdom came to their defense before everyone: the crowned monarch sheltered them with his imperial shield from the heights of his inaccessible throne.

Let us march on more boldly! And let the spirit not flinch from censure, but let it gratefully accept it when its faults are pointed out, not losing heart even when it is denied higher feelings or the sacred love of humanity! The world is like a whirlpool: opinions and comments perpetually circulate in it; but time grinds everything down. Like chaff, the false ones fly away, while, like sound seed, the immutable truths remain. What was considered empty may later appear invested with austere significance. And in the depths of cold laughter one can seek out the burning sparks of an ever powerful love. And who knows—perhaps everyone will then recognize the force of those laws, as a result of which a proud and powerful individual cuts a frail and insignificant figure in grief, while a weak person grows like a giant among disaster—as a result of those same laws, he who sheds deep, heartfelt tears, he, it seems laughs most heartily of all on earth!...

Translated by Isabel Heaman

Essays

Woman

"The devil's creation! Olympic Zeus! Oh, you are implacable in your rage! You wished to send a scourge on the world, you extracted all the poison that was imperceptibly spilled into the bowels of your fine earth, squeezed it into one drop, angrily threw it with your light-giving hand and poisoned with it your marvelous creation: you created woman! You became envious of our poor happiness, you did not wish for man to pour forth an eternal blessing from the bottom of his grateful heart: better that a curse flash across his sinful lips... You created woman!" Thus spoke Plato's young pupil Telecles, having appeared before his master. His eyes were throwing flames, a fire raged in his cheeks, and his quivering lips revealed the impassioned storm of a lacerated soul. His hand threw back with indignation the purple waves of his rich clothing, and an unbuckled clasp carelessly lay on the youth's virgin chest. "Well, my divine teacher? Was it not you who presented her to us in such heavenly, god-like robes? Were they not your fragrant lips that poured forth glorious speeches about her gentle beauty? Was it not you who taught us to love her so passionately, so non-corporeally? No, teacher! Your divine wisdom is still an infant in its knowledge of the bottomless abyss that is an insidious heart. No, no! And the shadow of vicious experience has not surrounded your clear thoughts; you do not know woman." Fiery tears fell from his eyes; cloaking his head with his tunic and covering his face with his hands, he leaned against the marble column on which a splendid Corinthian capital luxuriously rested, covered with sparks from the sun's rays. A deep, heavy sigh tore out of the youth's heart, as if all the secret nerves of the soul, all the feelings, all that is found inside a man gave out mournful sounds in him, and these sounds passed as a tremor through his whole system, and nature, observable through feelings, in its helplessness to tell of the deathless, eternal torments of the soul, was transformed into a single, painful moan. Meanwhile, the inspired sage looked at him closely in silence, revealing on his face the thoughts that were still imprinted there by his last lofty reflections. In just such a way the remains of a strange dream do not go away for a long time but mix with the beginnings of ideas until a person completely enters the world of reality. The light poured in through the bold opening in the dome and covered him with radiance; it seemed as if ideas and lofty feelings shone in every inspired feature of his face. "Do you know how to love, Telecles?" he asked in a calm voice. "Do I know how to love!" the youth quickly chimed back. "Ask Zeus if he knows how to rock the earth with a movement of his brow. Ask Phidias[1] if he can ignite marble with feelings and embody life in a lifeless block. When not blood but a sharp flame seethes through my veins, when all feelings, all thoughts and I myself transform into sound, when this sound burns and the soul resounds only with love, when my speeches are storms, and my breath—fire.... No, no! I don't know how to love! So tell me, where is the wondrous mortal who possesses this feeling? Has not the most wise Pythias[2] revealed this marvel between people?"

"Poor youth! So this is what people call love! So this is the fate prepared for that gentle being through which the gods wished to reflect their beauty and offer their blessing to the world, and in which they would show their presence on earth! Poor youth! With your scorching breath you would burn up this gentle being; with this storm of passions you would disturb this pure radiance! I know you wish to speak to me of Alcinoe's betrayal. Your own eyes were witnesses... but were they witnesses to the passionate movements taking place at that time in the depths of your own soul? Did you look carefully before you? Did not the whole rebellion of passion seethe in your eyes? And when did the passions discover truth? What do people want? They thirst for lasting bliss, eternal happiness, and one minute of bitterness is enough to compel them to childishly destroy the entire slowly-built structure! Even if truth itself looked through your eyes, even if it is true that the beautiful Alcinoe sullied herself with her perfidious betrayal; still, ask your soul: what were you, what was she at the time you found life and happiness and a sea of ecstasies in Alcinoe's embraces? Turn the fiery pages of your life and will you find even one page more eloquent, more divine than this one? Would you want to take all the precious stones of the Persian rulers, all the gold of Libya in exchange for these heavenly moments? And what is the first honor in Athens and sovereign power among the people when set against them? And the creature who, like Prometheus, brought as a gift to you all that was beautiful that she could carry off from the gods, installed the heavens with their radiant inhabitants in your soul—you strike at her with a sinful curse when your whole life should regenerate into gratitude, when you ought to pour yourself out in tears, tenderness, and a humble hymn to the life-giver Zeus that he prolong her beautiful life and that he waft away the cloud of grief from her pure brow.

"Turn a searching eye upon yourself: what were you before and whom have you become now, from that time when you read eternity in the divine features of Alcinoe; how many secrets, how many revelations have you perceived and discovered with your eternal soul, and how much closer have you moved to the supreme Good? We mature and improve, but when? When we comprehend woman more deeply and more perfectly. Look at the splendid Persians: they transformed their women into slaves and what? Refined feeling, the endless sea of spiritual pleasures, is not accessible to them. A spark will not be lit in their hearts at the sight of Praxiteles's[3] goddess, their rapturous souls will not be able to speak to the eternal soul of marble and find there any responsive sounds. What is woman? The language of the gods! We marvel at the gentle, pure brow of a man, but we do not contemplate the likeness of gods in it: we see in him woman, we marvel at woman in him and only in her do we marvel at the gods! She is poetry! She is the Idea, and we are only her incarnation in reality. On us burn her impressions, and the stronger and more extensively they are reflected, the more exalted and more beautiful we become. While a painting is still incorporeal and is still being created, turning about in the head of the artist—that is woman; when it turns into matter and becomes tangible—it is man. Why does the artist with such insatiable desire strive to turn eternal idea into crude matter, subjugating it to our ordinary feelings? Because he is ruled by one lofty feeling—to express the divine in matter itself, to make at least a part of the boundless world of his soul accessible to people, to embody woman in man. And if the eyes of a youth who ardently understands art inadvertently fall upon it, what do they catch in the artist's immortal painting? Do they see matter in it? No! It disappears, and before them opens up the boundless, eternal, incorporeal idea of the artist. With what lively songs will his soul's strings then begin to speak! How clearly will answer in him, as if to the call of one's native land, both the irrevocable past and the irresistible future! How incorporeally will his soul embrace the divine soul of the artist! How they will merge in an inexpressible spiritual kiss!... What would the lofty virtues of man be if they were not be ensconced and transformed by the tender, gentle virtues of a woman? Hardness, courage, proud contempt for vice would turn into bestiality. Take away the rays from the world—and the bright variety of colors would disappear: earth and sky would merge into darkness, even darker than the shores of Hades. What is love? The homeland of the soul, the beautiful nostalgia of man for the past, where the unblemished beginning of his life took place, when the inexpressible, indelible trace of innocent childhood remained on everything, where all is one's native land. And when the soul sinks into the ethereal womb of a woman's soul, when it finds there its father—an eternal god, and its brothers—the feelings and phenomena hitherto inexpressible by the world—what then? Then it repeats within itself the former sounds, the former paradisical life in the breast of a god, extending it to infinity...." The wise man's inspired gaze stopped still: before him stood Alcinoe, who had entered the room unnoticed during their talk. Leaning against a statue, she seemed to have turned completely into silent attention, and on her fine brow appeared the proud movements of a god-like soul. A marble hand, through which shone light-blue veins, full of heavenly ambrosia, hung freely in the air; a slender foot wound with red ties, having cast off its jealous slipper, stepped forward in its naked, blinding splendor and seemed to not touch the contemptible earth; the high, divine breast rocked with her agitated breathing, and her gown, half-covering the two transparent clouds of her breasts, quivered and flowed in splendid, artistic lines onto the platform. It seemed that the thin, bright ether in which the gods bathe, along which a pink and blue flame streams and spills over into countless rays for which there isn't even a name on earth, and in which trembles a fragrant sea of ineffable music—it seemed this ether became visible and stood before them, sanctifying and idolizing the beautiful human form. The curls carelessly thrown back, dark, like inspired night, moved onto her lily brow and flowed in a dusky cascade onto her radiant shoulders. The lightning of her eyes poured forth her whole soul... No! Never was the queen of love herself so beautiful, even in that moment when she was miraculously born out of the foam of virgin waves!... In awe and wonder the youth threw himself at the proud beauty's feet, and a hot tear from the demi-goddess bending over him fell on his burning cheek.

Translated by Irene Kiedrowski

"Boris Godunov"
A Narrative Poem by Alexander Pushkin

Dedicated to Pyotr Alexandrovich Pletnyov

The second floor of the bookstore shone in *** Street, the lamps cast a warm light on the walls of books stacked up high, vividly and sharply illuminating the titles of gilt-edged blue and red books, as well as the dusty and buried ones, a sign of the power and powerlessness of man's creations. The crowd kept growing and getting denser. The thunder of the road and carriages on the street was echoed by the rattling of window panes, and a slight trembling seemed to run through the lamps, books, people, everything, thereby doubling the motley nature of the picture. Those seated were fussing about. "A glorious work! A splendid work!" reverberated on all sides. "So, my dear fellow, you've read *Boris Godunov*, have you? Well, you haven't read anything good," murmured a coffee-colored overcoat to an out-of-breath square figure. "What Pushkin?" said a newly-made Hussar cornet, after quickly turning around to his neighbor, who had impatiently cut the last pages. "Yes, there are some remarkable bits!" "Well now, *Godunov* has appeared at last!" "What, *Boris Godunov* is out?" "Tell me, what is this *Boris Godunov*? What do you think of this new work?" "Unique. It's unique! If only a certain scene... Oh, Pushkin has gone far!" "The mastery, that's the chief thing—the mastery; look, look how skillfully he...," chirped a chubby block with merry little eyes, who in front of these same eyes was turning around his hand with the fingers slightly cupped, as if a ripe, transparent apple lay in it. "Yes, great merit, great merit!" affirmed a lean expert, putting half an ounce of tobacco in one go into his Roman tobacco pouch. "Of course, there are places which severe criticism... Well, you know... he's still young... Nevertheless, the work is almost first class!" "As far as that's concerned, allow me to report," added the bookseller with a satisfied look: "booming sales vouch for its durability...." "But is the work itself really sensitively written?" stammered a meek-looking hazel grouse, who'd just come in. "Of course, it is!" the bookseller caught him up, throwing a murderous glance at his faded overcoat: "If it weren't, they wouldn't have bought up 400 copies in two hours!" Meanwhile, the faces kept changing ceaselessly, leaving with satisfied looks and the little book in their hands. At this point Elladius walked up to his friend Pollior, who had been absentmindedly watching the greedy crowd of buyers. "Isn't it true, dear Pollior! Isn't it true that nothing can compare with the quiet ecstasy that suffuses the soul upon seeing how a great work, which we passionately love, incessantly strikes a chord and resounds in all hearts, and people who seem to have fled forever from their nonspiritual world, hidden within them and incomprehensible to them, perforce return to its realm!" Pollior silently and mutely shook his hand. They left. But neither the oppressive light of the moon, a fusion of joy and sadness, which so beautifully evokes from the depths of the soul a silver assembly of visions when the night sky is incorporeally embraced by inspiration and the earth is full of incomprehensible love for the sky, nor those lively feelings that suddenly awaken us when the wondrous city thunders and shines, bridges shake, crowds of people and shadows flash along the streets and along the pale yellow walls of the gigantic houses, whose windows, like innumerable fiery eyes, throw flaming trails on the snowy roadway, merging so strangely with the silvery light of the moon—nothing was capable of arousing him from a solemn thoughtfulness; his features retained a quiet indignation as if in his soul he had heard a prophecy of eternity, as if his soul were enduring inexpressible tortures, incomprehensible to the earthly.... "How come," asked Elladius as they entered his lonely room, lit by a solitary, fluttering lamp, "you still haven't given our great creation its due, haven't contributed a gifted expression—an interpretation of your feelings to the cup of general opinion?"

"You understand me, Elladius. Why do you ask me that pointless question? What can I contribute? Who needs, who wishes to know my secret impulses? Often, upon hearing how they publicly judge and discuss a poet, when their debate raises a storm and the foaming mouths yell in the marketplaces—in the depths of my soul I think: isn't it heresy? Isn't it the same thing as if someone took it into his head to burst rough-and-tumble into a square where the rabble teem and bustle, performing its usual rites, and he, falling to his knees, offered up passionate prayers to heaven? And what would I say? 'Beautiful! Incomparable! Unique!' But will these words express even one stream of the boundless ocean of feelings? They're powerless! They've lost even their meager proper meaning from people's frequent repetition of them. But people who endorse poets with paltry epithets, as if ranking them, who call them first class, as if poets like plants or inanimate minerals demand a classification in order to stay in our heads—these people seem even more ridiculous, more laughable. Almighty! When I unfold your marvelous creation, when your immortal verse thunders and the lightning of fiery sounds shoots at me, a sacred coldness courses through my veins and my soul trembles with awe, summoning God out of His boundless bosom... What then? If the sky, the sun, the sea, the fires that devour our earth's interior, the infinite air encompassing worlds, the angels, the blazing planets were transformed into words and letters—even then I would not express through them a tenth of the phenomena that took place at that moment in the bosom of Him whom I cannot see. And what are they all in comparison to man's soul? In comparison to the incarnation of God? Into what sounds, what bright sounds is the soul transformed, as it gives birth to everything that bears the image of the expressible and finite, and in a powerful rush penetrates into its incorporeal breast! How the frail, long-suffering composition burns, how it grows parched! How the powerless earthly element trembles, how it moans, until everything merges into the spiritual sea, until the flood of grateful tears washes like rain the tortured breast, shedding reconciliation between the two antagonistic natures of man. How futile are these people who demand a report of the impressions produced by a great poet's creation, knowing beforehand that it will not correspond to their irrational desire! When they extract a result from the featureless earthly skull it is a dazzling gem, when they extort sounds from strings—what sort of result do they wish to extract from sounds? Perhaps this wish will be fulfilled, but when? When man disappears and the soul is raised up on his dilapidated ruins in the majestic, unbounded dwelling."

"Then, in your opinion," Elladius asked after a momentary silence, "people shouldn't share their impressions and communicate revelations, even fragmentary reports of their feelings, which perhaps would persuade others of the creation's spiritual elegance?"

"No, Elladius, no. Your attempts to arouse the soul of whomever requires persuasion will be unavailing. Uncover the great creation before him. Read it together, and if its wonderful letters do not at once have an impact on the secret strings of your hearts, which sets your nerves aquiver, if you do not gush with responsive tears, and if your souls sense a separation—close the book and don't waste empty words. But if you encounter a feeling that ardently understands you—the beautiful half to your beautiful soul—will you demand an accounting from each other? What good would it serve you, when you already are so wonderfully merged into one? And what sort of contemptible joy can compare with that moment when the work is read in you at one stroke? How do you understand it? 'My God!' I often say to myself, 'what a sublime, what a marvelous pleasure you give a person, when you inspire in one soul the answer to another's passionate question! How quickly these souls search each other out, the chasms that divide them notwithstanding!'

"It is as if I am riveted to the spot, having destroyed my surroundings, not hearing, not listening, not remembering anything, I devour your pages, wondrous poet! And when the past slowly moves before me and silver shadows all flicker and in a marvelous brilliance stretch in an endless row out of the grave in their formidable silent grandeur, when all life in me responds and the passions are experienced anew in my soul—what wouldn't I give then just to read in someone else a replica of my entire self.... There seem to be no treasures with which I wouldn't part for such a blessing. 'Take, take everything I have,' I would exclaim then with my hands raised to the heavens, 'and send me this being who understands me. Almighty! Why have you given me an incomplete soul? Either make it whole or take this remaining half to yourself.'

"Oh, how great is this regal sufferer! How much good, how much benefit, how much happiness has he given the world—and nobody understood him... A decision thunders over his head... His former life, as if in answer to the sad ringing of a bell, all comes together around him! The dead live!... And your wonderful pictures sparkle and resound ever more expansively, expansively, expansively... And torments again in my breast!... Responsive strings of the soul thunder... The peal of the silvery heavens with their radiant cherubim pulses through my veins... Oh, give me, give me still more, more of these torments and through them I shall flow out into the Creator's bosom, not leaving the contemptible body a single drop....

"Almighty! I swear on your eternal creation!... I am still pure, not one contemptible feeling of self-interest, servility or petty pride has yet sparked in my soul. If the deadening coldness of the soulless world heretically wrests from out of my soul even a portion of its substance, if flint takes hold of my quietly ardent heart, if contemptible, worthless laziness fetters me, if I bear the wondrous moments of the soul to the marketplace of popular praises, if I disgrace in myself the sounds forced out by you... Oh! then let it be washed by a ceaseless stream of poison, let it drive its millions of strings into my visible self, let it wind an inextinguishable flame of reproaches around my soul and engulf me with that piercing howl from which all the joints would ache and the eternal soul itself would start to moan, having returned like an unanswered echo to its desert... But no! It is like a creator, like a blessing! Should it burn in punishment? It will again embrace the soul with its sea of bright rays and sounds and with a tear of reconciliation it will quiver in the clouded eyes of the transformed criminal!..."

Translated by Ronald Meyer

On Kozlov's Poetry

The luminous, ample world of the ancient Greeks—the expansive sea of life—lacked the power to give direction to Kozlov's poetry.[1] When all the brilliance, all the diversity of the ever-luminous life of nature, which manifests itself in countless forms, merges for him into one terrible unity—that of darkness—could his soul live according to the former, clear phenomena? As if in a frenzy, as if overcome by grief, in fits, with an unquenchable thirst—to exult, to rise above its own happiness, it sought another encounter and in amazement it stopped before Byron, whose gigantic dark soul had so wonderfully encompassed the world's whole life and had so impudently laughed at the world, perhaps because it was powerless to communicate its individual brightness and greatness. Our poet's soul wished to entwine itself around this proudly solitary soul, which monstrously schemed to possess the soul's own world, created by it, dissonant and wonderful, as a substitute for that which it had rejected; and once entwined around it, the poet's soul wished to smile bitterly at the former *Iliad* of life that no longer existed. The meek Christian sublimity of faith, so accessible to man in that terrible moment of his rebirth, permeated and enveloped in its own pure radiance everything he had received by associating with the soul of this giant, with whom he did not have sufficient power to measure strength, and it conveyed to him his individuality, without which he would have been only a feeble imitator. But even in the quiet transport of his religious soul, when he is blessing his heavy cross of misfortune, a sorrow bursts forth, one might even call it a malicious enjoyment of his own torments. He powerfully lets us feel all his great, bitter losses; he often brings together in one moment all that has vanished, he vividly presents it in all its blinding brilliance in order to show simultaneously what it cost him to forget and dismiss the thought of it. Looking at the rainbow colors and hues with which his sumptuous pictures of nature seethe and shine, you immediately recognize with sadness that they are lost to him forever: they would never appear to a person who can see in such a bright and even heightened brilliance. They can only be the achievement of a person who has long ceased to admire them, but who has faithfully and powerfully preserved his memory of them, which has grown and become magnified in his feverish imagination and shone even in the darkness that is inseparable from him. But even in these creations, in which he seems to try to forget everything melancholy concerning his own soul, when he tries to capture with invisible eyes a visible nature, even here, even behind the colors, burns a quiet sadness. He is completely immersed in himself. He carries his entire inseparable world in his soul and is powerless to break away from it. Sometimes his attempt is centrifugal, as if he wants to spill to the outside, but only so that he can again, with greater force, turn toward his center, to himself, as if surmising that his life is only there, only there will he find his answer. If he dwells for a long time on some external object, he deprives it of its individuality, he reveals himself in it, he sees and develops in it the world of his own soul. Even now many remarks and reproaches concerning Kozlov seem strange to me—that there is an everlasting celebration and monotony of life in his narrative poems, that his characters do not have a full novelistic finish and do not live their own life, that *The Mad Girl* does not resemble a Russian peasant woman at all; in a word they demand from Kozlov that which we can rightly demand only from Pushkin, forgetting that for Kozlov an external life full of diversity does not exist, that his entire world became concentrated in him and that he is capable of following only it in its multifarious guises. And his characters and heroes are only images, conventional signs, in which he envelops the phenomena of his soul. That to embrace in its entirety internal and external life is the province of universal genius and that, finally, Kozlov stands in relation to Pushkin as a part to the whole. The poet understands all the value of the latter. It is more complimentary to his passionate soul than flattery and uncontrolled praise. And who would not find this glorious, who would not envy this fate: to be a part of the boundless Pushkin!!

Translated by Ronald Meyer

ON THE TREND OF JOURNAL LITERATURE IN 1834 AND 1835

Journal literature, that living, fresh, garrulous, keen literature, is just as essential in the sphere of science and art as a means of communication for a nation, as are fairs and stock exchanges for the merchants and trade. It controls the taste of the crowd; it directs and sets in motion all that comes to light in the world of books, which, without it, would be in both senses dead capital. It is a rapid, capricious exchange of general opinions, a lively conversation of all that is pressed by typographical plates; its voice is a true representative of the opinions of an entire epoch and time, opinions that would silently disappear without it. Willingly or unwillingly it attracts and embraces in its sphere nine-tenths of all that becomes the property of literature. How many people there are who make judgments, discuss and interpret, because all their opinions are presented to them almost whole, and who, on their own, would never interpret, voice an opinion or discuss. Thus, journal literature has, in any case, a right to demand our closest attention.

Perhaps it has been a long time since the absence of journal activity and a lively contemporary movement has been as sharply noticeable with us as in the past two years. The idiom of the greater part of the periodical press was blandness. Many of the old journals ceased publication, others dragged on slowly and indolently; new ones, other than *The Library for Reading*[1] and afterwards *The Moscow Observer*,[2] did not appear, while just at this time a general demand for food for thought was noticeable, and the number of readers significantly increased. However poor this period is, it has the same right to our attention as would one in which activity seethed, because it also belongs to the history of our literature. The readers were within their rights to complain about the slender lenten appearance of our journals: *The Telegraph*[3] long ago lost that sharp tone which gave it its militant position among the Petersburg journals; *The Telescope*[4] was filled with essays in which there was nothing fresh and stirring. During this period the bookseller Smirdin, long famous for his activity and conscientiousness, who alone, to the shame of his short-sighted comrades, showed enterprise and whose ventures stimulated the book trade—the bookseller

Smirdin decided to publish a voluminous, encyclopedic journal, to capture all the literary people there are in Russia and have them participate in his undertaking.[5] The names of nearly all our writers were displayed in the program. Mr. Senkovsky, professor of Arabic literature, was chosen to be the journal's manager; in addition, the editor, who was to be Mr. Grech,[6] well known for the regular publication of two journals, *The Northern Bee*[7] and *Son of the Fatherland*.[8] We do not know whether they took this task upon themselves or whether they were persuaded by Mr. Smirdin; but in either case the bookseller, according to the general opinion, acted rather incautiously. Having succeeded in uniting such a large number of literary people for his publication, he should have left the choice of editor to their judgment.

At the time no one worried about the extremely important question: should a journal have one definite tone, one authorized opinion, or should it be a warehouse for all opinions and interpretations. On this count the journal answered remotely with the usual announcement that the criticism would be the most well-intentioned and dispassionate, independent of personalities or unpleasantnesses—a promise that every journalist makes. With the publication of the first issue the public clearly saw that one tone dominated in the journal, the opinion and thought of one person, that the names of the writers which filled one half of the title page in a shining rank were only hired to attract a greater number of subscribers.

The bookseller Smirdin on his part did all that the public could rightfully demand *from him*. In the publication of the journal he showed the same honor for which he was always distinguished. The journal appeared with unusual punctuality: the subscribers were greeted the first day of each month with a fat book such as formerly not one of our presses could put together in two months. Instead of the promised number of eighteen signatures a month, sometimes twice as many were published. Now we will examine whether or not those to whom he entrusted the internal management of the journal fulfilled their obligation. The journal's central figure and mainspring was Mr. Senkovsky. The name of Mr. Grech was displayed only as a matter of form—at least there was no noticeable activity on his part. For some time now Mr. Grech has been an honorary and essential editor of every periodical publication that is undertaken: thus, people usually invite an honorable, middle-aged man to preside at all weddings. But what was the goal of the editorship of this journal, what problem did it propose to resolve? Here we are forced to ponder the situation, which, no doubt, the reader will also do. In his platform Mr. Senkovsky said nothing about what path he had set for himself, what goal he had chosen for himself; everyone saw only that he entered unnoticed in the first issue and at the end of it showed himself to be the complete master.

Incidentally, we cannot complain about this: let us assume that a biting tone is necessary for a journalist—and even some impertinence (of which, however, we do not approve, although we know that journalists with such qualities always win in the opinion of the crowd); but on what was the attention of this master predominantely focused, which of his thoughts overpowered all others, where was his bias directed, and were those unbending principles, without which any man becomes characterless, anywhere noticeable, those principles which give a man originality and define his physiognomy?

Having read everything he placed in this journal, following every word that he has said, we involuntarily stop in amazement: What is this? What makes this person write? We see a person who certainly is not taking money for nothing, who works until his face perspires, who is not only concerned with his own essays, but even corrects those of other people—in a word, he is indefatigable. What is the goal of all of this activity? We will follow the manager in all genres of his writings and we will say a few words about the principal characteristics of his articles. This is absolutely essential.

Mr. Senkovsky appears in his journal as critic, storyteller, scholar, satirist, town crier of the news and so on and so forth. He appears in the form of Brambeus, Morozov, Tjutjundzu-Oglu, A. Belkin, and finally, under his own name. As a scholar Mr. Senkovsky included a rather long essay on the sagas—an essay replete with hypotheses not his own, but snatched at random from sundry cursorily read books—hypotheses which do not at all appertain to Russian history. These sagas which the incisive Schloezer[9] (who to this day has no equal in his scrupulous and profound critical views) acknowledged to be fables unworthy of any attention—these are the sagas he sets as the cornerstones of Russian history and he doesn't present one piece of evidence verified by criticism. He doesn't at all define their true and singular value. The sagas are essentially a poetical creation of the people who have played a great role in history. This essay, speckled with rhetorical figures, pleased decent but limited people, and Mr. Bulgarin even wrote a review in which he placed Mr. Senkovsky higher than Schloezer, Humboldt and all scholars who ever lived. Another extremely important pretension of Mr. Senkovsky, his real hobby-horse, is the East. Here he has always raised his voice, and the instant any work about the East appeared or the East was referred to anywhere, even if it be only in a poem, he became angry and asserted that the author could not judge and should not judge about the East, that he did not know the East. A word pronounced with passion is very excusable in a man who is in love with his subject and who at the same time sees how little others understand it: but this person should at least establish his authority. It behooves Mr. Senkovsky to publish something about the East. It is difficult to believe the word of a man who has done nothing, especially when his opinions are so lightweight and permeated by the spirit of impatience; and in his few fragments about the East the same shortcomings for which he constantly reproaches others are visible. He has said nothing new about the East—not one sharp feature, astute thought or brilliant proposition! One cannot deny that Mr. Senkovsky is informed; on the contrary, it is very obvious that he has read a great deal. But that motivating, dominant force, which would direct him towards some goal, is nowhere apparent in his work. All those facts in his work exist in a kind of fermentation; they contradict each other, do not harmonize together. Let us examine his opinions that relate directly to contemporary literature. In his criticism Mr. Senkovsky displays an absence of any opinion, so that not one of his readers can say for sure what the reviewer liked the most and seized his soul the most, what harmonized with his feelings: in his reviews there is *no positive, or negative taste—there is no taste at all.* That which pleases him today, tomorrow becomes the object of his sneers. He first placed Mr. Kukolnik with Goethe, and he himself announced that he had done this only because it suddenly occurred to him to do so.[10] It must be that a review for him is not a matter of conviction and feeling, but is simply a consequence of mood and circumstances. Walter Scott, that great genius whose immortal creations embrace life with such fullness, Walter Scott is called a charlatan.[11] And Russia read this, this was said to people who are already educated, who have already read Walter Scott. One may be sure that Mr. Senkovsky said this unintentionally, from hastiness alone—because he never pays any attention to what he is saying, and in the next essay doesn't recall anything that he wrote in the preceding one.

In his studies and criticism Mr. Senkovsky also never mentioned the internal character of the composition that he was examining; he didn't define the true and exact characteristic feature of its virtue. His criticism was either unconditional praise, in which the reviewer from his very soul comforted himself with his own sentences, or detraction, in which a kind of strange bitterness was heard. It consisted of trifles, was limited to the quotation of two or three sentences and a sneer. Nothing was said about what the author of the work being examined set as a goal for himself, how he achieved that goal and, if he didn't achieve it, what he should have done to achieve it. For the most part, Mr. Senkovsky occupied himself with the examination of sundry literary garbage, a multitude of all kinds of empty books; he joked about them, made fun of them and displayed that wit which so pleases some readers. Finally, he even instigated the whole business about the two pronouns *sej* and *onyj*, which for some unknown reason seemed to him out of place in Russian. He wrote entire treatises about these pronouns, and his essays, no matter what subject they were discussing, always ended with the fact that the pronouns *sej* and *onyj* were absolutely disgraceful. This is reminiscent of Trediakovsky's old case for the letter *izhitsa* and the *desyaterichnoe i*, which subsequently was supported by a certain professor not so long ago. A book in which Mr. Senkovsky met with these two particles was triumphantly proclaimed to be written in a bad style.

His own compositions, stories and the like, appeared under the guise of Brambeus. These stories and essays written like stories, produced general amazement by their close, immoderate imitation of present-day French writers, because Mr. Senkovsky publicly denigrted all contemporary French literature. It is incomprehensible why in this case he had so little keen-wittedness and to what degree he considered his readers simpleminded. It is also unknown why he called some of his essays fantastic. The absence of any truth, naturalness and probability cannot be considered fantastic. The fantastic works of Baron Brambeus recall the sorts of books that used to be very numerous at one time: "If it isn't pleasant, don't listen, but don't question the lies," and the like. The same absence of control and even less striving to prove any idea are present. Experienced readers noticed an unusual number of abductions, completed suddenly at full gallop: the author troubled himself little about their connection. That which in the originals made sense, had no meaning in the copy.

Such were the work and activities of the manager of *The Library for Reading*. We considered it necessary to mention them rather detailedly because he alone legislated in *The Library for Reading* and because his opinions spread extremely rapidly, along with the 4,000 copies of the journal, across the whole face of Russia.

It is impossible that a journal published with the means provided by the bookseller Smirdin would be bad. It benefited by the simple fact that it was published in a large format, in thick volumes. For the subscribers, especially the inhabitants of our cities and rural landowners, this was a pleasant innovation. Translations of occasionally interesting essays from foreign journals were found in *The Library*, and the names of the luminaries of the Russian Parnassus in the poetry section. But the Miscellaneous was consistently the best section, including a great many sundry bits of fresh news; it was a lively, purely journalistic section. The artistic prose, both original and in translation—stories, etc.—showed very little taste and selection. Yet one other thing took place in *The Library for Reading*, which until then had been unheard of in Russia. Its manager began to correct and rework almost all of the essays that were published in it, and it is curious that he rather daringly and frankly announced this himself. "*The Library for Reading*," he says, "is not like other journals; we do not leave a single story in its original form, we rework every one: sometimes we make one from two, sometimes from three, and the essay is significantly improved by our alterations." Such strange guardianship never existed before in Russia.

Many writers began to fear that the public would not accept as their own articles that were often included without credit or under a pseudonym; and therefore they began to refuse to participate in the publication of this journal. The number of contributors so diminished that the following year the publishers did not exhibit the long list of names and mentioned vaguely that the best literary people participated, not specifying anybody. Although the size and plan of the journal did not change, the essays began to be noticeably worse, less effort was apparent. Already *The Library* was being read less in the capitals, but still just as much in the provinces, and its opinions circulated just as rapidly. Let us turn to the other journals.

The Northern Bee included the official news and in this respect served its purpose. It included political news, foreign and national news. Its editor, Mr. Grech, led it to strict punctuality: it always came out at the set time; but in a literary sense it had no definite tone and displayed no strong hand guiding its opinions. It was a kind of basket into which everyone tossed what he wished. The book reviews, almost all favorable, were written by friends of the authors, and sometimes by the authors themselves. In *The Northern Bee* wit of the pen was attempted by various unknowns under sundry initials—undoubtedly young people, because considerable boldness was evident in the essays. They attacked what is probably the most defenseless and forlorn orphans. Witty barbs, somewhat similar to each other, appeared concerning slovenly publications. The essence of the review consisted in praising the book and at the end removing all sin from oneself with a reservation such as: "However, it is desirable that the author correct small errors in language and style," or "A good book demands a good production," and so on—by which the author of the book being reviewed was occasionally offended and complained about the reviewer's prejudice. The books were often discussed by the same reviewers who wrote the news about new tobacco factories that had opened in the capital, about pomade, etc.; these news items were sometimes rather witty and from their jokes it was apparent that the writers were adroit and well-educated people, no doubt having substantial reason to be satisfied with the factory owners. Incidentally, one could demand nothing more of *The Northern Bee*; it always was a punctual daily poster, its business was to invite the public, it left it to the public to judge for themselves.

The journal carrying the name *Son of the Fatherland and Northern Archive* was virtually invisible the whole time. No one spoke about it, no one made reference to it, despite the fact that it came out punctually every week and that it printed on its cover a huge program the like of which it would be difficult to encounter anywhere else. In *Son of the Fatherland* (said the program) there would be archaeology, medicine, jurisprudence, statistics, Russian history, world history, Russian literature, foreign literature, finally simply literature, geography, ethnography, historical portraits, etc. Another would oh and ah, having read such a frightful program, and would think that this was the hugest encyclopedic publication that had ever existed. But there was nothing even remotely like that: what appeared was a slim, thin little booklet of three signatures, which began with an essay about some kind of disease that even the doctors didn't read. The critical essay, which was more lively and contemporary, did not appear every time. The political news was the same dry facts taken from The *Northern Bee*, consequently already known to everybody. The original stories that were included were rather strange, extremely short and absolutely colorless. If some worthwhile observation found itself there, it remained unnoticed. The names of the editors, Messrs. Bulgarin and Grech, appeared only on the title page and no activity on their part was evident. However, the journal did exist, so there must have been readers and subscribers. These readers and subscribers were respectable middle-aged people living in the provinces, for whom it is just as essential to read as it is to take an after-dinner nap and shave twice a week.

Throughout this period a purely literary paper was published in Petersburg, free from any intrusion of the sciences or important news—not political, not statistical, not encyclopedic, a fancier of the old things, but for all that having a special character. The title of this paper: *Literary Supplements to the Invalid*. Included in it were light stories, conversations of rural landowners about literature, conversations that were rather ordinary, but in places occasionally pierced with barbs close to the truth: to his surprise the reader saw that towards the end of the articles the landowners had become accomplished literary people, took current literature completely to their hearts and seasoned their opinions with a caustic sneer. This journal constantly opposed any happy horseman, although its whole tactic often consisted only in citing one passage, demonstrating a journalistic precipitancy and adding only a rather caustic remark, not longer than one line, with an exclamation point. Mr. Voeikov[12] was an extremely active fisherman and, like a fisherman, he sat on the bank with his line, not losing his patience, although, for the most part, only small fish happened onto his line, while the large ones got away. A purely literary life was evidenced by the editor, who with undampened ardor did not take his eyes off the field of journalism. I don't know if the journal had many regular readers, but it was very worthwhile to look at occasionally.

Only *The Telescope* was published in Moscow, with a few supplementary pages under the title *Talk*. The journal at first showed liveliness but quickly cooled, being unselectively filled with randomly selected essays, devoid of any literary impulse. It was apparent that the publishers did not put any effort into it and churned out the issues carelessly.

The monopoly seized by *The Library for Reading* could not but bury alive the other journals. But *The Northern Bee* was published by that same Mr. Grech, whose name was for a short time on the title page of *The Library* as its editor-in-chief, although this title, as we have already seen, was purely honorary, and therefore it was very natural that *The Northern Bee* had to praise everything included in *The Library* and call its real moving force, appearing under a multitude of various names, a Russian Humboldt. But even without that it could hardly have been a strong opponent, because it was not run by a single will; various literary people looked there only when they felt the need. *The Son of the Fatherland* had to repeat the words of *The Bee.* Thus, only two journals could rise up against its opinions. In *Literary Supplements* Mr. Voeikov exhibited something that looked like opposition; but this opposition consisted of light comments on journalistic blunders and an occasional successful witticism expressed curtly in a few words with a sneer—comprehensible to a few literary men, but unintelligible for the unenlightened. Nowhere did he feature circumstantial and fundamental criticism that would in some way define the direction of the new journal. *The Telescope,* in collaboration with *Talk,* operated against *The Library for Reading,* but operated ineffectively, without consistency, patience and the essential composure. The critical articles were often full of indignation at a new lucky person, joked about the baronry of Mr. Senkovsky, made a few just remarks concerning his strange imitation of French writers, but did not see the matter in all its clarity. The same hints about Brambeus were repeated in *Talk,* often in connection with an examination of works completely peripheral to the subject. Besides this, *The Telescope* injured itself considerably with the lateness of its issues, the sloppiness of the publication, and because of this the critical articles were talked about even less.

It is obvious that the strength and resources of these journals were too weak compared with those of *The Library for Reading,* which towered over them like an elephant among small animals. Their battle was too unequal, and, it seems, they didn't take into consideration the fact that *The Library for Reading* had approximately 5,000 subscribers, that the opinions of *The Library for Reading* were carried into classes of society which did not even suspect that *The Telescope* and *Literary Supplements* existed, that the opinions and works placed in *The Library for Reading* were lavished with praise by the publishers of that same *Library for Reading,* who were hiding under various names, and lavished with enthusiastic praise, which always has an influence on the greater part of the public, because that which is amusing for the enlightened reader is believed with complete simpleheartedness by the limited reader, who, judging by the number of subscribers, we may suppose to dominate the readers of *The Library,* and furthermore the majority of the subscribers were new people who until then had not been familiar with journals and, therefore, were taking everything for the purest truth, and that, finally, *The Library for Reading* had the firm support of 4,000 copies of *The Northern Bee.*

A strong murmur was made against such an unheard-of monopoly. Finally, in Moscow a few literary men decided to publish a journal of their own. The new journal was not needed by the public, that is, by the majority of readers, but particularly by the literary people themselves, who were variously oppressed by *The Library*. It was needed (1) by those who wanted to have some shelter for their ideas, because *The Library for Reading* did not accept any critical essays which were not to the editor-in-chief's taste; (2) by those who looked on in amazement at how the hand of the editor-in-chief was laid on their own works, because Mr. Senkovsky had already begun to correct indiscriminately all articles published in *The Library*. He rewrote military, historical, and literary articles, those relating to political economy, etc., and he did all this without any bad intent, even without any account of it, unguided by any feeling of necessity or decency. He even added his own ending to Fonvizin's comedy, without looking to see that it already had an ending.

All this was very annoying to the writers, who had no place where they could present their complaint to the world and their readers.

But just the rumor of a new journal aroused the indignation of *The Library for Reading* and impelled it to an unexpected step: its readers and subscribers were assured with extraordinary passion that the new journal would be abusive and disloyal. It seemed that the article placed in *The Northern Bee* on this occasion was written by a man who in desperation foresaw his own final demise. In it the public was informed that the new journal intended to injure *The Library for Reading* simply because its publishers had announced that they would print the same number of pages as *The Library for Reading*. An extremely imprudent act! In such a situation it is essential to conceal one's petty feelings skillfully and then, having waited for a convenient moment, deliver a well-considered blow. If I publish a journal, why should another not publish one? And how can I become angry if the other says he is going to take me as a model? Shouldn't I, on the contrary, thank him? Doesn't he display by this the degree of respect that I have earned in the public's eye? The more competition, the more gain for the readers and for the literary people.

But let us see to what degree *The Moscow Observer* has fulfilled the expectations of a public thirsty for novelty, the expectations of educated readers, the expectations of the literary people, and the fears of *The Library for Reading*.

Despite its earnest efforts to be known throughout Russia, the journal didn't have the means to announce its appearance in all corners of Russia, because the solitary heralds of this news were its opponents—*The Northern Bee* and *The Library for Reading*, which, of course, would not print favorable announcements about it. It began rather late, not with the new year, therefore, not at that time when subscriptions usually begin; finally, it neglected to publish the issues quickly and put them on sale as scheduled. But the most important reasons for its lack of success can be attributed to the nature of the journal itself. From the first published issues one could already see that the journal's intention was the result of a single heated moment. *The Moscow Observer* also had no visible mainspring capable of directing the entire journal's direction. Its editor was visible only on the title page. His name was almost unknown. Before this he had written only a few statistical studies, which had much worth, but with which the purely literary public was not at all familiar. His literary ideas were unknown. This was a big mistake on the part of the publishers of *The Moscow Observer*. They forgot that an editor should always be a well-known person. The entire credit of a journal is based on him, on the originality of his ideas, on the liveliness of his style, on the general intelligibility and interest of his language, on his constant fresh activity. But Mr. Androsov was a completely invisible person in *The Moscow Observer*. If it was the publishers' desire to set up a purely honorary editor, as has become customary with us in indolent Russia, they should have taken the tasks of editorship upon themselves; but they left all the responsibility with the editor, and *The Moscow Observer* resembled those learned societies in which the members do nothing and don't even attend the meetings, while the president appears every day in his chair and orders that the minutes of his lonely sessions be written. There were some rather good essays in the journal, it was graced by the poetry of Yazykov and Baratynsky, those pearls of Russian poetry, but for all that no contemporary liveliness, no bustling enterprise was in evidence; there was none of the variety essential to a periodical publication. The outstanding essays that appeared in the journal were like oases flourishing in the middle of a sea of sandy steppes. In addition, it seems the publishers had little knowledge about what pleases and does not please the public. The good articles often became boring only because they dragged on from one issue to the next with the unbearable signature: to be continued. Such was the journal that was supposed to do battle with *The Library for Reading*.

The Observer began with an opposition essay by Mr. Shevyryov about the commerce that has arisen in our literature. In it the author attacks commerce in the scholarly world, the all-pervasive tendency to draw profit from literary activity. The first mistake here was that the author didn't focus his attention on the main point. Second, he thundered against those who write for money, but didn't destroy the public's opinion about the product's intrinsic value. This essay, comprehensible only to literary people, angered *The Library for Reading*, but didn't inform the public, which didn't even understand what was going on. Furthermore, these attacks were unjust, because they were directed at the unchangeable law of every action. Literature had to become commercial, because the readers and the need to read increased. In such a case it is always natural that enterprising people without great talent gain more, because in any trade where the buyers are still simpleminded, merchants are more resourceful, push more, and gain more. It is necessary to show where the deception lies and not to enumerate the profits. It is not a misfortune that a writer buys a profitable house or a pair of horses; what is bad is that some people have purchased bad goods and nevertheless boast about their purchase. Mr. Shevyryov should have drawn attention to the poor buyers and not to the merchants. Merchants are often traveling people: here today—God knows where tomorrow. In this case an unjust reproach was made to the totally innocent bookseller Smirdin, who deserves only thanks for his enterprisingness and honorable actions. There is no question that he gave a great deal of freedom to people for whom it would have been more seemly to engage simply in commerce and not literature. Talent is not sychophantic, but greed is. It would be just as ridiculous to complain about that as it would be strange to complain about a government after you have met a shortsighted civil servant. For talent there is posterity, that incorruptible jeweller who mounts only pure stones. In his essay Mr. Shevyryov displayed his noble burst of indignation against the prosaic, abased trend of literature, but this essay made absolutely no impression on the public at large. *The Library* answered curtly, in the spirit of its usual tactic: turning to the viewers, that is, to the subscribers, it said: "Look what baseness of spirit Mr. Shevyryov has shown, indecency, and absence of lofty feelings—reproaching us with the fact that we work for money, while," etc. That's the usual politics of the Petersburg journals and newspapers. As soon as anyone reproaches them for greed and idleness, they complain to the public about their opponent's indecency of expression and baseness of spirit, they say that the essay was written with the sole aim of hoodwinking the public and taking money from the readers, that, for their part, they consider it their sacred duty to forewarn the public.

Thus, *The Moscow Observer*'s escapade glanced off *The Library for Reading* like a bullet off the hide of a rhinoceros and didn't even make the corpulent beast sneeze. Having let loose this bullet, *The Moscow Observer* fell silent—proof that it hadn't outlined for itself a well-thought-out plan of action and that it definitely did not know how or where to start. They should have either not started at all, or, once they did start, they shouldn't have stopped. Only by steadfast action could *The Moscow Observer* have gained circulation and made its name known to the public, as *The Telegraph* had made its known, acting in the same manner and in almost identical circumstances. After this *The Observer* published several issues, but not in one of them did it say anything in defense and support of its opinions. Finally, after several issues an essay dedicated to Brambeus appeared, concerning an essay printed a long time ago in *The Library*, entitled "Brambeus and Young Literature," in which Brambeus called himself the lawgiver of some kind of new school and the harbinger of a new era in Russian literature.

This was in fact extremely strange. It sometimes happens that literary people occasionally praise themselves either under the name of their friends or even under their own name, but still with some humility, and afterwards, feeling a bit guilty, they try to brush this away with their own hands. But never before has an author praised himself so freely and with so little constraint as Baron

Brambeus. This original essay stood out too much not to be noticed. *The Telescope* took it up and joked about it rather amusingly, but casually; Mr. Voeikov also hinted about it with his usual keenness; it gave birth to an essay in *The Moscow Observer*, too. The purpose of this essay was to show from where Baron Brambeus drew his talent and fame; which works of other masters he had used as his own; in other words, from whose rags Baron Brambeus had sewn his housecoat. The several mute issues that came out after this completely consigned *The Moscow Observer* to oblivion. Even *The Library for Reading* finally stopped referring to it as a powerless opponent, continuing to joke about the important and unimportant and saying the first thing that came to mind.

Such were the activities of our journals. Having given an account of them, let us now see what they did in these two years that should be written into the history of our literature, what should leave its original imprint on our literature; what opinions and trends they approved, what they defined and what thought they gave to civil law.

A long program, promising statistics, medicine, literature, means nothing. The announcement that the criticism would be conscientious, independent of personalities and parties, doesn't show an aim either. That should be the essential requirement of every journal. Even a multitude of essays published in a journal means nothing if the journal doesn't have its own idea and does not display a tendency, even a one-sided one, to some goal. *The Telegraph* was published, it seems, in order to topple over the decrepit, worn out, almost mechanical ideas of our old-timers, the classicists of the time; *The Moscow Herald*, one of the best journals, despite the fact that there was little contemporary activity in it, was published in order to acquaint the public with the most remarkable works of Europe, to broaden the field of our literature, to provide us with fresh ideas about the writers of all times and peoples. This is not the place to speak about the degree to which both of these journals fulfilled their aims; at least their striving for this was sensed by the readers. But carefully examine the journals published in the last two years; catch the main thread of each—you can't detect those threads. Opening them you will be struck by the pettiness of the subjects that gave rise to their comments. You would think that not one important event took place in the literary world. And meanwhile:

(1) The famed Scot died, the great writer of the heart, nature and life—the most complete and sweeping genius of the nineteenth century.

(2) A restless, exciting taste in literature spread throughout Europe.[13] Rash, foolish, youthful creations appeared, but they were often ecstatic, passionate—as a result of the political disturbances in the country where they were given birth. Strange, rebellious and unorganized, like a comet, this literature agitated Europe and rapidly flew to all corners of the reading world. Admittedly, these manifestations were universal European ones, although they were reflected in Russia,

too; we will examine the purely Russian events.

(3) The reading of novels and cold, boring short stories was popularized to a large degree, and a general indifference to poetry was clearly felt.

(4) New editions of Derzhavin and Karamzin appeared, openly demanding commentary and truly reliable evaluation—like all of our other old writers, for there is no death in the literary world, and the dead mix in our work and interact with us just as much as living writers. They demand the return of that which is really due them; they demand the destruction of incorrect accusations, incorrect commentary, which have been repeated senselessly over the course of several years, and are repeated to the present day.

But did our journals, guided by strict reasoning, say who Walter Scott was, what his influence was, what contemporary French literature is, from whence it evolved, what the reason for the incorrect deviation of taste was and in what its character consisted? Why was poetry replaced by prose works? What is the Russian public and what is the level of its education? What is the originality and virtue of our writers?

In this respect the reader will in vain seek new ideas or any traces of thorough, conscientious study. They have only cursed Walter Scott. They accepted French literature with childish enthusiasm, asserting that the fashionable writers had pierced the secrets of the human heart, until now the reserve of Cervantes, of Shakespeare... Others abused it uncontrollably, while they themselves were writing in the style of the very same school with even greater absurdities. They didn't bother themselves at all with the question of why diluted novels and tales are so popular with us, issuing instead still more of their own works. Of the public they said only that it is a respectable public and that it should subscribe to all the journals and various publications, because the father of a family, and a merchant and a soldier could read them; about Derzhavin, Karamzin and Krylov they either said nothing or said the same thing a provincial teacher says to his pupil, and escaped with a few banal phrases.

What did our journalists talk about? They talked about their dearest and most favorite subjects: they talked about themselves, they praised their own works in their own journals; they were entirely concerned only with themselves; they paid cold, passionless attention to everything else. It was as if the great and amazing were invisible. Their indifferent criticism was directed at those subjects which scarcely deserved attention.

What was the general nature of this criticism? One clearly noticed:

(1) Disregard for their own opinion. It was almost never noticeable that the critic considered his business to be important and undertook it reverentially, with preliminary consideration in order that, while guiding his pen, he would think about the small number of highly educated contemporaries before whom he must answer with his every word. For the most part, journal criticism was

some kind of buffoonery. How did they praise an author who was patronized? They didn't simply say that such-and-such a book was good and worthy of attention in such-and-such a regard—not at all. "This book," said the reviewers, "is amazing, unusual, unheard-of genius, the best in Russia, the price is fifteen rubles, the author is superior to Walter Scott, Humboldt, Goethe, Byron. Get it, bind it, and put it in your library; it doesn't hurt to have two copies of a good thing."

Most of the books were praised and praised indiscriminately and completely senselessly. If you counted all those that fell into the first-class category, you would think that there is no literature in the world richer than Russian literature, but after only a short time contradictory opinions of those same reviewers about the same books make you pause and become bewildered. That same absence of measure was apparent in the reproaches to writers the reviewer was ill disposed towards or hated. He poured out his anger just as senselessly, satisfying a momentary feeling.

(2) Literary faithlessness and literary ignorance. These two characteristics have particularly spread in our literature recently. Nowhere will you encounter passages which mention the names of writers who have already finished their careers, who watch us in rays of fame from above. Not one of our critics has raised his eyes reverentially to note them. The names of Derzhavin, Lomonosov, Fonvizin, Bogdanovich, Batyushkov almost never appear on the pages of our journals. Nothing about their influence that remains, that is still discernible. They have never even been compared with the present era, so that our era seems as if it were cut from its roots, as if we had no beginning, as if the history of the past does not exist for us. This literary ignorance is spreading especially among our young reviewers so that, in general, contemporary literary criticism is quite superficial. A year hardly passes before trends which were rather strongly voiced are already mute, voiceless—like a sound without any echo, like words said at yesterday's ball. The names of writers who have already consolidated their fame and the names of those demanding it have become nothing but toys. One reviewer drops those which his opponent raises, and all this is done without any discretion, without any ideas. Another name owes its fame to the squabble of two reviewers. Saying nothing about our national writers, the reviewer of any book, no matter how empty it might be, inevitably begins with Shakespeare, whom he has never read. But it has become fashionable to mention Shakespeare—give them Shakespeare! He says: "From this point we will now begin to examine the book before us. We will see how our author corresponds to Shakespeare," but meanwhile the book which is being examined is trash, written entirely without any pretension to comparisons with Shakespeare and corresponds only to the reviewer's spirit and manner of expression.

(3) Absence of purely aesthetic pleasure and taste. In the Moscow journals you will still occasionally see some taste, something resembling love for art; in contrast the critics of the Petersburg journals, especially the so-called decent ones, are extremely vacuous. The works examined are elevated higher than Byron, Goethe, etc.! But nowhere does the reader see that this is a sign of taste, a sign of understanding, that it flowed from the depth of a grateful, touched soul. Their style, often in spite of an external pretentiousness and shining decorativeness, breathes a deathly coldness. Liveliness and a passionate manner are found only when a reviewer touches on something lively and when the matter is related to his own worth. Fairness demands that we make reference to Shevyryov's criticism as a comforting exception. He communicates impressions to us in the manner in which his soul received them. A thinking man, who is occasionally attracted by a first impression, is always visible in his essays.

(4) Trivial ideas and trivial dandyism. We have already seen that criticism has not been concerned with important questions. The reviewers' attention was aimed at a whole rank of empty books and not at all in order to examine them, but to sparkle with civility and make the reader laugh. To what degree the criticism was concerned with trifles and senseless quarrels the reader has already seen from the famous proceedings about the pronouns *sei* and *onyi*. That is what Russian criticism has finally achieved.

Who among us spoke about literature? During this period neither Zhukovsky, nor Krylov, nor Prince Vyazemsky, nor even those who not so long ago published journals, who had their voice and had shown taste and knowledge in their essays, voiced their opinions: is it any wonder that our literature has reached such a state?

Why haven't those writers who have displayed profound aesthetic feeling in their works spoken? Did they consider it beneath them to descend to the sphere of journalism, where warriors of all sorts normally conduct their noisy battle? We don't have the right to decide this. We must only note that criticism based on profound taste and intellect, criticism of superior talent has an equal value to all original writings: in it the writer who is being studied is visible, in it even more visible is the one who is doing the examination. Criticism inscribed with talent outlives the ephemerality of a journal's existence. It is invaluable for the history of literature. Our literature is young. It has had few leading figures, but for thinking criticism it presents a whole field, work for many years. Our writers have been cast completely in a special form, and, in spite of the general feature of our literature, that of imitation, they incorporate purely Russian elements; and our imitation carries a completely northern original character; it constitutes a manifestation remarkable even for European literature.

But enough. We will conclude with a sincere desire that in the coming year there will be more activity and that with a greater number of journals there will be more independence from monopoly and through that more attempts by all to conform to their ideal. At least a certain comforting tendency is already noticeable in that several journals promise next year to publish with more diligence than was the former state of affairs. The publishers of *The Son of the Fatherland* and the publisher of *The Telescope* have begun to speak of improvements. It cannot be doubted that with more effort something more can be done. In any case, we, with all candor and a warm prayer, state our desire: let the efforts of each and every one be generously rewarded, and the less greedy and more conscientious his work is, the greater may he be paid homage by the attention and gratitude he deserves.

Translated by Carl R. Proffer and Ronald Meyer

Book Reviews

Reviews from *The Contemporary*

The Historical Aphorisms of Mikhail Pogodin.[1]
Moscow, 1836.

Mr. Pogodin is, in many respects, one of our noteworthy literary figures. He stands alone among our writers, not attracting the favor of the majority. But he draws attention to himself more than any of those who have dedicated themselves to history. He was the first to say that "history ought to create one individual, one person out of all mankind and present the biography of this person through all the stages of his life"; that the "innumerable peoples who have lived and worked during a span of one thousand years, would each furnish a single feature for such a biography. A great historian recognizes this feature." He was the first to speak about the great writers who in their works had pointed to the true meaning of history. He has translated excerpts from these for his journal; and, finally, he has translated many of them in full, hardly bothering whether their importance had been recognized. The following is a list of his published works:

1. A study of Cyril and Methodius by Jozef Dobrovsky[2]
2. On the dwellings of the ancient Russians—his own composition
3. The critical works of Evers[3]
4. An outline of ancient geography—his own composition
5. Lectures about Heeren[4]
6. Bettiger's outline of world history
7. A. Schloezer's[5] introduction to history for children
8. A Russian history for use in schools
9. Ritter's maps of Europe
10. Goethe's *Goetz von Berlichingen*
11. *Marfa Posadnitsa*, a play
12. *Dmitri, the Pretender*, a historical drama
13. Dobrovsky's Slavonic grammar, translated together with Mr. Shevyryov[6]

Besides this he has published: *The Moscow Messenger*, for the years 1827, 1828, 1829, 1830; *Urania*, an almanac for the year 1826.

His historical critiques evidence much intelligence, deliberate moderation and sometimes a youthful passion in pursuit of an original idea.

The present book collects individual ideas and comments, recorded by him at different times. These ideas have been put together without any kind of order and are not always clearly expressed. But one senses in them a striving for generalities. The boundaries that he has marked out for history are extensive. He embraces history not only in political events, but also sees it in commerce, literature, religion, artistic development—in all the sundry phenomena in which humanity is to be found. These are his thoughts about history in general:

> Each man acts for himself, according to his own plan, but a general course of action results, a higher plan is fulfilled, and from these raw, delicate, disintegrating biographical threads is woven the durable fabric of history.

> History for us is still a narrative poem in a foreign language that we don't understand and we only aspire to the meaning of some words, of many, many episodes. And how many passages have been distorted in our manuscripts due to the scribes' ignorance and limitations! History must be restored (restaurare) like a statue discovered in the ruins of Athens, like Virgil's text in a monastery copy.

> Imagine (I'm asking what is possible only in imagination) that a person who doesn't have any understanding of music, but who is naturally endowed with all the faculties to feel and understand it, receives a score of some great oratorio and all the musical instruments on which it can be played; with this he is told only that the conventional signs (notes) that he sees represent different sounds made by the instruments. He wants to imagine on the basis of these two facts the performance (execution) of this great musical work. He must first of all try all the instruments and learn all their possible sounds, mark them all down and put his new notation in order, search out by means of trial and error the relationship between his notation and what he was given (as if by means of a false mathematical rule), thereby learn what sound and what instrument is represented by one or another note, play the score by parts and so on and so on. How much mental effort is required to find these means, how much labor to use these means! Entire generations would pass before the grandchildren's grandson would finally succeed in accomplishing the distant goal of his forefathers and would enjoy the divine harmony.

> The historian is given a most difficult task: he himself must catch all the sounds (the chronicles, the Nestors,[7] the Gregorys of Tours[8]), distinguish the false ones from the true (historical criticism—the Schloezers, Krug), the insignificant from the important, combine all of this into one heap (histories, collections of events—the Rollains), set out these heaps according to the types of history (individual histories of religion, commerce—the Heerens), foresee that there must be some sort of system, order and harmony in these heaps (the Schloezers, Herders, Schillers), prove a priori that it is positive (the Schellings), conduct experiments to find this system (the Asts and Schtussmans), and, finally, find the system and read history in the same way that the deaf Beethoven read scores.

Mr. Pogodin sees in the Byzantine Empire the continuation of the history of ancient Greece. The genius of Plato and Aristotle is resurrected in John Chrysostom[9] and Gregory of Nazianzen.[10]

He supposes France to be the spring of everything social, civic and political, a country that is continually undergoing experimentation. The events with which he substantiates this claim evidence careful observation. He writes that the Franks were the first to accept the Christian Catholic faith and it became a state religion earlier; the Franks were the first to institute and develop feudalism; the crowned Frank, Charlemagne, was the first to elevate the Pope; having recalled the Pope to Avignon, France was partially responsible for his fall; the first attempts against papal power (Albigenses[11]) took place in France; chivalry developed more splendidly in France; the Crusades were advanced by a Frenchman, the hermit of Amiens; ravaged feudalism was organized into autocracy first in France; a standing regular army began in France; permanent taxes and the royal court began in France; the idea of a balance of power had its source in the Italian wars engendered by France; the institution of embassies, political journals, coffeehouses, encyclopedias, language, fashion, cards—everything was begotten in France. Public opinion is nowhere so strong as in France; France brought a stop to revolution by its terrifying example; the cause of today's close union of the European powers is France and her Napoleon.

Many aphorisms merely bring together similar and contrasting events that took place in different corners of the world or in one and the same land; the bringing together of a remote, almost distant cause with its colossal consequences reverberating throughout several centuries is always striking. Other aphorisms are merely questions in answer to questions. Everywhere you see a person possessed by the greatness of his subject. This reverential amazement breathes on every page. Sometimes, struck by the infinity of science, it is as if he senses the powerlessness of the spirit and exclaims: "How difficult it is to recognize from what something originates, what the direction of something is! How interwoven are the causes and effects! I repeat my question—is it possible to represent history? Where is there a form for it? History in its fullness can only be felt."

The ordinary reader will glance through this book carelessly and absentmindedly, and having found two or three insignificant thoughts poorly stated, will perhaps laugh at it with a childish levity; but the reader in whose soul burns a passionate love for science and whose thought grasps its profound significance, will read these pages with sympathy, will be filled with gratitude for the stirring of reflection in his soul and will say: this man saw and felt in history that which is not given to everyone to see and feel.

Ya. Ozeretskovsky, *Sailing the White Sea and Solovetsky Monastery.*
St. Petersburg, 1836.

A few entertaining remarks on the nature of the north. One would like to have heard more about this gloomy and famous monastery of our chronicles, where in ancient times disgraced patriarchs and bishops languished in seclusion.

The Field Notes of an Artilleryman, 1812-1816, The Artillery of Lieutenant Colonel I.R...[12]
Moscow, 1835-1836.

When our forces returned from their glorious journey to Paris, each officer brought with him his own store of reminiscences. All their stories, without exception, were entertaining; everything had been observed with the fresh and curious feelings of a novice; even the billeting of a Russian officer in a German apartment was material for a novel. Until now, if an officer who had been in Paris, now a veteran in evening clothes with graying hair, started talking about the campaigns he participated in, an interested circle would gather around him. But until now none of our officers had thought to write down his stories with that truthfulness and simplicity with which they pour forth in an oral telling. They consider what had happened to them as private individuals to be too insignificant, and they are gravely mistaken. Their simple stories sometimes bring to history that feature that cannot be found anywhere. Take this book, for example: it is not distinguished by the brilliant style and manner of an experienced writer, but everything in it is alive and the witness's voice is heard throughout. It will be read by those who read just for entertainment and by those who extract new riches for the mind.

The Letters of Lady Rondeau,[13] *Wife of the British Minister at the Russian Court During the Reign of Empress Anna Ioanovna.*
Translated from the English by M. K.
St. Petersburg, 1836.

This book is wonderful. Lady Rondeau writes to her friend about herself, her feelings, about things that are interesting only to her, but, in passing, touch on history. A few fleeting words about Peter II, Empress Anna Ioanovna and Biron add some new details to their portraits.

Journey Around the World.
Compiled from the Journeys and Discoveries of Magellan, Tasman, Dampier, etc.[14]
St. Petersburg, 1836.

There are books written for that public which, like children, needs to be forced to read. In this respect the English have acted more selflessly. With all their national pride, they are distinguished by their philanthropy in forming societies for the propagation of morals, temperance and the like, and they publish and distribute without cost, or at an exceedingly low price, many useful books for the people. What the English invent, the French add depth to, enlarge upon, and spread all over the world. Hardly had one cheap publication appeared in France, when a flood of cheap publications poured in the next year. The book cited above belongs to this multitude of publications. It stands out more than the others, because it's more useful. This is a compilation of all the journeys, a depiction of the entire world in its current geographical, political and physical state; in a word, this is a book which above all has found an audience, because a journey and stories of journeys have more impact than anything else on the developing mind. The information supplied by the most recent travelers is put into the mouth of one person in this book. Maybe the very exacting reader will be vexed by the idea that he's told all this by a person who does not exist—the freshness of impressions retained by the eye-witness has no substitute. The translation is clear and lively. The illustrations are very good. A rather large volume in quarto, printed in two columns, is being published each month. Mr. Polevoi has begun translating this same work in Moscow. He's already published the first volume; if the remaining five volumes come out, then his edition will be a bargain.

An Atlas of Cosmography.
Published by Obodovsky.[15]
St. Petersburg, 1836.

This atlas appertains to Mr. Obodovsky's cosmography, which was published two years before the present work.

My Housewarming.
An Almanac for 1836 by V. Krylovsky.
St. Petersburg.

This is an almanac? What a strange feeling we experience when we look at it: it seems as if we see before us an emaciated wailing cat on the roof of an abandoned house, where at one time things were gay and noisy.[16] An almanac! Once upon a time Delvig published his aromatic almanac.[17] In it flowered the names of Zhukovsky, Prince Vyazemsky, Baratynsky, Yazykov, Pletnyov, Tumansky, Kozlov. Now everything's new, you won't recognize anybody: different people, different faces. In the table of contents provided at the beginning stand the names of Messrs. Kurut, Bargasov, Krylovsky, Gren; apart from them, the letters S, Sh and Shch have written some poems. We read the poems—similar poems were around before; but at least everything was more even and flowing in them, writers babbled in imitation of the talents. Oh, for the old days!

Forty-One Stories by the Best Foreign Writers.
Published by Nikolai Nadezhdin.[18]

Moscow, 1836.

Stories printed in various issues of *The Telescope*. The publisher has done a good thing by selecting and issuing them as individual books. They are better in this format than in the other. Collected together they offer something truly diverse: Russian peddlers will carry them along the first wintry road to all our far-flung cities and villages; they will help our provincial ladies pass long evenings and nights pleasantly, at least more pleasantly than do our home-grown novels.

Reviews Not Published in *The Contemporary*

Chronicles of Russian Glory from the Time of the Blessed House of Romanov's Accession to the Throne.
St. Petersburg, 1836.

A memorandum-book in the form of a calendar in which are recorded under every day of each month the battles that took place on that day and all the victories of our triumphant forces. In addition, portraits of the emperors and famous generals are included.

A Children's Karamzin.
St. Petersburg, 1836.

A periodical publication—up to two issues per month. The lithographs are mediocre, but are suitable for children.

Russian Classics. Part I: Kantemir. [1]
St. Petersburg, 1836.

The intention is a very good one—to publish Kantemir and other writers of the past. But it is published very peculiarly: each month one or two signatures are issued. The reader pays one ruble for these signatures and the cover, for which the reader has absolutely no use. Fairly expensive and inconvenient. Expensive because a small volume of Kantemir will cost a good deal more than ten rubles. Inconvenient because we're not accustomed to such a small format and everyone will wait to buy the whole book. In Europe large books are divided into booklets to make it easier for the readers to pay (N.B. almost all of whom are poor people). Furthermore, the installment published by the French is never just a single signature—for one ruble they give you a quantity of letters that exceeds all of Kantemir. Plyushar is publishing Dumont-Durville's *Journey Around the World.* Ten signatures of small print are issued each month; and in addition, with a multitude of illustrations and the entire booklet sells for two rubles. We can call that inexpensive. Besides, the publishers are drawing out this book. Kantemir, who could be printed in all of two weeks, will be published over a span of half a year. Who wants to wait every month for a single signature?

The History of Poetry.
Readings by Stepan Shevyryov,[2] Post-graduate Fellow at Moscow University. Volume I. Moscow, 1835.

This is a remarkable event in our literature. For the first time we have an original Russian study of the history of world poetry. The study is written by a thoughtful writer, whose critical insight is vast. Of all the writers heretofore who have principally worked in criticism, Shevyryov is indisputably the first whose name will remain in the annals of our literature. We will place a comprehensive analysis of this important work in the next issue.

He and She. A Novel.[3]
Moscow, 1836.

Three types of novels have now been established in our literature: fifteen-ruble novels which are almost always thick, long, and solid, in four parts with 300 pages in each; other novels, which are of medium quality, are the eight- or six-ruble ones, which are also sometimes in four parts, but are found in two parts as well. Each of these parts consists of only 160 pages, and sometimes even fewer. Cheap novels of this sort are usually written by young people; there is a lot of romanticism in them—no lack of exclamation points and an extraordinary number of ellipsis points. Finally, there are the five- or four-ruble novels: these consist primarily of three parts, sometimes of two, but these parts are never more than sixty or ninety pages, and sometimes some part is done so peculiarly that altogether it has only thirty-six pages. For the most part, they are written by elderly people who are not professionals by any means. These are naturally-gifted Russians and the leader of this disabled troop is A.A. Orlov, whom the Petersburg journals like to ridicule so much.

The novel under review belongs to the first type, that is, to the fifteen-ruble novels, though the author, as is apparent from the opening pages, is often very impatient and will not stay in one place and deal with one character for very long. I didn't remember anything after I'd read half of the first part. I remember only that some count and some student wander the streets of some city, maybe Moscow, seize Katya, abduct her, then seize her again and, it seems, abduct her again. However, anyone who wants to can read it himself and find out what happens later.

The Malcontents. A Comedy in Four Acts.
By M.N. Zagoskin.[4]
Moscow, 1836.

The plan is rather weakly conceived. There's no action at all. Therefore scenic requirements are not met. The verse in places is good, everywhere almost natural, but there is almost no comic element and that's the main thing. The characters are not drawn from nature.

A Journey to the Holy Land, Made in the Seventeenth Century by the Archdeacon of the Trinity Monastery.
Moscow, 1836.

Journeys to Jerusalem produce a magical effect in our country. This is one of those books that is read more than any other kind and more reverently. Almost the same impression is produced by a journey to Constantinople, as if the Russians preserved an instinctive gratitude preserved for that world which in the old days emanated from there. Often a Russian merchant with some education would quit his business and set off for Jerusalem or Constantinople and would even publish a book, which people eagerly bought from peddlers, passing over the many pictures strung from the peddler's shoulders, regardless of the fact that these pictures were drawn with all sorts of colors. The Russian reads other kind of books only to read something for the chance to show himself and others that he can read just the high points of that which another reads a lot of—without the slightest attention to the book's content. And that is why it is so exceedingly difficult for the people to choose their reading.

A Description of the Prussian Government. Geographical and Political Aspects.
Compiled by Ardalion Ivanov, Educator and Tutor of the Imperial School of Jurisprudence.
St. Petersburg, 1836.

This book is the sort of geography that is found all over Russia and from which our children are taught. Whoever wants to possess a complete political and satisfactory understanding of Prussia will not find it in this book. It's somewhere in between: as a book for a pupil it's too big, for someone who has completed his education it smacks of a pointer.

An Index of the Provincial and District Post Roads in the Russian Empire.
Compiled by Mr. Savinkov According to the New Department of Post Roads and Stations.
St. Petersburg, 1836.

The book is published rather compactly for the road, although it could be published even more compactly. The map is unnecessary, especially such a large one—it would be impossible to unfold it while traveling—it would be better to think of a way to put it in the pages of the book, if only in sections, and it would be still better to combine the description with the topography.

The Founding of Moscow, or the Death of the Boyar Stepan Ivanovich Kuchka.
A Historical Novel, Taken from the Times of the Reign of Izyaslav Mstislavovich. Written by I. K...
St. Petersburg, 1836.

One of those kinds of novels that are published a great deal and particularly in Moscow. Their plot is usually taken from national history. They are usually slim, slight, but divided into four parts, and are sold very cheaply. Their authors are often timid, young, not yet tested by fire as writers; therefore they put only the first initials of their name and end it with dots. The author usually has his characters speak like Russian peasants and merchants, because over the past ten years, since the appearance of novels in a Russian caftan, the notion has arisen that our historical figures and, in general, all heroes from the past must without fail speak the language of today's simple folk and use as many proverbs as possible. In approximately the last two or three years a new French school, given voice here in many translated excerpts and melodramas for the theater, has manifested its appreciable influence even on them. An exceedingly large number of the strange phenomena in our novels have resulted from this. Sometimes a Russian peasant will come out with a theatrical trick that even a Roman would not be capable of. He gets up from his wooden plank or stove and comes forward with a walk resembling Napoleon's; some Vassily, Ulita or Stepan Ivanovich Kuchka, after showing us some Russian ways and letting loose with a folk proverb, suddenly roars "death and hell!" Elsewhere the reader is prepared for the fact that these peasants roll up their sleeves and punch each other, but instead of this he sees them throw each other a dark glance and!! Here the author usually puts several dots and adds: "And they understood each other." And sometimes he even adds: and a terrible drama took place in that silence, and the like. One cannot even reproach them for the fact that the character is a bit like a Spaniard or Frenchman; our big novels have not been able to escape this flaw and.... The general character of these little novels, which are proliferating in such abundance and so quickly in Russia, is their complete immaturity. It would be very unjust if we were to say that one sees only foolishness in them, for which our journalists often reproach them. It's not foolishness at all, but the creation of the most immature child, who takes up one thing and then another, who wants one thing and then another—there is no continuity. And therefore he has as many incongruities on one page as someone else has in an entire volume. Every line is either a whole octave lower or higher. In the untalented but experienced writer, who has become a practiced hand at writing, incongruities become apparent only after one reads several pages: in the untalented but inexperienced and young writer, so many accumulate on a single page that on this basis the reader can come to an accurate conclusion about the entire work.

If we were to cite an example of a few pages from such a work, it could make the reader smile; but there's no sense in filling a page of our journal with poor writing when we can use that space for an excerpt from something good. An innocent wish to write without fail some sort of little novel is apparent in all these books. May God forgive them their unwitting transgressions! There's no reason for us to be annoyed with them and get angry because they are published in a slovenly way and so forth. And that's why it has been necessary here to say a few words about them respectfully, so that with a similar novel we need say absolutely nothing at all, but refer to what we have stated above.

A Murderous Encounter.
A Novella by Ya. A.
St. Petersburg, 1836.

This little book has appeared, consequently somewhere in this wide world there must be a reader for it.

134   Book Reviews

Pictures of the World, or Useful and Pleasant Reading for Young People. Part II.
St. Petersburg, 1836.

The title of this book shows that it fell into the literature books by mistake.

Several years ago in Russia, as in Europe, there was in general a noticeable liking for moralistic reading, which took the form of long discourses and tracts. Readers demanded edifying and wholesome works. Psychological works, printed in a number of huge volumes, significantly outnumbered everything else. Everything else, everything practical, everything light taken from life was considered empty and unworthy. An extraordinary number of books of this kind appeared in Russia during this period. This was a sedate time; however, one should note here that despite all this, the morality of this time was not very pure, and that those who read wholesome books secretly played tricks and pranks, which now would be too obvious to everyone. It is remarkable that at the same time that so many moralistic works appeared, so did ones so immoral that now even the most courageous of the French writers would be ashamed to write them. All the old people then read devotional books; all the youth, on the contrary, read the Foublases and others and a careful examination reveals that the old people almost surpassed the youth in their domestic affairs. Such a discrepancy between theory and practice prevailed at the end of the eighteenth century. In the nineteenth century masonic and other sects and abstract mysticism supported the existence of similar philosophical works, discourses, exhortations and tracts, although already clothed in different guises. They, one could say, were responsible for the limited desire for reading in our society, because they demanded a fixed degree of some intellectual effort, and thus were the province of a few. When Kant, Schelling, Hegel, Oken, as artists, cultivated science, clothing it in the concise terminology of determinants, anatomically dividing, separating and uniting into a whole the great sphere of thought, their opinions circulated only among a small circle of their listeners, who understood their difficult, laconic, almost mathematical language. But when their thoughts began to be disseminated, the German writers, if one can call them that, people of the middle class, who for the most part were rather intelligent but lacked a penetrating mind and talent, when these people began to develop these thoughts with their own standards of understanding, when they clothed these discourses in eloquent phrases, common language, often even with the lyrical ardor of the soul, then these creations gained popularity everywhere among the reading public—and the readers schooled by mysticism gladly started reading these books. In our time the indispensability of realizing every thought in practice has been acknowledged with almost universal sympathy. It should always celebrate as a wonderful epoch the incipient connection between theory and practice, following the great but simple truth that actions speak louder than words. A living example is more powerful than discourse, and thought never seems so elevated to us, so strikingly elevated, so stunning in its greatness, as when it is endowed with a visible form, when it is created before our eyes by a living, familiar world, when it is read, one might say, with our spiritual eyes from the poet's entire creation. Our divine teacher and Savior was the first to disclose this lofty mystery, clothing his holy divine thoughts in parables, which thousands of nations have heard and understood. Therefore, we, having engaged in such great evasions for thousands of years, are finally returning to that truth which was already uttered in the depths of our infant hearts. And now history is demonstrating to the intellect the union with philosophy and is forming a great edifice. And now everywhere, in all the current attempts of ours at novels and stories, one can see the striving to realize, to prove or lend wings to some idea, and only mediocrity is to blame when an elegant, incorrect idea is sometimes preferred to a profound and simple one.

A Children's Pavilion.
Compiled by B. Fyodorov.
St. Petersburg, 1836.

A children's almanac is a small store, without a doubt, of very pleasant things for them. B. M. Fyodorov is one of our oldest authors; he has written tragedies and novels, he has written and translated many genres of poetry, but finally, sensing that everything in this world is vanity and that one has to have too much to rouse our adult generation, he took to publishing books for children. And of our writers nobody in this regard has done his work as assiduously as he. He published a magazine for children fairly punctually and regularly, and has always prepared some present in the form of an almanac for the new year. The Russian Academy has elected him to membership, although he has not written a learned discourse of six pages in which it is usually stated that someone says this, someone says that, whereas I think that this subject needs clarification. But, nevertheless, his labors were useful and his works quickly sold out. His name earned no reproach. His current almanac has the same merits as the previous ones and all children can get some good reading out of it.

The Beautiful Woman of Astrakhan, or A Hut on the Bank of the River Oka.
A Novel Based on a True Event. A Russian Composition.
Moscow, 1836.

Not a novel, but a novella, because the first part is only forty-two pages long, and the second is seventy-six.

Review of Agriculture of the Imperial Estates in 1832 and 1833.
Published by the Department of Imperial Estates.
St. Petersburg, 1836.

The book is remarkable in many respects in that it throws some statistical light on the central provinces of our Russia. All of the imperial estates are now concentrated and contained in the central region. There are none either in the south or the north. For the most part they begin in a narrow wedge from Moscow and extend eastward, drawing apart in proportion to their approach to the Ural mountain range, encompassing the lands of the following provinces: Moscow, Vladimir, Kostroma, Nizhegorod, Kazan, Simbirsk, Penza, Saratov, Vyatsk, Perm, Orenburg. Besides these there are also imperial lands in the Baltic provinces.

We'll say a couple of words about the soil and land, as the first natural law of the organization of the government's estates. The central lands, that is, those not far from Moscow, the provinces of Moscow and Vladimir, and in part the lands of Kostroma and Nizhegorod, contain a sandy, clay soil alternating with tundra, silt, tussocks; you almost never see black earth—these are lands that require tilling more than any other kind. Further to the southeast the type of soil changes; the southern part of the Kostroma and Nizhegorod provinces, and the northern provinces, Kazan, Simbirsk and Penza, comprise another type; the soil contains less clay and tundra, more black earth that is immeasurably deeper, up to twelve inches. This soil requires less tilling than the former. The southern estates, the Kazan, Simbirsk and Penza provinces, and particularly the entire Saratov province, are comprised of almost steppe-like expanses. The soil is now pure black earth, rich, extending deep into the ground; sand and salt marshes are an exception and are to be found only in the Saratov province; the soil produces almost without any fertilization. The lands of the colossal Perm, Vyatsk and Orenburg provinces offer a completely superior kind of soil. In Perm and Vyatsk the forest dominates, in Orenburg the force of vegetable nature casts the tribute of its fodder grass all over its huge expanse. The proximity of the Urals and the ravaging mountain nature give new powers to vegetation. The large quantity of marl offers a means of fertilization. With little labor the soil can exceed expectations. But in examining in this remarkable book the people's work efforts, we see that agriculture is still in its early infancy, despite the resources available to the government. Manual labor in relation to the expanse of the land is incomparably small. Tools are still not very light; habit and long held custom still take precedence over tested experience. The plow today is still heavy, the lazy slow sickle, still not displaced by the scythe, is powerless before such great expanses.

The efforts of labor are more noticeable in the central provinces, where the soil is poorer; they are weaker where the soil is richer and finally disappear altogether in the Perm, Vyatsk and Orenburg provinces, where there are few people in proportion to the land, where the untamed nature of the soil leaves its imprint of wildness on man himself.

So, what is the cause behind this state of agriculture? The cause is found first in the land: not in the soil, but in the extraordinary expanse that still disproportionately exceeds the population. On a small corner of land, even if the soil is infertile, agriculture springs up quickly; at first the consequence of basic necessity, it becomes increasingly necessary as it is developed by demand. Land and people progress at the same pace; the land, testing all of man's strength, forms and triples man's development, his keen-wittedness. Man continually finds means to enrich it. So, it's natural that agriculture in Russia will progress slowly for a long time yet, despite all of the measures introduced by the government, because this is the work of centuries. And who thinks that one man in a short time can accomplish what is accomplished by masses of people and by centuries?

The second, major cause is found in the people. What is a Russian peasant? He is stretched out, or to put it better, he is scattered sparsely, like seeds over a broad field from which thick grain will be reaped, but not soon. He lives isolated in villages separated by large distances, far away from the cities: cities, moreover, that are not much richer than some villages. Deprived of personal, quick communication, he is still rather coarse and underdeveloped and has only the most basic needs. Take the land laborer from the northern and central regions. His food is monotonous: rye bread and cabbage soup, the one and same cabbage soup that he eats every day. He doesn't even have a garden by his house. He has no need whatever of pleasure. He doesn't need to expend a lot of work and effort to get such food and what other desire could occupy him after he satisfies this primary need, when the profound simplicity around him cannot offer him any idea. He is capable of suddenly changing his life, but only when his surroundings are improved—whereas a Russian who has spent some

138   Book Reviews

time in the city will quit agriculture and become an industrial manufacturer, and suddenly his vocation is developed and his vital bustling nature manifests itself; with the aid of vitality and sharpness he becomes a rich man in a short time. This is how a Russian peasant positively becomes a citizen of all Russia, without becoming strong in any one area.

Is it any wonder, then, that our agriculture is still in its infancy? One often hears questions as to why agriculture here is poorer than in Europe and opinions as to how we can catch up with Europe. That's easy to say, especially for those who don't have the brains to see the terrible dominance of the European population over the land and the terrible dominance of the land over the inhabitants of Russia. In any case the government is taking measures; guided by a profound wisdom, it is focusing its primary attention on agriculture. The agricultural laborer is the kind, solid root of the government in both the political and moral sense. The merchant is a mercenary person, the artisan is a mercenary person; every manufacturer is a mobile person, here today, gone tomorrow, but the agricultural laborer is a stationary element in the government. One of the government's best actions in this regard is its publication of the results of the agricultural reports, among which in some respects one can include this book. These reports always show the situation clearly and suggest ideas as to what needs to be undertaken and how to improve the situation.

Guidelines for the Construction of Sea and River Steamboats.
Translated from the English by the Boatbuilder Vasily Berkov.
St. Petersburg, 1835.

A fairly comprehensive manual on the building of steamship vessels with a brief look at the beginning and advanced levels of this art.

A Complete Manual for the Eating-House Establishment.
Compiled from the personal experiences of Gerasim Stepanov.[5]
Moscow, 1835.

If you used all of these recipes and directions, you could cook up a porridge for which there'd be no takers.

A Business Calendar with Addresses, or the General Commercial Index of the Russian Government for the Year 1836.
Compiled by Vikenty Zhgersky
St. Petersburg, 1836.

The business address book-calendar—as a calendar with addresses—is far from complete and is unsatisfactorily compiled. Despite this, the articles on industry and even the plans that are included are not without value, but they are presented here only in excerpts and don't show any planning in the edition. It's expensive, considering the size of the book.

A Review from *The Muscovite*

Dawn. An Almanac for 1842.
Published by V. Vladislavlev.[1]
St. Petersburg, 1842.

Let's begin with this brilliant item of typographical splendor, this light, sparkling flower, greeting the coming year of 1842.

Dawn is published more magnificently with each year. Now it is adorned with portraits of the Petersburg beauties. The portrait of Her Imperial Highness, Maria Alexandrovna, is the leader among these. Expression and thought shine through, and most likely every Russian on the eve of the New Year will look at it carefully, as at something bright and prophetic. The rest of the portraits are wonderful. One examines them not without a certain secret pride, seeing that the beauties of the North almost outshine the beauties adorning European keepsakes. The portrait of Countess Elena Mikhailovna Zavadskaya shines with all the splendor of her unfading beauty. The light clarity of simplicity is reflected in the face of Countess Sofia Alexandrovna Benkendorf. A southern plentitude of mien illuminates the face of Baroness Ekaterina Nikolaevna Mengden. Finally, the purely Slavic type of beauty is seen in the profile of Princess Maria Ivanovna Baryatinskaya. The inclusion of portraits of our radiant female contemporaries is still a new thing for us. They will be greedily pored over by the inhabitants of some of the remote parts of Russia, where rumors of our capital scarcely reach, and more than one person, endowed with high artistic taste will admire them, as Pushkin said, "Revering devoutly/Before the sacredness of beauty." And everyone this year will be even happier to give or receive *Dawn*.

It's a pity to subject this brilliant article to the callous pen of stringent criticism. Criticism will halt before it as before a gentle butterfly or flower, afraid to deprive it of freshness with a breath. Its contents correspond wholly to its significance. It is light boudoir reading for beauties. There is a worldly style, smoothness of language, and strict decorum in many of the tales, a light grace in some of the poems, in a word, it is a shiny toy. The publisher's tales sparkle with liveliness and lightness. They have the same art, as is usual for him, of turning an insignificant object into an entertaining one. Zhukova's Cartesian monastery and Nadezhdin's Montenegrins stand out more than the others... As for the poetry, the reader will probably pause over Lermontov's "A Dead Man's Love" and Vyazemsky's "Traveling Ballad." Besides these, the names of Koltsov, Benediktov, Count Sollogub, Kukolnik appear in *Dawn*. But why talk about what the reader will find here? Better that this sparkling butterfly be carried to every corner of Russia and brightly greet everyone from Kamchatka to the shores of the Tavrida with the New Year.

Translated by Ronald Meyer

LETTERS

1. M. I. Gogol.[1] April 17, 1827. Nezhin.

...I passed the time rather boringly. I didn't have any books. Our theater had been stopped for the meantime, and I was forced to sit motionlessly in one place hanging my head and thumbing through my old lessons. The fine weather of spring was beginning to entice me; it was gay at first, but gaiety is good when you share it; and then it got boring. Only the dream of my joy, of you, sometimes sends rays of light through my gloomy thoughts.

Man is strange with regard to his internal desires. He catches sight of something in the distance, and the dream of it doesn't leave him for a minute. It disturbs his peace and makes him employ all his efforts towards acquisition of what is important. Occasionally what seems to be the smallest trifle, but which is precious to me personally, torments me with anguish and vexation because I haven't the means to possess it...

2. M. P. Pogodin.[1] December 14, 1834. St. Petersburg.

I have received your letter of November 20. I was talking to you about Heeren[2] in jest, between us; but for all that I respect him much more than many, although he doesn't possess such deep genius as to stand alongside the first-class thinkers. And I would be sincerely happy if we were given a few more Heerens. You can drag things out of them with both hands. I have long since been in accord with your thoughts. And if you think that I am cutting peoples off from humanity, you are wrong. Don't look at my historical excerpts; they are young, they were written long ago; don't look at the essay "On the Middle Ages" in the departmental journal either.[3] It was said only so as to say something, and will only provoke something of a need in the listeners to find out about what else must be said, what it is. With each month, with each day I see new things, and I see my mistakes. Don't think that I was just trying to arouse feelings and imagination either. I swear I have a higher goal. Perhaps I am still little experienced, I am young in my thoughts, but some day I will be old. Why is it that in a week I already see my mistake? Why are nature and man unfolding before me? Do you know what it means not to meet compassion, not to meet a response? I lecture alone in this university, absolutely alone. No one listens to me, not at one lecture have I once met anyone who was struck by a glaring truth. And that's why I am giving up absolutely any artistic polishing now, and even more so the desire to rouse the sleepy listeners. I express myself in fragments and just look into the distance and I see it in the system in which I will have it molded in a year. If only one student-creature understood me! They are a people as colorless as Petersburg. But all that to the side. You ask what I am publishing. I am publishing a miscellany.[4] All the works and fragments and thoughts that have ever interested me. Among them there are historical ones—some already known and some unknown.[5] I ask you only to look at them a little condescendingly. Much in them is young...

3. M. S. Shchepkin.[1] May 14, 1836. St. Petersburg.

I cannot, my kind and esteemed countryman, there is no way I can visit you in Moscow. My departure has already been decided. I know that you would all receive me with love. My thankful heart feels this. But for my part I don't want to seem boresome to you or unappreciative of your interest—which is precious for me. Better, I will carry this enlightened gratitude of the old capital of the fatherland in my soul with pride, and in a foreign land I will treasure it like a holy thing. Besides, even if I came I couldn't be as useful to you as you think. I would read it to you badly, without interest in my characters. First, because I have become cold to it, second, because I am dissatisfied with much in it, though absolutely not with what I was accused of by my short-sighted and unreasonable critics.

I know that you will understand everything in it as it ought to be understood, and in the present circumstances you will stage it even better than if I were there myself...

Farewell. May God love you and assist you with your arrangements; and on the road I am going to ponder carefully a play which I have planned. I am going to write it in Switzerland this winter, and in the spring I will moor right in Moscow with it and Moscow will hear it first. Farewell again! I kiss you several times. You love your Gogol always too.

It seems to me you would do better to put off the play until fall or winter...

4. A. S. Danilevsky.[1] October 23, 1836 (New Style). Lausanne.

...Well, aren't you ashamed, have you no conscience? How could you give absolutely no news of yourself until now! I wrote and wrote, I wrote to Kreuzny, dispersed letters to you in all the German road towns; with charcoal and pencil, I wrote my address on all the monuments and places and streets of note, I left letters for you in all the hotels, finally I wrote to the innkeepers to make inquiries to the travelers about you... and all in vain! As a punishment to make up for that you will squander a fair amount of centimes if you get all my letters. But then we are given small pleasures as a reward for worry. I don't know if I would have been as happy if I had received a million rubles as I was made by your letter. During the course of almost an entire month I constantly dreamed about you, and always in the most unfavorable situations, so that I began to seek information about you with fear; and I already wondered if it wouldn't be better if I remained in the dark; but, praise God, you're alive and well, and when I send this letter to you I will fly after it to Paris myself. I have spent the time somehow or other, God knows how. I lived in Geneva for more than a month (if you are ever in that city you will see an epistle to you traced in Russian letters on the monument to Rousseau). In that city I was in a *pension* where I had begun to jabber rakishly in French, but realizing that you and I are a little too old for *pensions*, and becoming incensed at the Irkutsk climate of Geneva and at the vile season, I whipped out of there to Vevey where I also spent almost a month. I found almost no Russians there, but I liked the town. I made friends with the light and dark blue clouds that surround it; every day a shady old avenue of chestnut trees right over the lake saw me sitting on a bench and bent over slightly to the right side letting my stomach digest—it was completely conquered by the same murderously abundant table that you had such just cause to complain about. Every day at exactly three o'clock I went together with the not numerous inhabitants of Vevey to gape at the steamship tying up at the shore, where I expected to meet you every time; and every time only Limeys with long legs climbed out, after which I felt a kind of insensate boredom for almost an hour and went off to my beautiful mountains to air out. I even became more a Russian than a Frenchman in Vevey, and this all happened here because I began to write and continue my *Dead Souls* which I had left off. But... I will tell you the rest when we see each other...

5. A. S. Danilevsky. April 15, 1837 (New Style). Rome.
...What should I tell you about Italy in general? It seems to me as if I had dropped in to see old-time Ukrainian landowners. The houses have the same dilapidated doors (with a multitude of useless holes) that smear your clothes with whitewash; ancient candleholders and lamps like those in church. The platters are all unusual, all in the ancient manner. Up till now I had seen a picture of changes everywhere. Here everything has stopped in one place and goes no further. When I entered Rome for the first time I couldn't give myself a clear picture. It seemed small. But the longer I have been here, the larger and larger it seems to me; and the buildings seem huger, the sights more beautiful, the sky finer; and there are enough paintings, ruins, and antiquities to look at for a lifetime. One falls in love with Rome slowly, little by little—and for a lifetime. In a word, all Europe is to look at, but Italy is to live in. All those who have stayed to live here say this. And it's true that in addition to the other things you will hardly find another country where you could live as cheaply.

There are no trifles and that which in Paris hungry taste invents for amusement.[1] In the stores there are only antiques. But on the other hand there are artistic pleasures... You cannot have any idea of what Raphael is. You will stand before him just as speechlessly and turned all into eyes as you once sat in front of Grisi.[2] But dammit! I got an apartment ready for you and I got ready to be your ciceroni and instead... At least write where you are planning to be in a month and a half, for in a month and a half I will leave Italy to have a look at some German waters. Certainly I should direct my [...][3] on a straight road at some time. By God, it's even funny when I imagine you sitting and freezing at Janin's. At first I couldn't even figure what Annenkov[4] you were writing about, and I wondered if, God forbid, you had popped a switch saying that I had lived at his home. But at the end of the letter, seeing no address or anything I guessed it was *aux eaux vives*. I hardly think you'll be able to stay there for a month. But in any case please write a little more often and inform me of all changes that you venture—not a few of which, I think, must happen to you. We ought to look at something good together. Or are you purposely making a fool of me? Last year, having given your word to come to see me in Switzerland, you pushed off to Paris. Now, having promised for sure to come to Italy, you pushed off to Switzerland. Apparently you have a devil sitting in you that turns you around. You should have, you should certainly experience the artistic-monastic life in Italy, take in the marble and plaster of which there is plenty here, drink in the stars of the night which glitter here with an extraordinary glitter, have your fill of looking at monks and abbots who are strewn about the streets like poppy seeds. I arrived here just the day before Easter, and the first thing I saw was the Pope. Thus I fulfilled an old rule. I attended the liturgy in the boundless Peter which still seemed empty no matter how many people there were in it...

6. N. Ya. Prokopovich.[1] July 21/9, 1837. Baden-Baden.

A request of you! An urgent request! Take 1500 from the bank and send it to me. I hope to return it to you in half a year without fail. At the beginning of next year I am sending my big thing to be printed, one which I think will reward my labors and troubles over it.[2] Please send it quickly; I've run through all my money. I thought I would finish my work much earlier, but that didn't happen! Now I'm sitting at the waters undergoing treatment...

7. N. M. Smirnov.[1] September 3, 1837 (New Style). Frankfurt.

I've hauled your box to Frankfurt. I gave it to Zarg in good shape; he promised to carry out your wish to the letter. As for the slow pace of your journey, I'm not moving any faster myself. The steamer presented me with a pleasant surprise—that of taking two days instead of one. Rain, the faithful fellow-traveler of a journey on the Rhine, redoubled the pleasure. All the passengers crowded in one cabin, and the German odor got so thick you could hang 700 axes in the air. The round windows of our cabin screeched so and were so drenched with sweat that melancholy possessed me from head to heel. And I still have dreams about the wet umbrellas, the greasy boots, and the universal head cold. Finally I got to Frankfurt and for three days now I have been admiring the vilest weather the world has ever seen and the noble physiognomies of the Jews. Because you, I think, already know that Frankfurt smells terribly of the Jew, including Germans. Oh, I almost forgot to tell you, in Frankfurt I met Turgenev[2] with whom I spent a half a day... Turgenev, incidentally, uttered an important truth which perhaps Alexandra Osipovna partly knows—that living abroad one gets sick for Russia, but you no sooner manage to reach Russia than you get sick of Russia. Incidentally I received a short little letter from Zhukovsky[3] which he wrote back in March. Five or six lines, but filled with such grief over the recent great loss[4] that I couldn't read them without emotion. He is still just as kind and loves me just as much, and says that he thinks of me very often. I still haven't received anything in answer to the letter I wrote from Rome. It is probably still lying in the Winter Palace awaiting his arrival from the journey. At Turgenev's I saw the completely finished printing of the first book of *The Contemporary*. In it there are verses by Pushkin with the title "A Fragment," in which he tells how he visited his country estate where he hadn't been for ten years, how his little house seemed to him—and his room (beyond the wall of which the heavy footsteps of his poor nanny were no longer heard), and the same trees with new young ones. Amazing simplicity and such quiet but at the same time deep sadness that I could not even copy it I became so sad. I am leaving today. I am setting off for Geneva...

8. M. P. Balabina. November 7, 1838. Rome.

...My feelings are alive again. You awakened them with your letter, you awakened them pleasantly. I love to read your letters very much. Although the grammatical cases in them are occasionally great liberals and occasionally do not obey your legal power, your thought is always clear and occasionally expressed so felicitously that I envy you. I have already stolen two places, two entire sentences, from them—which ones I won't tell you because I intend to possess them completely... But let's turn to the first point of your letter. You seemed to me very attached to Germany. Of course, I don't argue, occasionally there are moments when one would like to fly out of the environment of tobacco smoke and German cooking to the moon, sitting on the magic cloak of a German student as, it seems, you expressed yourself. But I doubt whether that is the same Germany which we imagine to ourselves. Doesn't it seem like this to us only in the tales of Hoffmann? At least I didn't see anything of it except boring *tables d'hôte* and eternal waiters all with one and the same face and endless discussions about what dishes made up dinner and in what city they eat the best; and the idea of a wonderful and fantastic Germany which I carried in my mind disappeared when I saw Germany in reality...

9. M. P. Pogodin. December 1, 1838 (New Style). Rome.

My dear fellow, I received your letter which you wrote in care of Valentini[1] in September, along with the copies of the money orders. I didn't answer it immediately because I waited for your first letter which searched for me all over Naples and Rome and, as often happens, not at all where it should have sought me. I have finally received it and am writing to you. I thank you, my kind, faithful fellow! I thank you very, very much. Your concern for me touched me deeply, to the very bottom of my soul! So much love! So much solicitude! Why does God love me so much? But at the same time it was sad for me to see, painful, unbearably painful to my heart to feel... God! I am unworthy of such beautiful love. I haven't done anything! How poor my talent is. Why haven't I been given good health? Something has been piled up in this head and soul, and can it be I won't have the opportunity to reveal and express at least half of it? I confess: I have little hope for my health. But that to the side. It saddened me to learn from your letter that you live not without unpleasantnesses and disappointments. Various literary dirty tricks, especially now when those on whom our hope rests are no longer here, have the power to reduce one to great sadness, perhaps even to poison the solemn and inspired moments of the soul. I can't tell you anything by way of consolation. As you know yourself it is impossible for one who is nobly armed with just a sword, that defender of honor, to conduct a battle against those who are armed with cudgels and truncheons. The field will have to remain in the hands of the brawlers. But like the first Christians we can consummate our works in catacombs and cells. Believe it, they will be purer, more beautiful, more elevated. You moved me to great pity for Shchepkin.[2] I am very sorry for him myself. I think about him often. I confess that I even intend to gather all the rough scraps that I have of the comedy I destroyed, and I want to sew something together from them for him.[3]

Apropos of *The Inspector General*, out of your unusual goodness and love for me you want to print *The Inspector General*. I confess that I would like to put it off for a while... I began to rework and correct several scenes which were written rather carelessly and thoughtlessly. Now I would like to publish it revised and improved. But if you find that a second edition is absolutely necessary—and without postponement—arrange it on your own accord. I don't think that it would bring in a lot of money now. But if 2000 or more is collected I will be very happy, because the money you sent me, I confess, weighs upon me. It still seems to me that you have gone without yourself and that you are in need. If all of a sudden people will give money for *The Inspector General*, please fill up the emptiness that I caused your pocketbook, or give it to whomever you borrowed from for me...

10. M. I. Gogol. December 10-11, 1838 (New Style). Rome.

...I even found it a little funny when I got to the place in your letter where you argued with several of your friends about me. Please, don't talk about me too often with them, and especially don't strike up any arguments because of me. It will be much better for you and for me if you will answer observations and remarks about my literary works: "I cannot be a judge of his works, my judgments will always be prejudiced because I am his mother; but I can only say that he is a good son who loves me—and that is enough for me." And be assured that the respect of others for you will be redoubled—as will that for me, because such a response from a mother is the best reputation that a man can have. But parents who brag about the works of their sons—are [...], extremely naive and ridiculous in their naivete. I knew a few who I thought were very ridiculous. I mentioned this because there are many, many sins in my works, and those who argue with you are sometimes very, very correct. I advise you to read the analyses of my works in *The Library for Reading* or *The Northern Bee* sometime, and you will see that they are not at all praised as you think they are.[1] And these remarks are almost always correct. But we will talk about this point some other time...

11. A. S. Danilevsky. December 31, 1838. Rome.

...What is there to tell you about Rome? It is just as beautiful, huge, the same luxurious abundance of objects for spiritual life—or any other. But, alas, my feelings are getting dull, my [...] are not as lively. There are swarms, a horrible crowd of foreigners here, among them not a few Russians. Of my acquaintances Shevyryov[1] and Chertkov are here; the others are not noteworthy, for me that is. The other day the heir to the throne arrived, and with him Zhukovsky. He is still just as kind, loves me just as much. Our meeting was touching; he is all full of Pushkin. The heir, as you know, has a kind soul. All the Russians were invited to his table the second day after he arrived.

You ask about my health... Bad, brother, bad; it keeps getting worse—the more time passes, the worse it gets. Such is the law of Nature. My indisposition absolutely prevents my work. I don't do anything, and often don't know what to do with the time. I might pass the time gaily now, but I am not up on things at all, and my friends themselves are bored with me; and often I, too, have nothing to talk about with them. It seems that some kind of devil is sitting in my belly; it positively keeps me from doing anything, now drawing some seductive picture of an indigestible dinner, now... You ask what I have for breakfast. Imagine it—nothing. I have no appetite in the morning, and not until I have dinner at five o'clock do I drink tea, prepared at my own place, just like that which we drank in the Cafe Anglais with butter and other appurtenances. I don't dine at the Lepre, where they don't always have the finest material, but at Falcon's—you know, the one near the Pantheon—where their roast mutton may compete with that of the Caucasus; the veal is more filling, and some kind of crostata with cherries can produce three days of mouthwatering in the most inveterate glutton. But, alas, there is no one to share such a dinner with. My God, if I were rich I would desire—what would I desire? That I would spend my remaining days together with you, to offer sacrifices in the same temple, to compete at billiards occasionally after tea as—do you remember—we played not so long ago; and suddenly what a distance there is between us. Afterwards I played billiards here, but somehow it didn't seem the same and I gave it up. I don't want to play with anyone except you. I feel that you would fill my days which seem empty now. But why be desperate? Why so many times we almost bade farewell forever, and nevertheless we met again and thanked God. God will grant that we meet again and live together again...

I got a letter from mama. She writes that they stayed in Poltava very long in order to wait until *The Inspector General* was given at some theater there, and that the peasant dolt who was sent to find out about it garbled and mixed things up, finding out nothing, and that instead of *The Inspector General* they got into *Hamlet*, which they listened to until the end; and the next day, to their unutterable pleasure (that is, mama's and sister's), they learned that *The Inspector General* was going to be given and they set out that same evening. I imagine that *The Inspector General* must have been played in all respects in a barbarous manner, because even mama herself, a woman, as you know, who is very condescending, says that they played the servant pretty well and the others, according to their abilities, they played as they could—what wealth they had, they gave. From a few words dropped by chance in mama's letter I could also note that my countrymen, that is, Poltava Province, cannot stand me...

12. A. S. Danilevsky. March 25, 1839 (New Style). Rome.

...I already wrote you that Zhukovsky left Rome. But I am unusually happy; in his place Pogodin came to see me. We now live together. His room is with mine; we breakfast and talk together. In a month I will send him off to you in Paris, straight to the benefactress m-me Hochard. He will spend a month in Paris and perhaps two weeks in London. I have commissioned him to drag you to Marienbad, where I also plan to plod, where he will be and where, it seems to me, it wouldn't hurt you to be; one of your main illnesses, it seems, is analogous to mine and is connected directly to the stomach; and it is said Marienbad is very good for that. Pogodin brought me news of Lukashevich.[1] He met him in Prague. This odd ball and friend of ours will be in Marienbad this summer. Besides him Pogodin invited a pack of sundry Slavs there for the summer so that we can have good company, make up our own table, and in this way slip away from pernicious *tables d'hôte*—in a word, undergo treatment seriously, methodically and gaily, strengthening and supporting each other; and at the waters that is certainly not the least important thing. Not long ago at the post office I pulled a letter from mama out of the vaults destined for oblivion, one written back in the month of July where among other things there is one very remarkable line about how rumors are still being spread about the letter (you know about it) written by me to the Tsar two years before. Among other things mama writes that she received a letter from Varvara Petrovna, formerly Kosyarovskaya, now Beryozina, who reports that she knows for sure that I wrote a letter to Zhukovsky asking him to borrow 3000 for me somewhere, but that the letter was written so humorously that Zhukovsky showed it to the sovereign, and that the sovereign grabbed both his sides, rolled with laughter for a full quarter of an hour, and ordered that I be given not 3000 but 4000 and said: "Let him write another letter like this to me—I'll give him another 4000." Mama said that she didn't doubt this, although I never, she says, talked or wrote about such things. But that she does not agree on one point, that it is more correct to suppose the sovereign gave me 6000 and not four, because even a certain (I don't remember his name) good and respectable man who served at one time in Petersburg and who is very well read and knowledgeable in literature, says that it was six. But let's forget the rumors...

13. S. P. Shevyryov. May, 1839. Rome.

I thank you a million times for your kind letter and I kiss and embrace you for it. I am very happy that you are satisfied with your dwelling and are completely at ease; without that it is impossible to begin one's observations properly. Incidentally, don't forget to make inquiries and find Turgenev if he is in Paris. He will be very useful to you. Danilevsky should know his address. If you happen to meet Mickiewicz,[1] embrace him firmly for me. Your news about Uvarov reached here too.[2] Of course, nothing could be better. So far as I recall this is the first consoling news from Russia. It seems the vengeful shadow of

Pushkin interfered in this affair, and defending the rights of literature and enlightenment dear to it from beyond the grave, it finally overtook the plunder inexorably. Everyone here has a different story about it, but no one knows the real truth. I see a miracle here and nothing else...

14. S. P. Shevyryov. August 25, 1839 (New Style). Vienna.

...Now about myself. That I am in Marienbad you already knew. Whether I am better or worse—God knows. Time will decide that. They say that the results of the waters can be seen only afterwards. But what is the main thing and what will perhaps interest you (for you love me as I love you) is the visitation which inspiration has made to me. The times of the Cossacks are becoming clear before my eyes and passing by in poetic ranks, and if I don't make anything of this I will be a great fool.[1] I don't know whether the Ukrainian songs which I have at hand now cast them over me or whether clairvoyance of the past came over my soul of its own accord—but I feel much that rarely happens nowadays. Bless me!...

15. M. I. Gogol. October 24, 1839. Vienna [Moscow][1]

I am leaving today. It is decided; I am coming to Russia for a short time, for the time that my health will allow me to spend. But in any case I will try to see you, and if my journey exhausts me too much and I am not in condition to come to see you on the first winter road, I will invite you to come to my place. I think Moscow will be the place of our meeting. I plan to take my sisters there too. I plan to take them before the examination. I don't want them to wait for that puppet comedy. Especially when they have little to show off in public. So much the better. What is good for boys does not become girls.

16. M. P. Pogodin. November 4, 1839. St. Petersburg.

...I don't approve of your intention to publish supplements to *The Moscow News* at all, and I am even surprised how you happened on the idea.[1] If one is going to publish, and especially you and at this time, one must publish seriously, efficiently, weightily, powerfully. If one must, then a real, serious journal is better. But what can these supplements be? No matter what you do—shallow little articles and all kinds of petty squabbles! And if there happens to be a significant essay among them it will be completely lost. And besides—to waste on them the first fire of the assault, the hot zeal of the beginning, and lastly, the essays which if saved up would give full weight and thickness to a serious future journal. And you yourself want to affirm the opinion of you that is unjustly going around society—that you are incapable of long and truly serious work, that you hastily take up everything at once, etc. For God's sake, think it over carefully and study it from all sides. Keep this firmly in mind: you must begin now in such a manner that it will be done once and for all, so that it will be unchanging and irresistible. I know that in your present intention you have been tempted by what seems at first glance to be a profit, and isn't it true that you imagine these pages will sell in a large quantity? I swear you are deceiving yourself cruelly here. If you had a place in *The Moscow News* itself that would be another matter. You would sell a lot. But you are publishing for a special price, separate from the news. Of the 15,000 subscribers to *The Moscow News* there are perhaps only fifty who have literary demands. Be assured that none of the rest will add ten rubles for anything. If, on the other hand, you are placing hope on the readers who do not subscribe to *The Moscow News*, you are deceiving yourself still more. Why the very name *Supplements to the Moscow News* will not attract anyone. There is nothing electric in it, not even a splashy effect. On top of that these are not political pages filled with current events, which is the only thing that can sell large numbers; and there has never yet been a case where pages devoted strictly to literature, a tiny literary newspaper, has had any success in our country. Of course even for such an undertaking there is a probability of success—but when? When the publisher sacrifices everything and gives up everything for it, when he turns into a never-silent buffoon, who will catch all the changing tendencies of the crowd, look ceaselessly into its eyes, guess all its desires and slightest changing tendencies, make it gay, make it laugh. But, fortunately, you are incapable of all that. And failing that, then what? Do you really think that solid essays placed on newspaper pages will interest anyone and last for long? Their life will be the life of the newspaper; after reading them the crowd will put them to the well-known use—with the only difference that maybe this will happen even before they are read. An intelligent, forceful, deep essay in a daily paper! Doesn't that strike your eye sharply? That's the same as Pushkin at a party at Grech's—in with Stroev[2] and other literary rubbish. Even this comparison isn't strong enough and does not reach the real truth. The question arises what need literature has of being weekly, and in our country where does news come up in the course of three or four days, especially at present? And why have a paper without what is current? You know yourself that in our country the reading of books is more in fashion than the reading of journals, and that in order to sell well journals are forced to assume the external appearance of books (only, unfortunately, in the literal sense). And point out to me any country where any purely literary newspaper is in fashion. All the Paris *Revues* are published in book form. What is destined to be bound should be bound; what is for toilet paper is for toilet paper. Don't ever mix up these two things which are never joined together. You can't do anything to change this.

154   Letters

No, you simply haven't examined the matter. I never expected to hear this from you. You have simply perplexed me. No, no matter what, I have been sent by God to oppose you in this. If only you knew how you have sent a chill through me and upset me with this news. I had formed and was carrying in my mind the idea of a carefully considered and indisputable journal, a source and sower of truths and good. I was even prepared to write a few essays for it myself, using the time of spring and next summer which will be free for me—I who had taken an oath never to contribute to any journal and not to submit my essays anywhere. But now my spirit has fallen; you will begin these supplements, you will ruin and wreck yourself on them, and afterwards you will be cold to the publication of a serious undertaking. For God's sake, study this matter carefully and soundly from all sides. What is this restless spirit that seethes in you now, which is dragging you to a journal when you still haven't even looked around yourself since the time of your arrival. No, this will lay on my conscience. I am going to beg you on my knees, I am going to cast myself at your feet. My life and soul, you know you are dear to me, that you are, precisely, my life. There will not, I swear it, there will not be any success in your undertaking. And seeing your failures I won't be able to bear it, and it will poison my stay in Moscow before I get there, and it can bring a state of torpor upon me. Give in to me. Let us discuss it, let us study it carefully, let us use a significant amount of time for the preparations, because really this is a significant business and, I swear, then it will be good. I have talked a lot, but, it seems, not enough yet. I will stay here another week and a half, and around the 20th of November I will certainly be in Moscow together with Aksakov...

17. V. A. Zhukovsky. May 3, 1840. Moscow.

I write you hastily. Before departure. I am late for both the latter and the former. I made an agreement of sorts about the third part of my works. I won't get the money all at once and not now—but it is a sure thing. This year you will get from Pogodin half of the loan which you gave to me thanks to your generous love. My soul is more at rest now, and I even feel what I have not felt for a long time—a kind of secret disposition for work. Oh, if only my last anxieties would leave me and be carried away. My spirit needs peace now, absolute peace. Now I must cast a request at your feet. A request which, as if from inspiration, both Prince Vyazemsky[1] and Turgenev[2] advised me to make at the same time. As you know, Krivtsov[3] received the post of director (with a salary of 20,000 rubles per year) of our Academy of Arts which is presently being founded in Rome. Since directors always have a conference-secretary, why shouldn't I become his secretary? I can even be useful in this, I, utterly useless in everything else. And this would certainly be useful for me, because then I would be given a salary of perhaps 1000 silver rubles. Oh, how many black and troublesome thoughts that would remove from me. And when everyone profits in some way from service, why am I, poor wretch that I am, the only one that is refused. If this worked out I would be the happiest person in the world, not because I got a means of subsistence, to hell with that; I wouldn't give a penny for my subsistence if I knew that my existence would drag itself on without practical work. But because then I would return myself to myself. I am completely exhausted by the burden of the most onerous troubles which have not left my shoulders for more than a year. Now hope has revived me, and I feel a readiness for work; I don't even know—something like inspiration, which I haven't had for a long time, is beginning to stir within me. Oh, if only I had peace and seclusion now! What are you doing now? Will I see you on the way? How I would like to chat with you. But you can even see to this matter yourself and do a great deal. Something inside me tells me that you would do a very good deed by this. You can present this situation to the heir to the throne and dispose him in my favor and write a letter about it from yourself to Krivtsov. If the crown prince sees Krivtsov, which will surely happen, and expresses even his slightest desire to him, I am confident that Krivtsov would then use all his efforts to request that I be given him as secretary. If you knew how my poor conscience is tormented that my existence hangs on the shoulders of my generous friends. Although I know that they have shared with me joyfully and willingly, I also know that all goodness and generosity in the world is in itself nakedness; and like a tsar on the chest or Anna on the neck,[4] rags are given to it for works. Not daring to believe anything and almost trembling in anticipation, I am sending you this letter, which is probably not coherent enough for you to be able to see the situation clearly from it; but I am writing it to you, and you see soul and sense where an intelligent person without a heart finds neither soul nor sense. Farewell. If you want to let me know about something quickly, address it to Vienna, *poste restante* (until July). If after this time (in August), then to Rome.

Yours to the grave and beyond the grave,
on this side of life and on the other,
Gogol.

18. A. P. Elagina.[1] June 28, 1840 (New Style). Vienna.

I simply cannot understand how it happened that I didn't visit you just before my departure. I don't understand, I don't understand, I swear I don't understand. Every day I came to the Arbat Gates to the house in the basement of which lives the cobbler who bears such a graceful surname to inquire whether you had arrived and when you would be in town, and every time the servant who came out to open the door for me met me with the same answer that you hadn't arrived and that it was not known when you would be in town. I learned to know that servant and his frock coat by heart so that I even know where there is a spot on it and which button is missing. I asked him in great detail about your address three or four times. I communicated all this to my coachman in great detail and for all that I still didn't visit you. Along the road I felt in all my pockets constantly; I kept on sensing that I had forgotten some very necessary thing, but just what I couldn't remember; and only the next day I recalled that I was a horse and struck myself on the forehead, but that didn't help anything at all. It was too late to correct matters; the vehicle I was sitting in had already reached Vyazma... I still had so much, so very much to tell you—just what I don't know, but I know I would have told it to you and that it would have been pleasant for me. In a word, I got so vexed that then I was ready to wipe my mug with the nastiest rag and thumb my nose at myself in front of everyone, publicly uttering, "There, take that you fool!" But the whole public consisted of one stationmaster who probably would have taken it on his own account and a cat which was sitting in his cap and which without any doubt would have paid no attention. The only thing consoling in my failure to say good-bye to you is, naturally, the fact that we will soon see each other; at least one must draw such a conclusion. But for God's sake, stay healthy! Why do you want to get ill so often? If only you knew how sad that is for me! I can just imagine you sitting on the divan with your angelic patience trying not to show that you are suffering. Fulfill my request if you love me even a bit, and if not I will again wipe my mug with a nasty rag, so nasty, that is, that I will sneeze all the way to Rome itself. Apropos of the latter circumstance. At the Russian border I took final leave of all things which engender sneezing. What air! Holy skies, what air! There is something of Italy floating in it. My nose even senses the little tail of sirocco. And where is this from? What beneficent winds have brought it? Is it meeting me on purpose? If it is for me, then surely it is worth it; of course I am not a general, but who can love like this... You get so intoxicated, you close your eyes, and you regret only that your nose is still small and short—if only it were a little bit longer!...

19. M. P. Pogodin. October 17, 1840 (New Style). Rome.
Aren't you ashamed? Only because I didn't write to you, you concluded and thought about me that... Who am I? So you didn't even know me enough to keep from concluding... I swear, I have more right to be angry with you than you with me. So if, let's suppose, someone were to tell a pack of lies about me,

tell a cock-and-bull story not resembling my character or manner of thinking, you would believe it. Aren't you ashamed! Why didn't I write to you? You could have found the reason yourself, to wit, the one why a person is silent for several hours at a time when left alone with his truest friend, while he immediately starts talking occasionally very hastily and finds material for conversation with a person who is more of an outsider. You should have at least adduced this reason and excused me in your mind. Now more than ever I am completely submissive to my mental disposition, though (alas!) it is sometimes unhealthy. I didn't have a sincere inclination to write you then and I didn't write. Once there was an inclination to write you, but (God!) at what a moment. I wrote but didn't send the letter—and did well not to. But you shouldn't have started thinking in any respect. Leave that to someone else. I would sooner forgive someone else, perhaps any other person no matter who else. But not you...

20. P. A. Pletnyov.[1] October 30, 1840 (New Style). Rome.

Hello, priceless Pyotr Alexandrovich. Write me even a brief line. I have had no news from Petersburg, absolutely none. I am writing you because the day before yesterday I saw you in a dream in such an unusual and doleful state that it frightened me and I cannot be at ease until I hear something from you. Also inform me how my project is going. Can I hope for the post in Rome about which I wrote to you? I need to know this now, more than ever now. I got cruelly ill; God how ill I got. I am to blame myself. I was gladdened by my aroused powers which were refreshed after the waters and journey; and I started to work with all my powers, sensing the awakening inspiration which had already been asleep in me for a long time. I overdid it and paid terribly for straining at the wrong time, when I needed repose. I don't want to tell and relate to you how dangerous my sickness was. The hemorrhoid threw itself onto my chest; a nervous irritation such as I had never in my life known befell me so that I couldn't lie down or sit or stand. The physicians were already about to throw up their hands, but one unexpected medicine saved me. I ordered myself put in the stage-barouche or a *vetturino*. The road saved me. The three days that I spent on the road made me recover somewhat. But I don't know myself whether I have yet got completely out of danger. The slightest movement, insignificant effort, and the devil knows what happens to me. It's terrifying, simply terrifying. I am afraid. And my task was about to begin so well. Really, I had begun a thing such as I had never had before—and now from the very clouds and into the dirt...

21. A. A. Ivanov.¹ October 20, 1841. Moscow.

...I'm surprised that you haven't received the money yet. It was sent to Krivtsov, and as early as August Krivtsov informed Pogodin that he sent an order to Rome for its immediate payment. Only I don't know to whom he sent the order: Valentini or someone else. Therefore I ask you to locate and pick up the money. There is 2000 rubles; give Valentini 200, take a hundred for yourself... Farewell, I embrace you, don't forget to write. Apprise me of everything that you're doing, of all your needs; and God prevent you from ever falling in spirit. There is nothing that can't be helped. Believe my word—my word does not deceive...

22. N. Ya. Prokopovich. November 25, 1841. Moscow.

I am writing you after a long illness which almost overcame me, the start of which I got in Petersburg. Now, praise God, I am much better though I have become very thin. Are you well? Write me a couple of words about yourself. I have been very worried about you. There were rumors here that there was something like a small flood in Petersburg and water appeared on Vasiliev Island. I feared for your little house and your living on the lower floor. Please, let me know if it hurt anything at your place. Because of illness my business has hardly begun. Only now has my manuscript started being copied. If my shirt-fronts are ready, send them—and with them my rubber boots that I ordered Platosha to put in the carriage—but he didn't think of putting them there. We ransacked everything in the carriage but didn't find them. And now I can't get boots like that anywhere...

23. M. P. Balabina. January, 1842. Moscow.

I will write you at least a few words. I didn't want to, really. I didn't want to take up my pen. To poke my nose out of this snowy cave and write besides? Bears usually tuck their noses more deeply into their fur coats and sleep at this time. You already know what a stupid role my strange figure plays in our native whirlpool, and I don't know why I happened to land in it. Since the moment I set foot in my native land it seems to me that I have turned up in an alien land.¹ I see dear familiar faces, but it seems to me they weren't born here; it seems I saw them in some other place; and in my stunned mind I imagine many ridiculous things incomprehensible to me myself. But what is terrible is that there is not one thought in this head, and if you need a dummy to put your hat or bonnet on, I am entirely at your service now. You can put a hat on me and anything that you wish; and you can brush the dust from me, sweep under my nose with a brush and I won't sneeze, and not even snort, I won't move.

24. P. A. Pletnyov. February 6, 1842. Moscow.
Among other things I learned from Prokopovich's letter that you want to submit the manuscript to Uvarov. Dissuade yourself from doing that. Uvarov was always against me, though I don't know at all how I aroused his hostile disposition. I think it began with *The Inspector General*. Given the present circumstances, it seems impossible to do anything else either, so therefore curtail the matter. I see it is not the fate of my creation to be published now.[1] And besides, the time has passed. I know how to be humble. I will try to bear more want and poverty, to be patient. But your generous sympathy hasn't lost any value through this; tell that to everyone: Alexandra Osipovna, Count Vielgorsky, Prince Odoevsky, Prince Vyazemsky. I will bear this gesture of their souls in the depth of my thankful heart everywhere, no matter where my wandering fate draws me. It will eternally refresh me, and awaken love to the fine treasures preserved in Russia. No, desperation will not enter into my soul. The higher will is incomprehensible to man, and what seems ruin is our salvation. Let us postpone the publication of my work for a while. And now I already begin to see many shortcomings, and when I compare this first part to those which are to be forthcoming, I see that it is necessary to soften much, to make other things stand out more strongly, and to deepen yet others. Oh, how I need my quiet corner in Rome now, where no agitations and disturbances reach me! But what was to be done: I had no money left. I thought I would arrange matters here and return—it turned out differently. But I am firm. So far as I can, I am mastering myself and my sickness. My faith in a bright future is irrepressible, and an unknown power tells me I will be given the means to complete my work. Convey my gratitude, my intense gratitude to all. Calm them, tell them they have already done much for me. I swear, only my heart knows and feels this. Perhaps in the future I will need more of their generosity. For the sake of God, calm them and return my manuscript to me. But first the main thing—read it all together, i.e., the five of you, and let each of you immediately write your observations in pencil on a small scrap of paper, note all the mistakes and incongruities. It will be a sin for whoever doesn't do this. You must tell me everything; it is necessary to point out my shortcomings to me more than anyone else. But you can understand all this yourself. Have them hand all these scraps over to you and you send them to me immediately. Deliver this short note to Alexandra Osipovna. May heaven preserve you all! It will preserve you for the noble fineness of your souls.

Eternally yours,
Gogol

P. S. Will there be room in *The Contemporary* for a piece about seven printer's sheets long, and will you agree to put off the printing of the issue, not to put it out at the beginning of April, but at the end, i.e., near the holiday? If so, I'll send it to you the first part of April.² Let me know.

25. P. A. Pletnyov. April 10, 1842. Moscow.

The destruction of Kopeikin¹ disturbed me greatly. It is one of the best places in the poem, and without it there is a tear which I don't have the strength to patch and sew up. I decided it was better to redo it than to be deprived of it completely. I threw out all the generals, marked out Kopeikin's character more strongly, so that now it is clearly apparent that he himself is the cause of everything and that he was well treated...

26. N. Ya. Prokopovich. April 15, 1842. Moscow.

...First of all: to Pletnyov about Kopeikin. I fear it will be delayed, and I cannot even think of publishing the manuscript without Kopeikin. Say that I implore him to defend it no matter what. It's simply shame on the censorship, because the way I redid it and sent it to Pletnyov, no censorship can hold it up. If the name Kopeikin makes them pause, I'm ready to call him Pyatkin or anything else.¹ However the censorship left the name Kopeikin alone everywhere in other passages...

27. V. A. Zhukovsky. July 20, 1842 (New Style). Gastein.

...I still haven't heard anything about my *Dead Souls* and what effect it is having, except for some uncontrolled praises, which (I swear) have never been as vexing and unbearable for me as now. Sins, an indication of sins—that is what my soul now desires and thirsts for! If only you knew what a celebration takes place within me now when I discover in myself a vice which until now was unnoticed by me. No one can present me with a better gift...

28. N. Ya. Prokopovich. July 27/15, 1842. Gastein.

I am still not sending you the two remaining pieces because much has to be corrected, especially in *Leaving the Theater after the Presentation of a New Comedy*. It was written hastily soon after the presentation of *The Inspector General*, and therefore it is somewhat immodest in relation to the author. It is necessary to make it somewhat more ideal, i.e., so that it could be applied to any play scoring social evils; and therefore I request you not to give any hint and not to issue it as written on the occasion of *The Inspector General*. During the proofreading of the second volume I request you to act as arbitrarily and autocratically as possible: in *Taras Bulba* there are many errors of the copyist. He often loves the letter "i" where it is out of place—toss it out; in two or three places I have noticed bad grammar and almost an absence of sense. Please, correct it everywhere with the same freedom that you correct the notebooks of your students. If there is a frequent repetition of the same sentence structure anywhere, give them another, and have no doubts at all and don't start to wonder if it will be good; it will all be good. But here is the main thing: in the current list the word *slyshu* [hear] pronounced by Taras at Ostap's execution has been replaced by the word *chuyu* [I hear]. It is necessary to leave it as it was before, i.e., "Father, where are you? Do you hear this? I hear." I lost sight of the fact that the readers have already gotten used to this word and therefore they will be dissatisfied with the change even if it would be better. And if it is going to be in *Notes of the Fatherland* please ask Belinsky to make special offprints of the criticism of *Dead Souls* for me—if possible on paper which is a little lighter so it can be sent to me right in a letter...

29. S. P. Shevyryov. August 15, 1842 (New Style). Gastein.
...Then in Gastein at Yazykov's I found last year's *The Muscovite* and read through all of your reviews and criticism voraciously; this gave me many pleasures and engendered an extremely strong request, of which, perhaps, you already have a premonition. It will be a sin on your soul if you don't write an analysis of *Dead Souls*.[1] There is hardly anyone besides you who can evaluate it accurately and properly. Here is something to work on, a double task. First to define and give the meaning of the work according to the impressions it produced on the mass of the public; check these for correctness and indicate the reasons for such impressions. (I think the first impressions will have to be unpleasant; at least it seems so to me just as a result of the subject itself; but everything which is related to the merit of the work is not seen at first.)... I recalled that to a certain extent, perhaps, even I myself gave my friends a reason to think of me as a proud person. Perhaps even some of the lyrical outbursts themselves in *Dead Souls*... But put all that aside, believe my words at this moment: perhaps not in all Russia is there a man so anxious to discover all his vices and shortcomings! I am saying this in a complete effusion of the heart, and there is no lie in my heart. There is an old belief that it is necessary to hide weak sides rather than display them before the public, that it cools the readers, drives away the buyers. This is not true. The voice of noble objectivity lives longer and reaches all souls equally...

30. M. V. Gogol.[1] August-September, 1842. Gastein.

...A beautiful soul is dear to me. And a prayer is nothing to me if it is superficial; on the contrary, it is even terrifying, because it brings punishment down on the head of those who say them in vain. If a man prays and is unable to keep himself from a feeling of pride and self-love and he complains and grumbles about offenses others have committed against him, if he prays and isn't able to feel love even for his enemies—his prayer will scream out against him.

I see from your letter that you pray and you are even teaching Kolya[2] to get down on his knees. It is fine and necessary to pray. But listen to the word of one who truly desires good for you, and try to pray as a Christian should. Has it ever occurred to you clearly to make an earnest confession without resorting to prayer? Are you able to remember all your actions and judge them severely? Are you able to blame yourself for everything and not others, because blaming others is not a Christian feeling, even though the others were truly guilty—and without Christian feeling it is impossible to pray. Are you able to say in place of the words: "Lord, forgive so-and-so who caused me evil," "Lord, forgive me for the fact that it seems to me that they caused me evil"? If you are able to do this, your prayer will be beautiful, it will carry straight to God; it will procure many deep spiritual comforts. I know that often the thought wanders through your head that I love you less than others. Know well that I am telling you the absolute truth at this minute—I have not yet loved any of you as I would like to love...

31. N. Ya. Prokopovich. September 10/August 29, 1842. Gastein.

Not receiving any letter from you yet I assume that our business is moving along constantly and in proper order. I've been slow in sending out the remaining pieces. But it was simply impossible; how many different corrections it was necessary to make! With great effort I corrected *The Gamblers* which I am sending now. The rough sheets were written so long ago and so illegibly that they gave me terrible work to decipher them. But the last play, *Leaving the Theater*, gave me the most trouble. There was so much that had to be redone in it that I swear it would be easier for me to write two new ones. But it is the concluding piece of the entire collection of works and therefore is very important and required careful polishing. I'm very glad I didn't touch it in Petersburg and didn't hurry with it. It would have been far from the significance it has now, and that would not have been good at all. The copying has still not been finished...

32. N. N. Sheremetieva.[1] February 18/6, 1843. Rome.

...Your letters are as sweet for me as a prayer in a temple; and their effect should be the same, for you wrote during a moment of sincere prayer; and it even seems to me that I perceive your very tears, engendered by prayer. I am fresh and cheerful. Often my soul is so firm that it seems no disappointments have the power to break me. And are there disappointments in the world? We call them disappointments when they are actually great goods and deep happinesses sent down to man. They are our guardians and the saviors of our souls. The deeper I look into my life and all the events that have been sent down to me until now, the more deeply I see the wonderful participation of higher powers in everything that concerns me; and I lack the words, the tears, and the prayers for an effusion of my sincere gratitude. And my soul would like to turn into one complete eternal hymn of gratitude! That is the state of my heart, my good friend! Farewell...

33. S. T. Aksakov.[1] March 18, 1843 (New Style). Rome.

At last I received a letter from you, my good friend, and my soul was put at ease, because, I confess, such long silence from all sides was extremely painful for me. I thank you for your news, it is all interesting to me. The success at the theater and the reading of the plays is exactly what I thought it would be. The comments about *The Marriage* and *The Gamblers* are absolutely correct, and the public showed good sense in this.[2] Concerning the change in the roles of the actors—the directors have a perfect right and I am surprised that they didn't do it themselves.[3] Who besides the actor himself can know his strengths and capabilities? Thank Verstovsky[4] sincerely for his interest and arrangement. But, naturally, *Leaving*[5] should not be played—it would be improper, and it's not at all suitable for the stage. Ask Shchepkin if he received my two letters...[6]

Tell Konstantin Sergeevich that I didn't even think of getting angry at him for the little brochure; on the contrary, basically it is a remarkable thing.[7] But there is a terrible difference between dialectic and a written creation, and woe to him who announces any remarkable idea if this idea is still a child, hasn't matured and assumed a form visible to everyone, wherein every word can almost be touched with the finger. And in general the deeper the idea, the more it can be childish than the pettiest idea.

Concerning the second volume of *Dead Souls*—I already gave an answer to Shevyryov[8] who will retell it to you. As for people cursing me, thank God; that's much better than if people were praising me. By cursing one can nevertheless tell the truth and find shortcomings, but prejudice inevitably settles in those who go into raptures, and it inevitably covers up the shortcomings...

34. N. N. Yazykov.[1] May 28, 1843 (New Style). Munich.

...And from boredom during the rains read through *Dead Souls* one more time. The second time things will be more obvious and all the mistakes clearer. I need this very much. In two years, i.e., before the complete correction of the whole thing, I have to see all the holes and rents. Especially necessary for me now are the following comments: which chapter is stronger, which chapter is weaker than another, where, in what passage does the greatest strength accumulate, where does the author get tired, where is he lazy or—if from tact or your lack of farsightedness you don't agree with the latter word—at least where he is inferior to himself as he appeared in other passages. In a word, everything that relates to the whole carcass of the machine. And we must talk about this matter as about one which is altogether extraneous, altogether unconnected to any personal relationships, as if the author of *Dead Souls* were Oznobishin[2] who had slain a wild goat. You should do this all the more because I have the intention of attacking you also without any mercy, and not just between our two eyeballs, but publicly; for I have in mind saying something about Russian writers in general. I learned about the rather sad story of Bakunin here.[3] This philosopher simply did many stupid things, and his present situation is a sorry one. He couldn't get along in Berlin and, as I was told, he left (for where I don't recall) for the reason that he could have no serious influence. He got the idea (for what purpose God knows, perhaps to do a service to Schelling and the new philosophers of Berlin) of writing an article in some journal on the Hegelians whom he had utterly destroyed and accused of the most revolutionary tendency.[4] The article produced indignation. The Prussian king proscribed the journal and reported this to the Russian government. Bakunin had to go into hiding and now it is said he is in Zurich, totally without any guarantees for the future. I learned all this from Popov, a Moscow graduate student who is attending lectures in Berlin...

35. N. M. Yazykov. February 15, 1844 (New Style). Nice.

...Meanwhile here is what my advice is: every time, whether it's at a moment of grief, or at a moment when a state of firmness settles in your soul, or at a moment when a state of heartfelt spiritual emotion entirely embraces you, immediately cast it onto paper, even if it is just in the form of hieroglyphics and brief indefinite expressions. This is very important. Reading them at a difficult moment you will get yourself (by this very act), even if only halfway, into the state of heartfelt emotion that you were in before. In addition, this will be the nucleus of your poetry—not borrowed from anywhere and therefore highly original. It will be a precious gift to the world and humanity if you succeed to any extent in pouring out onto paper the state of your soul as it moved out of the inmost recesses of grief to consolation. The state of a suffering soul is by itself a sacred thing, and everything that emerges from there is precious; and the poetry which has come out of such inmost recesses is the highest of all poetry. Formerly, when I had not yet experienced deep emotional shocks and when the powers of my soul were still little awakened, I saw in the Psalms of David only an enraptured state of the soul during a lyrical mood free from the cares and worries of life; but now that my eyes have become more lucid, I perceive their source in every word, and I see that all these are nothing but the effusions of a tender soul which has deeply suffered, which has been shaken and agitated constantly, and which has not found tranquility anywhere, or shelter in any person. All this is a sincere outcry and unfeigned enrapturement over God. That is why they have remained the best prayers, and through thousands of years to this time they have brought comfort to the soul. Reread them attentively or, better, at the first moment of grief break open the book at random and the first psalm which turns up will probably fit the state of your soul. And different psalms should be wrenched from your soul, psalms which do not resemble the first ones, ones which have come from your own sufferings and sorrows which are perhaps more accessible to contemporary humanity, because both your sufferings and sorrows themselves are more accessible to contemporary humanity than the sufferings and sorrows of David. Reread carefully everything that I have written to you here, for it has been written with strong, sincere sympathy and all the aspiration of my heart, and therefore no matter how weak my words might be, God, who invests every sincere word and good aspiration with strength, will surely turn this to your use.

Also, it seems to me it would be good for you to divide the morning into two halves. Devote a quarter of an hour at the beginning of each half to regular reading of the same regular book—one short page at a time, no more; this should be a certain law like the obedience required of a novice in a monastery, the same as Stoikovich after dinner.[1] For the first reading (which should be in the morning, right after coffee), Shevyryov will deliver to you a book like the one I am also sending to them as a medicine for various spiritual worries and upsets (though ones not like yours) with the addition of a prescription which you also should read. For the second reading (after twelve o'clock) use the Bible, begin with the Book of Job. Such an hour should begin at the same time every day, at exactly the same minute. Through this both of the divided spaces of time will be best filled with all kinds of intelligent occupations and meditations. Farewell, I embrace you with all my soul...

36. S. P. Shevyryov. March 12, 1844 (New Style). Nice.

...First of all do what I am going to ask of you—keep a short notebook about me. Every time you happen to remember me, immediately note down, in brief words, every thought that has come to you. Almost like a diary—day, month and date. Today you seemed like the following to me... Day, month and date. Today I got angry at you for the following reason. Day, month and date. Here is what seemed to me inexplicable in your character or actions. Day, month and date. The following rumors about you have been going around—I didn't believe them, but a certain doubt crept into my soul. Day, month and date. To this day I still hide in my soul dissatisfaction with you for this and for this, etc. When even a half sheet of stationery has been collected, dispatch it to me in your letter. If you do this for me, you will render me a service greater than all your previous services. Help me now, and when I have become more organized and more intelligent, I will help you...

37. A. O. Smirnova.[1] March 26, 1844 (New Style). Strasbourg.

How do you do! I meant to write to you only after I had arrived at my destination. But the steamer which I boarded in order to set out from here along the Rhine to Frankfurt slammed against the arch of the bridge, broke its wheel, and all the passengers were unloaded again to their inns. I took this event, as well as the extra time given to me, as a sign that I should do something, and I decided to write little notes both to you in Paris and to the Vielgorskys in Nice. In my little note to you there will be a certain reminder and nothing else. But this reminder refreshes and pours courage into our souls, therefore, recall all my words and all our conversations, recall also God's grace which commanded us to meet each other, and, finally, the brotherly inclination of our souls to help each other mutually. And let all this merge into one quiet favorable breeze for you while you are preparing yourself for the sacrament. Among the Ravignans[2] and other new preachings don't forget the old, or to put it more accurately, the eternal preachings. Right away, without putting it off, buy Bossuet's *Oeuvres Philosophiques*,[3] a small volume published by Charpentier, and immediately read the last two essays which are at the end of the book: the first, *Elévation à Dieu sur les mystères de la religion Chrétienne*, and the second, *Traité de la concupiscence*. They can help you to succeed in loving God...

38. S. M. Sollogub.[1] September 24, 1844 (New Style). Frankfurt.

Hello, little sister of my soul, my most kind Sofia Mikhailovna. I am sending you one more brief word for the road. I forgot to tell you something very necessary. Although it is apparently a trifle, many big things depend on such trifles.

You are now going to a new home, a new life, a new household. First of all, from the very start, establish order in everything in the house and especially order in time. So that the hours for your tasks are defined, so that both of you, your husband just as you, know when you are supposed to occupy yourselves apart from each other, each in his own room, and when together. So that this doesn't get mixed up, so that you don't sit together too long without a task that keeps you both equally busy, but so that, on the contrary, you see each other only when you and he each finish your task separately. Through this the times you meet each other will be much better, more lively and gay, and you will be satisfied with each other. In a word, arrange it so that you have less chance to yawn in front of each other. Better each of you yawn privately in your own room than in each other's presence. And also: fix it between you so that neither of you goes straight to meet the other (no matter where you are coming from when you return home); but drop in to your dressing room first and have a look in the mirror in order to straighten yourself up in everything in an external and internal or mental sense, so that in neither respect do you appear as slovens before each other, but on the contrary, meet each other with a bright and gay appearance. So that if it happens for one of you to come with a vexed and bored expression on his face, better let him take out his vexation on something in his own room. There are many objects for this: one can fling a chair, pound a pillow, one can even smash a bottle or inkwell—in a word, it's better to ruin a thing than to ruin the face's radiant expression which you should always display to each other. Absolutely do not disdain any of what I am saying to you now; however petty it is I repeat to you again that much depends on this. All this will be much easier for you to arrange now, if only you take it up immediately without putting off the matter; besides, now you have gotten bored without each other, therefore you esteem each other more and are more inclined to do nice things for each other. Your words and requests will have weight now. He won't refuse you, and will willingly do even what would be hard for him to do at another time. This apparently insignificant and external order will save you from much that is unpleasant and will help you both to fulfill many real and important obligations. By this you will render great service and aid to your husband. It is hard for him to master himself, even if he wanted to. I have more character than he, I have more control over myself; but even for me it is hard to force and coerce myself in many things. It is always easier for two people; all it takes is for one to establish order in everything for himself, the other will start to conform to this involuntarily. Thus, for example, arriving in another country, no matter how we have become accustomed to dining at a certain hour, to going to bed at a certain hour at our own house, nevertheless we give up the former habit all at once, and we dine at a different hour, we go to bed at a different hour—in a word, we do everything differently—which would have been absolutely impossible for us in our own country and which happens of its own accord in a foreign country. And why does it happen? Because others are doing it, and it is boring and troublesome to maintain an old habit alone. Such a service can be done for a man only by a wife who is given to him to refresh him and urge him on to work, to a task, and to all that is beautiful. And so, do this trifling thing for the sake of your love for your spiritual brother, who prays constantly for you to our heavenly Father, Who loves us so tenderly and so inimitably that no one on earth has the power to love even a thousandth part as much. Just resolve to carry this out, and you will carry it out; the strength will be sent down to you. But nevertheless in the meantime while reading this letter you will reward me with a little smile, the very prettiest.

Farewell! I kiss you mentally. Your Gogol.

Don't forget about the alms that you must cast at least once a month, if not once a week, to the beggar of whom you know. Start keeping a little book of expenditures in which you note it down thus: such-and-such a month and date a kopeck was thrown to the beggar.

39. S. P. Shevyryov. December 14, 1844 (New Style). Frankfurt.

Friend, forgive me for my stupid letter; I understand what a bad time it came at and how offensive it was to your heart to read it.[1] Pogodin's misfortune would have hit me hard if I weren't sure there are no misfortunes for a Christian.[2] For my part, I will write him a letter comforting him as far as my weakness has the strength. Friend, I didn't say the slowing down of my works was due to the portrait, but due to those of my inner mental happenings, which apparently insignificant matters and things, the tail end of which was the portrait, have served in a strange way to compete in me. But God be blessed! First of all let us say: Everything that happened in my soul, everything that was quietly suffered in it and hidden from others was suffered for the good and so that I would really have the possibility of being useful to others. Friend, don't condemn me for this excessive (as it seems to you) coquetry either, or a tedious trifle regarding any of my appearances in society. They do not flow from the source which you ascribe to them. And before, even during moments of great self-assurance and confidence in myself, even then I felt that he who can have an influence on others and, generally speaking, on the world must be very careful about going out into society with his shortcomings and imperfections. People are so capable of mixing up the bad with the good in the same man in whom they have noted two or three good qualities (especially if these qualities are also picturesque); everything seems good to them. Even geniuses have caused harm rather than good because of this. The premature publication of my works was basically useful only to me alone—precisely because connected to it were inner happenings (taking place because of all this senseless confusion) such that just at the thought of it terror embraces me—what would I be without these happenings? My friend, there is much I am unable to explain, and in order to explain anything I would have to raise such a story from the depth of my soul that you couldn't write it even with many pages. And for the same reasons it also cannot be comprehensible to someone else why the publication of my portrait is so unpleasant for me. Some can ascribe it to excessive humility, others to caprice, others to the fact that nothing has any rhyme or reason with an eccentric, and the odd fellow must be seen in every act. I won't even hide the fact that the placing of my portrait in just that manner, i.e., lithographed from the portrait I gave to Pogodin, increased the unpleasantness still more. I am depicted there as I was in my own den several years ago. I gave this portrait to Pogodin as a friend, at his own urgent request, thinking that it really was dear to him as a friend, and in no way suspecting he would publish me. Judge for yourself whether it is useful to exhibit me before the world in a dressing gown, disheveled, with long rumpled hair and a moustache. Can it be you don't know yourself what importance people give to all this? But it is not grievous to me myself that I was exhibited like a debauchee. But, my friend, I knew I would be torn out of the journals. Believe me, youth is stupid. Many of them have pure aspirations, but they always feel a need to create some idols for themselves. It is still worse for them if the man who ends up among the idols really has merits. They will not recognize their very merits or evaluate them properly; they will not imitate these, but they will first of all throw themselves on the shortcomings and vices—it is so easy to imitate those! Believe it, first of all I will be imitated in frivolous and stupid things...

40. A. O. Smirnova. February 24, 1845. Paris.

...And pray for me, pray firmly and strongly; my health is weakening and I haven't enough strength to work. Pray God to help me in my work which is no longer undertaken for fame or anything else, but for His Holy Name, for the spiritual comforting of my brother, not for his amusement. I see more perceptively that the climate in Germany is not as salubrious for me as in Italy. There is a big difference in everything. And therefore when I have taken the treatment this summer at the cold waters or the sea waters, I plan to set off next winter for Italy, and from there without putting it off any longer to Jerusalem, feeling that only there can I acquire a complete cure...

41. A. O. Smirnova. June 4, 1845. Hamburg.

My kind and fine friend, I have received your letter of the 12th. There's nothing to say about the fact that my heart read it, not my eyes; there's also nothing to say of the fact that all of your sufferings were felt in the very depth of that same heart. This year is difficult for everyone, and—not without the special intentions of Providence—it is passing in mental anguish for almost everyone. Also, it is in vain that you think I am above what is characteristic of a very weak person, that I have found the secret of conquering sufferings and I live in God alone. Alas! Even in the former I am worthless, not to mention the latter. To live in God means to live outside the body itself, and this is impossible on earth for the body is with us. I don't even have the strength to bear submissively the sufferings of my illnesses; here it's been almost half a year I have been in uninterrupted battle with my ailments and with the powerlessness of my spirit to take control of my sick body. Not suffering from a single mental illness, stemming from my relations to and attitudes toward people (however, perhaps my pride is whispering this to me and it only seems to me to be so), I am suffering with all my soul from the sufferings of my body, and my soul is becoming totally exhausted from the terrible spleen which sickness brings; the soul fights against it and exhausts itself fighting. Really I have gotten just as thin as you, and you would be horrified to see me. During the course of the most difficult moments there wasn't a soul near me—when any human soul would have been a gift; and any sufferer who had called me to his aid, just by this would perhaps have cured my spirit at least temporarily. With each hour my health gets worse and worse...

42. A. O. Smirnova. October 24, 1845 (New Style). Rome.

My friend, Alexandra Osipovna, don't worry about me. I am much better. Anna Mikhailovna[1] wrote me that you were sad because you were not with me and couldn't take care of my sickness. I thank you from all the depth of a loving soul, but nothing is done without the will of God. Sometimes it's good that we suffer something and are left alone—and everything goes to profit and good! I am again in Rome; the long road again helped me. Eternal Peter is again before me; the Coliseum, Monte Pincio and all our old friends are with me. God is merciful, and my spirit will be revived, and strength will be restored!...

43. A. P. Tolstoy.[1] January 2, 1846. Rome.

Your little letter greatly touched me also; there is so much sympathy and goodness in it! What can I tell you about my health? Every minute we must say this: "Great is God who sends us everything!" Here is my present condition for you: I suffer so much from the cold now that neither the fire, nor moving about, nor walking warms me. I have to run about a great deal to warm my blood even a little, but now it is impossible to do that because my legs and my strength have become completely weak; my veins ache and puff up. In addition constipation has begun and all functioning of my bowels has stopped. But I thank merciful God that in spite of the unbearable painful feeling which my entire body (which is constantly in a fever) is experiencing, neither spleen nor melancholy have taken possession of me. I am getting thin, withering and weakening; but at the same time I perceive that there is something in me which just by the beck of the Higher Will will cast all of the infirmities out of me at once, even if death be flying over me. Let the Holy Will of Him who created us hold in everything and turn everything within us into eternal praise of Him; let the illnesses, and infirmities, and our entire existence be transformed into an unceasing hymn to Him! I thank you very, very much, my very kind Alexander Petrovich, for your prayers for me; thank the countess also. Your prayers are necessary for me—yours especially. My heart tells me that you will pray for me as you have prayed for no one before, and your prayers will bring down the grace and mercy of God both on me and on your own soul. God is all mercy and is wondrous in his acts of mercy. Of the Tsar I will tell you little.[2] I caught a glimpse of him two or three times. His external appearance was fine, and he produced a big impression on the Romans with it. Everywhere among the common people they called him simply *Imperatore* without the addition *di Russia*, so that a foreigner could think that he was the legal sovereign of this country. Of course, it is unknown what his conversation with the Pope was about, although, by the way, the results will probably be those which were expected, i.e., a softening of the measures with regard to the Catholics. The reports of the persecuted Uniate turned out to be lies, and she admitted that she had been instructed by the Polish party outside of Russia afterwards.[3] The sovereign was benevolent to the arts and crafts. He showed taste in his choices and orders—and even in the fact that he ordered little. The aid which he extended to the poor was also done with consideration. May God preserve him and inspire him with everything that he needs and which is truly needed for conveying happiness to his subjects. If he prays, and if he prays as fervently and openheartedly as he seems to pray, then surely God will inspire him with the entire course and proper law of actions. God's own word tells us: "The heart of the Tsar is in the hands of God." And if good which is obvious to all is slow in coming from the Tsar, then no doubt this is necessary, no doubt we deserve this for our sins, no doubt we are still far from worthy. Let's pray again, my good friend Alexander Petrovich, that God will grant us all His mercy and will remove His legitimate and righteous wrath from all our generations and will forgive us everything, showing that there are no sins in the world which his clemency cannot overcome. I embrace you and the countess also. Farewell, write about yourself and your health. Do not be disturbed by any squabbles about churches and by what is happening in the world. Now is the time to pray and not to squabble. God demands from us only a prayer from our contrite hearts, only tears and sighs from the very depth of our souls.

All yours,
G.

44. V. A. Zhukovsky. March 16, 1846. Rome.

...My health has greatly deteriorated. At times it is so painful for me that I have to call on all the strength of my soul to bear it, endure, and pray. How mean and base man is—especially me. I don't have the strength to endure nobly and magnanimously in spite of having already seen in myself so many examples of how everything turns into good for the soul. And He is so merciful and repays so richly for the smallest particle of patience and humbleness! And amid the gravest of my illnesses He rewarded me with such heavenly minutes that any grief is nothing compared to them. I even succeeded in writing a little of *Dead Souls* all of which will soon be read by you because I hope to see you... If you are going to send your things to Russia—and along with them my books, take two copies of *Dead Souls* out and keep them with you for me. They are all sold out in Russia; I couldn't get one anywhere, and I need the first part while I am writing the second; and besides it is necessary to make significant corrections in the first itself.

45. N. M. Yazykov. April 21-22, 1846. Rome.

I received your letter but didn't receive the books containing our new literary items, even though I waited two whole weeks after the receipt of the letter. It's a pity you didn't mention with whom they were sent. I would very much like to read the stories of our present-day writers now. They always have a stimulating effect on me, in spite of the heavy burden of my illness. The material and spiritual statistics of Russia appear in them now, and that I need very much. Therefore even those narratives which to others seem weak and insignificant with regard to artistic merit have much value for me. I would read all these journals with great appetite, but I don't have them; and I don't even know where and with whom they were sent by you and when I will receive them. I received a notice from Zhukovsky that he had actually received Ivan Aksakov's poems,[1] but that he retained them thinking it would be better to hand them to me personally upon my arrival. He finds much mysticism in them and reproaches our young poets for the desire to make a show of their originality. I do not share this latter opinion, although I do not read poetry. This trend is involuntary and is not a desire to show off. A present-day young man is thrown about without his will because he has an internal force which demands something to do, which is greedy to act, but does not know where, how, in what place... Nowadays it is difficult for a person to fall into his right place, i.e., the place which belongs just to him; for a long time he has to walk about in circles before falling into it. Try, however, to let Ivan Aksakov read my letters to you about the subjects which face our lyric poet—in connection with the poem "The Earthquake."[2] They direct one to reality, even if only a little bit. How do we know? Perhaps they will give him some idea about how to direct his efforts to the subjects which arise. The point is not in our scribblings. Apropos of these letters—save them. Having examined everything that I have written lately to various people who especially needed and requested spiritual aid from me, I see that a book useful to people suffering in various walks of life could be compiled from this.[3] The sufferings which I have suffered myself have been of use to me, and with their help I have succeeded in helping others. God knows, perhaps this will also be helpful to those who were not in the same circumstances, and even those who worry little about the sufferings of others. I will try to publish it after I have added something about literature in general. But for the meantime this is just between us.

46. S. P. Shevyryov. July 26, 1846. Schwalbach.

...Now I approach you with my request—an extremely urgent one: print a second edition of *Dead Souls* in the same form, on the same paper, in the same printing house, the same number of copies (2400) with the addition only of a foreword which I will send later when the printing is near the end. It will be necessary to finish it in a month, so that it can appear in no case later than the fifteenth of September. The copies will be bought up, this I know. After what I have to say before my departure for worship in the holy lands, they will begin buying them up.

47. P. A. Pletnyov. October 16, 1846. Frankfurt.

I hurry to send the fifth and concluding notebook to you. I am so tired that I have no strength; I completed things only with great effort, especially the essay on poetry which in the three periods of my life I have written and burned three times and now finally written specifically because it is essential to my book as part of the explanation of the characteristics of the Russian man.[1] Had it not been for this it would never have been written; it is so difficult for me to write anything about literature. I don't see myself what way it can be close to that task which is my basic task. It is painful for me to hear about the confusion resulting from Nikitenko's slowness.² But how can I be blamed, my good friend?... Nikitenko is lazy—even incredibly so—this I knew, but he has a good heart, and it is especially necessary to press him personally... If, however, Nikitenko is going to hesitate or is overcome by timidity—then my opinion is to print the book and take it all (in the proofs) to the Tsar for reading. My mission is truth and usefulness, and I believe that my entire book will be passed by him.

48. M. S. Shchepkin. October 24, 1846 (New Style). Strasbourg.

Mikhail Semyonovich! Here's what this is all about: for your benefit performance you must take *The Inspector General* in its complete form, i.e., following the edition which is published in the complete collection of my works, with the addition of the tail which I am sending now... Pay special attention to the final scene. It is absolutely essential that it come out like a picture, effective—startling even. The Mayor should be utterly perplexed and not at all amusing. His wife and daughter, in complete fright, should turn their eyes to him alone. The Inspector of Schools' knees should be shaking violently—Zemlyanika's also. The judge, as you already know, getting ready to sit down. The Postmaster, as you already know, turns to the spectators with a question mark. Bobchinsky and Dobchinsky should be asking each other the explanation of all this with their eyes. There are poisonous smirks on the faces of the lady guests, except Lukanchik's wife, who should be all fright, pale as death, and her mouth open. This mute scene must without fail continue for a minute or two, so that Korobkin, who has gotten bored, has time to offer Rastakovsky some tobacco, and someone from among the guests even blows his nose in his handkerchief rather loudly. As for the *Denouement of The Inspector General* (enclosed with this) which should follow immediately after *The Inspector General*—before giving it to the actors to learn, you yourself read it carefully, enter into the meaning and force of each word, each role, as if you had to play all these roles yourself; and when you understand all of them, gather the actors and read it to them, and don't read it just once—read it three or four times—or even five. Don't scorn the fact that the roles are small, of a few short lines each. These short lines should be said firmly, with complete conviction in their truth, because this is an argument, and a real argument—but not moralizing...

49. A. S. Danilevsky. November 8, 1846 (New Style). Florence.

You should be ashamed for forgetting me and not writing a line in the course of an entire year... But I forgive your carelessness and neglect, and as proof of this forgiveness I am sending you a copy of my book—tell me your opinion of it frankly and in detail, without concealing any of your impressions—out with everything! I think that now you can already sense for yourself that for me those observations are most pleasant which for anyone else would be unpleasant. Don't hide the opinions which you hear from any other people either. And therefore I beg you, whenever you meet people of any class or any education, try to start a conversation about my book, and so as not to forget, immediately note all this down in a letter and send it to me without delay. You will efface all of your previous misdeeds and non-answers to my letters only by doing this. But farewell! I embrace you. Write to Naples, *poste restante...*

50. A. A. Ivanov. December 19, 1846 (New Style). Naples.

Surely you are not praying or you are praying badly. If you prayed as one should my letter would have brought you joy, not chagrin. He who prays to God accepts everything which comes to him as coming from God Himself and he seeks and finds God's directions in all the words addressed to him. He who prays to God is not only saddened by the cruel words and rebukes which are showered upon him—but he seeks still more of them (even if they are not just from those who love him but even from those who hate him). I too pray badly, and I am still far from being able to pray as one should; but I would give a great deal if someone would write me exactly just such a letter—with the same content and in just the same harsh expressions. Verily I say unto you that I would reread it several times a day, and I would prick myself every minute with just these harsh words—not to mention the fact that I would thank the man who firmly told me to quit worrying about my own affairs and rely on him; he who speaks so firmly surely says this basing himself on firm grounds. But you did not even fathom the sense of the letter—a simple content easily understood by every simple person—because you see all things as your inflamed eyes present them to you and not as they are in reality. The letter written to you was not at all to strike a man who is down, but to raise one who is trying with all his strength to lie down and loll about.

G.

51. P. A. Pletnyov. February 6, 1847 (New Style). Naples.

I received your letter with the news of the publication of my book.[1] Why do you call the appearance of my book a great event? That is both immoderate and unjust. The appearance of my book would not be a great event, but, to be exact, a useful one—if everything had fallen into place and been arranged as it should be. Now, however, as far as I can judge by the number of pages which you announced in the letter, more than half were not passed—and on top of that it was the essential half for which the whole book was undertaken, and furthermore (as you note vaguely) there were many passages struck out even on the pages which were passed.² If that is the case, it would be better to hold the book back. You look at my book as a literary person, from the literary side; to you the strictly literary event is important. For me the important thing is that which aches and pains most of all at this minute. You do know what is going on in Russia, inside, what disease man is suffering there, where and in what places what screams of pain are ringing out. It is cozy living in Petersburg, enjoying conversations about art with friends and all other kinds of higher pleasures. But when you find out what the sufferings of man are—from which even the insensitive soul breaks, when you learn that one drop, one dewdrop of help can pour out refreshment and raise the spirit of the fallen—try to bear this destruction of my letters indifferently then. You do not know in exactly what respect my letters would be useful to those for whom they were written; you have not analyzed the soul of man, you have not, as one should, laid bare others or your own self, and therefore it is impossible for you to feel everything that I feel. Even these very words will seem strange to you. Not only my shirt, but my very skin has been stripped off me, but for the moment I alone sense this; and it seems to you that they are simply taking off just my overcoat without which, of course, it is cold—but not so much so that it is impossible to get along without it. Of course I and no one else am to blame for the muddle of this matter on the censorship's part. I should have informed Count Mikhail Yurevich Vielgorsky with detailed information in the very beginning. He would have brought the essays which were not passed to the attention of the sovereign long ago.

52. S. P. Shevyryov. February 11, 1847 (New Style). Naples.
I received your letters with the news that Yazykov has passed away. And so that heavenly, cloudless soul is already in the heavens! Of all my friends he had more of those certain qualities which were in my nature too, which, however, he did not reveal either in his works or even in his talks with others, and which were the reason that there was a close friendship between us. Our thoughts and tastes were almost identical. But at the same time reason and the purity of childhood, which I didn't have, glowed in his words. How good he was to me and how he loved me! Oh, may God consider us all worthy of fulfilling our duty on earth honorably so that we can be worthy of heavenly bliss and rejoicing together with him, whom it was so pleasant to talk to just here on earth, as if one were talking with an angel in the heavens. I thank you for finally starting to talk to me frankly and being bold enough to make reproaches to me. I expect them from everywhere; I seek them from everyone—although no one believes

my words; they think that I am fooling people. In your reproaches there is a just and an unjust side; but both are precious to me, because, first, they show me how I appear in your eyes, and, second, they make me look about and examine myself a little more severely once more...

53. A. O. Smirnova. February 22, 1847 (New Style). Naples.

...My entire book[1] was supposed to be a test; I wanted to test with it to see what condition minds and souls are in. I only wanted by means of it to plant in the mind the ideal of the possibility of doing good, because there are many people who truly desire good, who have grown tired from the struggle and been made gloomy by the thought that it is impossible to do anything. One must keep the idea of this possibility in mind, even if it be distant, because with it as with a lamp you will somehow find something to do; but without it you are left absolutely in the darkness. These letters would call forth answers. These answers would give me information. I must pile up a great deal of knowledge; I must know Russia well. My friend, don't forget that I have my constant work—those same *Dead Souls* whose beginning[2] was so unattractive. My friend, art is a great thing. Know that all those ideals, which French novels crammed into the head, can be driven out by other ideals. And the images of these can be produced with such life-like quality that they will remain irrepressibly in the thoughts and pursue a man to such an extent that all the social lionesses will desire to become another kind of lioness. The ability to create is a great ability only if it is animated by the higher blessing of God. I have a part of this ability, and I know that I will not be saved if I do not make good use of it as I should. And I have strength to make good use of it as I should only when my reason is illuminated by full knowledge of the good use. That is why I beg, I seek information with such greed, information which almost no one wants to furnish—or else they are too lazy to do so. My images will not be alive, if I do not compose them from our material, from our soil, so that everyone will feel that this is taken from his own body. Only then will he awaken, and only then can he become another person. My friend, there is the confession of my literary work for you. I am announcing it to you, because God has considered you worthy of understanding a great deal (so bless any illnesses or griefs which have brought your soul to this state). Don't discuss this with my Moscow friends. They are intelligent people, but they are verbose, and they beat the air for lack of anything to do. Because of this any woman's gossip can confuse them and become the subject of inexhaustible arguments for them. Let them get mixed up about me; I am not going to set them straight. But at the same time their opinions of me have the profitable aspect that they nevertheless make me look around at myself an extra time. And this does not hurt at all, and therefore I am curious to know everything they say about me. And don't you conceal anything from me, no matter whom you hear it from...

54. P. A. Vyazemsky. February 28, 1847 (New Style). Naples.

...The appearance of my book can be important if it just makes society become a little thoughtful about more essential matters. It is true that in it there is a kind of artificial tone and inappropriate rapture—which came about because this book really should have appeared after my death. Also working here was fear for my life and the possibility of completing the work I have begun *(Dead Souls)*, a fear which is excusable in my painful illnesses which were extremely difficult for me to bear. This fear made me start talking in advance about many things which should have been developed in the whole work so that they didn't resemble a confusion. That is why in some letters there are some inappropriate insertions which go outside the usual tone of the letters. That is why in some passages there are pomposities and expressions which show a man who is presumptuous or thinks too highly of himself. I cannot see them all, but you will notice them, because a mote in the eye of someone else is more visible and because your intellect is capable of embracing many sides of a matter... After a careful reading of my manuscript, arm yourself with pen and first erase the I from all places where it has thrust itself forward indecorously. And imagine my personality in all the opinions and thoughts in general about higher subjects and wherever you notice a civil servant of the eighth class has over-reported himself, fix it so that he won't forget he is a civil servant of the eighth class...

55. M. A. Konstantinovsky.[1] May 9, 1847 (New Style). Naples.

What can I say in answer to your frank letter? Gratitude! There is the first word I must say to you, although I would like very much to get a different letter from you. All of your words, about the meaning of charity in the Gospels as well as the other things, are holy truth. I am convinced of them; I do not argue against them, but at the same time things in my book are set forth as if I were against this. How can this phenomenon be explained? I will say more: I did not write the essay about the theater to give society a taste for the theater, but to ward it away from the depraved side of the theater, from all kinds of ballet danseuses, and a multitude of the strangest plays which people have started translating from French in heaps lately. I wanted to ward it away from this by pointing to better plays, and I expressed all this in such an absurd and inexact way that I gave you cause to think I am sending people to the theater and not to church. God preserve me from such a thought! I never had it even when I felt the sacredness of sacred truths much less. I only thought it is impossible to deprive society of all its amusements, but it is necessary to manage things so that after amusement the desire to go to God and thank Him and not go to the devil and serve him would revive in a man of its own accord. That was the basic idea of the essay which I was unable to write well. I will tell you frankly and unhypocritically that the cause of a multitude of the shortcomings of my book is not so much pride and self-willed blindness as my immaturity. I began my education late, during the years when other people think that they are already educated. Encouraged by the fact that I had succeeded in conquering much within myself, I imagined that I could teach other people too; I published my book, and in it I saw clearly that I am still a student. The desire and craving for good, not pride, prompted me to publish my book; but when my book came out I saw in it that there is pride in me—and blindness and much that I would not have seen if my book hadn't been published. This obstinacy and impertinent manner which so offended you in my book also derived from another source. Educating myself in the severe school of reproaches and defeats, and finding an essential usefulness to the soul in them, at one time I was seriously convinced that this would be useful to others too, and I expressed myself rudely and harshly. I forgot that when one wants to teach others something one must speak the language of love, and the more sacred the truth, the more humble the one who desires to proclaim it must be. I myself ended up with the same deficiencies for which I rebuked others. In a word, everything in my book exposes my lack of education. God has made a gift of a large estate, there is a multitude of all kinds of comforts and appurtenances to it, the land stretches out of sight; but the manager to whom this estate has been entrusted is not yet capable of managing it himself. There is my portrait for you! There are many powers, but too little ability to handle these powers—perhaps for the very reason that too many powers have been given. I cannot hide from you the fact that I was very frightened by your words that my book could have a harmful effect, and I would have to answer to God for it. For some time after these words I remained ready to fall in spirit, but the thought that God's mercy is infinite supported me. No, there is a preserving holy power which does not sleep in the world, which guides toward the good even that which man produces with a bad intention. But my book didn't come from a bad intention, my foolishness is the reason for everything; God punished me to make up for that, punished me by having everyone crying out against my book, although the reasons for these cries are infinitely varied. But how merciful is His very punishment! In punishment He lets me feel humility—the best thing that I could be given...

56. M. S. Shchepkin. About July 10, 1847 (New Style). Frankfurt.

Most kind Mikhail Semyonovich, your letter is so convincing and eloquent that if I had really wanted to take away from you the Mayor, Bobchinsky and the other heroes to whom you say you have gotten accustomed like blood relations, I would return them to you again, perhaps with the addition of an extra friend. But the point is that it seems you misunderstood my last letter. I wanted to read *The Inspector General* just to make Bobchinsky more Bobchinsky, Khlestakov—Khlestakov, and, in a word, each one what he ought to be. I had rewriting in mind only with regard to the play which concludes *The Inspector General*.[1] Do you understand? In that play I managed things so clumsily that the spectator must surely draw the conclusion that I want to make an allegory of *The Inspector General*. I don't have that in mind. *The Inspector General* is *The Inspector General* and its application to one's own self is the indispensable thing which every spectator ought to do—with everything even, not just *The Inspector General*, but which it is more fitting for him to do with regard to *The Inspector General*. That is what ought to have been proved by the words: "Can it be my mug is ugly?" Now everybody keeps what is theirs. The sheep are whole and the wolves are sated. An allegory is an allegory, but *The Inspector General* is *The Inspector General*. It was strange, however, that we didn't manage to see each other. For once in my life I wanted to read *The Inspector General* as it should be read; I felt that I would really read it well, and I didn't get to. Apparently God is not commanding me to occupy myself with the theater. Take one observation about the Mayor into consideration. The beginning of your first act is rather cold. Also, don't forget the Mayor's expression is somewhat ironic at the very moment of his vexation as, for example, in the words: "Apparently it ought to be like this. Until now they have sneaked up on other towns; now our turn has come." In the conversation with Khlestakov in the second act, there ought to be much more play in his face. At this point there are completely different expressions of sarcasm. Incidentally, this is more perceptible in the last edition published in my *Collected Works*...

57. P. V. Annenkov. September 7, 1847 (New Style). Ostend.

My conception of the divinity is not as narrow as you think, but at least it is much broader than the sense which you gave to my words. But this is a subject of lengthy speechs and commentaries, and therefore let's put if off. In the meantime the point is that we are all going toward the same goal, but we each have different roads; and therefore we cannot be completely understood by each other until we arrive. We are all seeking the same thing; at present every thinking person, if only he has a noble soul and elevated feelings, is seeking the lawful, desired *middle course*, the destruction of falsehood and exaggeration *in every* -

thing, and the removal of the coarse outer core, the coarse commentaries in which man is capable of enveloping the greatest—and at the same time simplest—truths. But we are all striving towards this on different roads, depending on the variety of abilities which we have been given and the qualities which function within us. One strives toward this on the road of religion and internal self-knowledge, another on the road of historical investigation and experiment (on others), a third on the road of natural sciences, a fourth on the road of poetic comprehension and an eagle-like consideration of things not circumscribed by the view of the common man, in a word—on different roads, depending on the greater or lesser development in himself of his preponderant ability. Anatomizing a man, one sees that in the brain and head there are organs of prominence and bumps on the head especially arranged for this. The organs have been given—it must be they are necessary so that each one will strive on his road and make discoveries in his field, discoveries impossible for one who has other organs. He can say many things that are excessive, he can be carried away by his subject; but he cannot lie, be carried away by a phantom, because he doesn't speak of his own volition; the ability enclosed in him speaks in him, and therefore some truth lies in every person. This truth can be envisaged only by a complete and all-sided genius who has received as his lot a complete organization in all respects. Other people will get mixed up, confused, confounded—they will attach themselves to words and fall into infinite misunderstandings. That is why no extraordinary man should reveal his inner process—and these are being completed everywhere now, and most of all in the people who stand in the forefront; his every word will be taken in a wrong sense, and what is a transitional state in him will be taken as the normal state by others. That is why every man who has been gifted with extraordinary talent should first arrange his own self to some extent...

58. S. P. Shevyryov. December 2, 1847 (New Style). Naples.

...To your observation that *Dead Souls* will sell out quickly if the second volume appears and that everyone is waiting for it, I will say only that it is absolutely true; but the point is that it is not at all a trifle to write the second volume. If it seems to some that this is a rather simple matter, perhaps let them get together and write it themselves, combining their efforts, and I will see what comes out of this. I will have to look at very many things in Russia personally before starting the second volume. It would be shameful to make a blunder now. You see (or at least you ought to see more than others) that the subject is not a trifle and that it would be a misfortune to take up this task without being completely ready and organized. If this task is done well, a great deal of good can be caused by it; but if it is done badly, *harm* can be caused. If my current book, *Correspondence* (in the opinion even of intelligent people and my friends), is capable of disseminating *falsehood* and *immorality* and has the quality of captivating, judge for yourself how much more I can captivate people and disseminate falsehood if I step out on the stage with my living images. Here, surely, I will be a bit more powerful than in *Correspondence*. In the latter both Pavlov[1] and Baron Rozen[2] could have pounded me into feathers, but in the former it isn't likely that either Pavlov or sundry other literary knights and horsemen will have the power to compete with me. In a word there is no reason even to look at all these childish expectations and demands for volume two. Of course, no one wanted to help me in the actual product which he awaits! I cannot get the notes of anyone's life. The notes of a contemporary would be a priceless thing for me, or better, the reminiscences of his earlier life, surrounded by all the characters with whom he came in contact. If I got to read the biographies of even two people from 1812 until now, the current year that is, many points which are giving me difficulty would be explained to me. But enough about all that. God is merciful and with Him everything is possible. Perhaps I will be given the health, the strength, and the opportunity to search out everything myself without relying on anyone...

59. M. A. Konstantinovsky. February 28/16, 1848. Jerusalem.

I am writing to you to tell you I am here. Through your prayers and the prayers of people who please God I arrived here safely. At the Sepulcher of the Lord I prayed for you; I prayed as best I could with my heart which does not know how to pray. My prayer consisted only in a weak expression of thankfulness to God for sending me you, my priceless friend and intercessor. I needed your letters very much; they made me examine myself better and analyze my actions more severely. Again, accept my thankfulness from here, from this place made sacred by the footsteps of Him who brought us our redemption. I will be unspeakably happy if in June or in August I embrace you personally. Farewell.

60. S. P. Shevyryov. March 30/18, 1848. Beirut.

Since the time of my departure from Naples I have had no news from anyone in Russia and do not know what is happening there. Are you well, and are all those close to us well? My journey, thank God, is going safely so far. With the aid of our General Consul in Syria, Bazili, my old schoolmate, I have completed the road through Sidon and ancient Tyre and Acre and from there through Nazareth to Jerusalem. Here in Beirut I am just waiting for the steamer to cross over to Constantinople via Smyrna where I will be in quarantine for twelve days. After having stayed a while in Constantinople—to Odessa, from

Odessa to the Ukraine which will happen perhaps at the end of June. I will spend the summer in the Ukraine. In the month of August I want to go to Moscow and embrace you there. Write to me in Poltava, adding: "thence to the village of Vasilevka." Your letters will be the best gift you could think up for me. Inform me in more detail, so far as possible, about yourself and all our acquaintances, with an announcement of who is moving where for the summer and who is staying in Moscow. Tell Pogodin I am impatiently waiting for news about everything he is doing. Give Sergei Timofeevich[1] the little note enclosed with this. Whoever writes to me about himself also will oblige me. It is as if I am in the dark and feel nothing but a thirst *to know*...

61. M. A. Konstantinovsky. April 21, 1848. Odessa.

...Often I wonder: why is God so merciful to me, and why is He giving me so much all of a sudden—and I can only explain this to myself by the fact that my position is really more dangerous than all others, and it is more difficult for me to be saved than anyone else. There is much I would like to tell you. But that would take up pages and extremely easily turn into prolixity, perhaps even into lies... The Tempter is so close to me and has deceived me so often by making me think that I already possessed that to which I was only still striving and which was so far just in the head and not in the heart. I will tell you that I was never so little satisfied with the state of my heart as in Jerusalem and after Jerusalem. Except perhaps that I saw more of my callousness and my egoism—that's the whole result...

62. M. P. Pogodin. Beginning of October 1848. St. Petersburg.

Here are a few short lines for you, my good and dear fellow! I can hardly find time. Petersburg takes so much time. I am going around looking for people from whom I can find out something about what is going on in our sinful world. Everything is so strange, so bizarre. Some unclean power has blinded peoples' eyes and God has permitted this blindness. It is as if I am in the position of a foreigner who has arrived to examine a new land which he has never before seen; everything surprised him, everything amazes and at every step some new unanticipated thing pops up. But there isn't room in a letter for all the stories about that. In a week, God willing, we will see each other in person and discuss everything...

63. V. A. Zhukovsky. December 16, 1850. Odessa.

My greetings to you for the approaching new year; God help you, good friend! Wherever you are, wherever my letter finds you, whatever work you are at, whatever task and thought you are occupied with—God help you! We have not written to each other for a long time; we didn't write because somehow we couldn't write, but no doubt we often thought about each other. The subject which has joined us more tightly than before is equally close to both our hearts, and thinking about it, it is impossible that we would not remember each other. Merciful God still preserves me, my strength is still not weakening in spite of the weakness of my health; my work goes along with its former constancy, and although it is still not finished, it is already close to completion. What is there to be done? While a man is young—he is a poet, even when he is not a writer; but when he matures he must recall that he is a man, even when he is a writer. And what is man? His significance is great: through the love of Christ Who suffered for us, he is ordained to stand higher than the heavenly angel. While a writer is young he writes much and rapidly. The imagination spurs him on ceaselessly. He creates, builds enchanting castles in the sky for himself, and it is no wonder that there is no end to the writing just as there isn't to the castles. But no sooner does pure truth alone become his subject and the task touches on lucidly reflecting life in its higher value, which it should have and can have on earth, which it already does have in a few chosen, better people; here the imagination moves him but little; he must struggle to elicit every characteristic. I would very much like to read you everything I have written. If God gives His blessing for you to return to Russia next summer, it would be good for us to get together wherever you intend to spend the summer—whether this is in Revel, Riga, or somewhere else.

Translated by Carl R. Proffer

NOTES

Notes to *Hanz Kuechelgarten* were supplied by Paul D. Putz; the majority of those to the Letters by Carl R. Proffer; the remainder by the editor.

INTRODUCTION
1. *The Moscow Telegraph* (June 1829). Quoted in V. V. Veresaev, *Gogol' v zhizni* (M-L, 1933; rpt. Ann Arbor, 1983), pp. 80-81.
   Unless noted otherwise, all translations from Russian sources are my own.
2. Ibid., p. 81.
3. See V. V. Gippius' *Gogol*, translated and edited by Robert A. Maguire (Ann Arbor, 1981), pp. 20-27, for a discussion of *Hanz Kuechelgarten*.
4. Vladimir Nabokov, *Nikolai Gogol* (New York, 1944), p. 9.
5. *Pushkin on Literature*, translated and edited by Tatiana Wolff, revised edition (Stanford, 1986), p. 299.
6. Veresaev, pp. 162-63.
7. Letter to M. P. Pogodin (May 10, 1836) in *Letters of Nikolai Gogol*, ed. Carl R. Proffer (Ann Arbor, 1967), pp. 55-56.
8. Gogol writes about the importance of *Leaving the Theater* in Letters 28 and 31 in the present collection.
   See also Carl R. Proffer's *The Simile and Gogol's "Dead Souls"* (The Hague, 1967), pp. 183-200, where he discusses the relationship between *Leaving the Theater* and both *The Inspector General* and *Dead Souls*.
9. As Gogol scholars have noted, earlier examples of a drama that turns on the critique of a drama are Molière's *La Critique de L'ecole des femmes* and Sheridan's *The Critic; or, A Tragedy Rehearsal*.
10. F. Bulgarin, *The Northern Bee* (1836).
11. Gogol, *Arabesques*, translated by Alexander Tulloch (Ann Arbor, 1982).
12. Gippius, p. 41.
13. See Simon Karlinsky's *The Sexual Labyrinth of Nikolai Gogol* (Cambridge, 1976), pp. 26-30.
14. Gogol's essay on Pushkin waited fifty years before it was published by I. S. Aksakov (*Rus*, 1881).
15. *Arabesques*, p. 114.
16. D. S. Mirsky characterizes Kozlov (1799-1840) as standing out "among the poets of the

186 Notes

Golden Age for the comparative inadequacy of his technique." For a summary of Kozlov's work see William Edward Brown's *A History of Russian Literature of the Romantic Period* (Ann Arbor, 1986), volume 3, pp. 241-65.

17. Gogol's participation in *The Contemporary* and his relationship with Pushkin are examined by Donald Fanger in his *The Creation of Nikolai Gogol* (Cambridge, 1979), pp. 72-79; M. I. Gillel'son, "Pushkinskii 'Sovremennik,'" in *Sovremennik. Prilozhenie k faksimil'nomu izdaniiu* (Moscow, 1987), pp. 5-11 and V. V. Gippius, *Gogol*, p. 94.

18. Quoted in Gippius, *Gogol*, p. 94.

19. The "Letter" is translated in full in *The Critical Prose of Alexander Pushkin*, translated by Carl R. Proffer (Bloomington, 1969), pp. 206-12.

20. Ibid., p. 212.

21. See the Commentary in Gogol, *Polnoe sobranie sochinenii*, volume 8 (Moscow, 1952), pp. 769-75.

22. Carl Proffer's Introduction remains one of the best surveys of Gogol's biography as well as a good overview of his letters.

HANZ KUECHELGARTEN

1. Tripods—the tripods of the oracle at Delphi.
2. Kandis—a Greek word denoting a type of caftan worn by ancient Persians.
3. Mangustan—probably the province of Mangu in southern China, mentioned by Marco Polo.
4. Kandahar—the ancient city of Kandahar, in present-day Afghanistan.
5. Hemasagara—perhaps Sagara, a Hindu deity.
6. Israzil—Israfil, an archangel of Islam, with four wings.
7. Khindara—perhaps the city of Chhindwara in central India.
8. The characters and events mentioned in the preceding lines were all current news in 1823. Kolokotroni: Theodore Kolokotronis (1770-1843), Greek general and folk hero in the Greek war for independence.
9. Johann Joachim Winckelmann (1717-68), classical archaeologist and authority on ancient art.

WOMAN

1. Phidias' (c. 500-c. 432 B.C.) statue of Zeus was one of the seven wonders of the world.
2. Pythias was condemned to death by the Syracusan tyrant, Dionysus the Elder. He was released to put his affairs in order on the condition that his friend Damon would remain as his pledge. Upon Pythias' return, Dionysus released them both. The story of the two friends' loyalty and trust has come to symbolize friendship.
3. Praxiteles of Athens (fl. 370-330 B.C.) was one of the great Attic sculptors. Aphrodite of Cnidus was his most celebrated work.

ON KOZLOV'S POETRY

1. The essay on Kozlov, never published during Gogol's lifetime, first appeared in 1890.

ON THE TREND OF JOURNAL LITERATURE IN 1834 AND 1835

First published in the inaugural issue of Alexander Pushkin's journal *The Contemporary* (Sovremennik, 1836).

1. *The Library for Reading* (Biblioteka dlia chteniia), founded in 1834, and its first editor Osip Senkovsky (1800-58) are the primary objects of Gogol's critical attack. In fact, Gogol widened the scope of his survey, which was originally conceived to cover only the year 1835, to include the year 1834 as well, and thus have more material in his summary of Senkovsky's sins.

Senkovsky, who published his own prose fiction under the pseudonym of Baron Brambeus, created an immensely popular journal with contributions from Pushkin, Lermontov, Bestuzhev-Marlinsky, and other leading writers. But, he was also somewhat despotic and unscrupulous in his editorial policies. A good introduction to Senkovsky's career as prose writer and journalist can be found in V. Zilber's "Senkovsky (Baron Brambeus)" in *Russian Prose*, edited by B. Eikhenbaum and Yu. Tynyanov, translated by Ray Parrott (Ann Arbor: Ardis, 1985).

2. Both Pushkin and Gogol viewed *The Moscow Observer* (Moskovskii nabliudatel', 1835-39) as their ally, which accounts for Gogol's reserved criticism of the main critic, Shevyryov, and the journal in general.

3. *The Moscow Telegraph* (Moskovskii telegraf, 1825-34), the first Russian encyclopedic journal, was closed in 1834.

4. *The Telescope* (Teleskop, 1831-36), edited by N. Nadezhdin, has the great distinction of being closed down after the publication of Pyotr Chaadaev's "Philosophical Letter."

5. Alexander Smirdin (1795-1857) was so well known for his publishing enterprises that Belinsky named the 1830s the "Smirdin period in Russian literature."

6. Nikolai Grech (1787-1867), together with Bulgarin and Senkovsky, formed the sometimes odious triumvirate opposed to new currents in Russian literature.

7. *The Northern Bee* (Severnaia pchela, 1825-64), edited by Grech and Bulgarin. The latter is known as prose writer, informer, and plagiarist.

8. *Son of the Fatherland* (Syn otechestva) was founded by Grech in 1825. Bulgarin was also on the staff.

9. August Ludwig von Schloezer (1735-1809) wrote on the history of the Russian chronicles.

10. Senkovsky compared Kukolnik with Goethe in his article on the former's *Torquato Tasso*: "This last act brings great honor to the poetic talents of our young Goethe" (*Library for Reading*, No. 1). Nestor Kukolnik (1809-68) authored Romantic tragedies, which enjoyed popularity in their time, but now, without exception, are unread.

11. Senkovsky's attack on Walter Scott was published in 1834 under the pseudonym "O. O...O!": "Seeing the decline of his [Scott's] fame won by verse, he rushed the other way, to another forced means of fame, or to put it simply, charlatanism, and created an artificial concoction of truth and imagination, so successfully spliced together that it is impossible to know for certain what is truth and what is imagination."

12. Alexander Voeikov (1779-1839), journalist, poet, and co-editor of *Literary Supplements*.

13. *L'école frénétique*.

BOOK REVIEWS

Reviews from *The Contemporary*

1. Mikhail Pogodin (1800-75), historian and journalist, editor of *The Moscow Herald* (1827-30) and *The Muscovite* (1841-56). Gogol, most likely at Pushkin's insistence, softened or deleted some of his remarks regarding Pogodin, because Pushkin hoped to enlist the latter's services for *The*

Contemporary.

2. The Czech Slavist Jozef Dobrovsky (1753-1829)—author of *Cyrill und Method, der Slaven Apostel* (1823) and *Mährische Legende von Cyrill und Method* (1826).

3. Johann Philip Evers (1781-1830)—historian of German origins who lived in Russia from 1803, known for his work on the Old Russian state and law.

4. Arnold Hermann Ludwig Heeren (1760-1842)—historian of the Goettigen school. See Gogol's letter (No. 2) to Pogodin about Heeren.

5. August Ludwig von Schloezer (1735-1809)—author of *Vorstellung der Universalhistorie* (1722). See Gogol's essay "Schloezer, Mueller and Herder" in *Arabesques*.

6. Stepan Shevyryov (1806-64)—professor of literature at the University of Moscow, where he was Pogodin's colleague.

7. Nestor (ca. 1056-1113)—compiler of the *Primary Chronicle*, author of *Reading on the Life and Slaying of the Blessed Passion-Sufferers Boris and Gleb*.

8. St. Gregory of Tours (538-94)—French historian and Bishop of Tours. Author of *History of the Franks*.

9. St. John Chrysostom (ca. 347-407)—Doctor of the Church, Patriarch of Constantinople.

10. St. Gregory Nazianzen (ca. 330-90)—Doctor of the Church, one of the Four Fathers of the Greek Church.

11. Albigenses—French religious sect (12th-13th centuries), which believed in the coexistence of the principles of good and evil.

12. The author of these memoirs was Ilya Radozhitsky (1788-1861).

13. Lady Rondeau (1699-1783) lived in Russia during the years 1731-39.

14. The French original of this compilation of various travels was published in 1834.

15. A. G. Obodovsky (1796-1852)—professor at the Main Pedagogical Institute.

16. The contributors to *My Housewarming* are, without exception, totally forgotten.

17. A reference to Baron Delvig's *Northern Flowers*, an almanac that published many of the outstanding figures of the Golden Age.

18. Nikolai Nadezhdin (1804-56)—editor of *The Telescope*. A translation of French, German and English prose works primarily of the Romantic school.

Reviews Not Published in *The Contemporary*

1. Prince Antiokh Kantemir (1709-44)—poet and satirist.

2. Stepan Shevyryov (1806-64)—critic and literary historian.

3. The first work of the prolific novelist Mikhail Voskresensky (d. 1867). Gogol's plot summary of the novel is factually inaccurate, but true in spirit.

4. Mikhail Zagoskin (1789-1852) is best known today for his historical novel *Yury Miloslavsky, or the Russians in 1812*, which was enthusiastically received by Pushkin.

5. The choice of this cookbook for review reflects Gogol's culinary interests.

A Review from *The Muscovite*

1. Gogol's review as published in Pogodin's journal (*The Muscovite*, 1842, No. 1) underwent considerable editorial alteration. The translation here is from Gogol's manuscript as published in *Polnoe sobranie sochinenii*.

LETTERS

Gogol is often prolix in his correspondence. In many cases, Carl Proffer has selected excerpts from longer letters. All cuts are marked by ellipsis.

Letter 1
1. Maria Ivanovna, Gogol's mother.

Letter 2
1. Mikhail Petrovich Pogodin (1800-75), writer, critic, publicist, professor of Russian history at the University of Moscow, editor of *The Moscow Herald* (1827-30) and *The Muscovite* (1841-56), was a friend of the literary circle of Pushkin and Gogol and an ardent Slavophile.

2. Arnold Hermann Ludwig Heeren (1760-1842)—the foremost historian of the Goettingen school.

3. This was Gogol's first lecture at St. Petersburg University. It was published in *Arabesques* (1835).

4. *Arabesques*.

5. Gogol's "Historical Fragments" were published in *The Journal of the Ministry of People's Enlightenment* in 1834.

Letter 3
1. Mikhail Semyonovich Shchepkin (1788-1863)—one of the first great Russian actors. Gogol met him in 1832. As his letters show, Gogol valued Shchepkin's talents highly and relied on him to keep *The Inspector General* from being played as a traditional farce.

Letter 4
1. Alexander Semyonovich Danilevsky (1809-88)—Gogol's Nezhin schoolmate.

Letter 5
1. A quotation from Alexander Pushkin's *Eugene Onegin*, I, XXIII.

2. Julietta Grisi (1811-69)—an Italian opera singer.

3. Censored in the Soviet edition.

4. Danilevsky's landlord's name happened to be Janin. Gogol thought he meant Pavel Annenkov whose nickname was Jules Janin.

Letter 6
1. Nikolai Yakovlevich Prokopovich (1810-57)—schoolmate in Nezhin.

2. *Dead Souls*.

Letter 7
1. Nikolai Mikhailovich Smirnov (1807-70) was the rich (6000 serfs) husband of A. O. Rosset.

2. Alexander Ivanovich Turgenev (1784-1845)—a friend of Karamzin, Zhukovsky, Pushkin and Vyazemsky. He lived for long periods in Western Europe, collecting materials about Russia from French and Italian archives.

3. Vasily Andreevich Zhukovsky (1783-1852)—dulcet-tongued sentimental poet, influenced strongly by German romantics; talented translator of everything from *The Odyssey* to *Lenore* and *The Prisoner of Chillon*; friend and protector of Pushkin and Gogol; tutor of the Tsar's children. His aesthetic and religious beliefs had considerable influence on Gogol.

4. The loss of Pushkin.

5. "Again I visited..." (Vnov' ia posetil...).

Letter 8
1. Maria Petrovna Balabina (1820-1901). In 1831 Pletnyov procured Gogol a position as tutor of the Balabin children, one of whom was Maria. Gogol remained a good friend of the family for years. His whimsical letters to Maria suggest that in his own peculiar way he felt particular affection for her.

Letter 9
1. A banker.
2. Shchepkin was engaged in a struggle in the theaters to present plays (comedy in particular) in a less traditional manner.
3. The comedy, *Vladimir of the Third Degree*, remained unfinished.
4. Gogol did make a number of changes. See Gogol, *Polnoe sobranie sochinenii* (M, 1937-52), V, 532ff.

Letter 10
1. Gogol refers to hostile articles by Senkovsky and Bulgarin.

Letter 11
1. Stepan Petrovich Shevyryov (1806-64) was professor of literature at the University of Moscow. Frequently attacked by radicals of his own age and our age, he was nevertheless one of the best critics of the time. His essays on Pushkin and Gogol are well worth reading. He was among Gogol's regular correspondents.

Letter 12
1. P. A. Lukashevich—a schoolmate in the Nezhin gymnasium.
2. The meaning of the word "vaults" (podvaly) here is not clear.

Letter 13
1. Adam Mickiewicz (1798-1855)—Poland's greatest poet. His epic, *Pan Tadeusz*, was published in 1834. Gogol made the acquaintance of Mickiewicz in Paris in late 1836 and during the winter of 1836-37 he saw him regularly.
2. Sergei Semyonovich Uvarov (1786-1855)—president of the Academy of Sciences and director of the Ministry of People's Enlightenment. It is not known what "news about Uvarov" Gogol has in mind.

Letter 14
1. Gogol didn't make anything of it. Only a few fragments of a play based on Ukrainian history have survived.

Letter 15
1. Gogol had already been in Moscow for a month, but he did not wish to be bothered by his mother and family, so he pretended to be in Vienna.

Letter 16
1. Pogodin's plan for a supplement to *The Moscow News* was not carried out. He began *The Muscovite* in 1841.
2. Pavel Mikhailovich Stroev (1796-1876)—bibliographer and publisher of Old Russian texts.

Letter 17
1. Prince Pyotr Vyazemsky (1792-1878)—graceless but witty poet and critic, staunch defender of romanticism, one of Pushkin's closest friends and cleverest correspondents.
2. A. I. Turgenev.
3. P. I. Krivtsov—a relative of Gogol's friends, the Repnins. Gogol's efforts to be appointed secretary were fruitless. In 1841 Gogol refused the proffered post as librarian in the Academy.
4. An "Anna" was one of the honorary awards (a medal) given for service to the government.

Letter 18
1. Avdotya Elagina—Zhukovsky's niece. Her sons by a first marriage, Ivan and Peter Kireevsky, became well-known Slavophile essayists.
2. In Moscow.

Letter 20
1. Pyotr Alexandrovich Pletnyov (1792-1865)—close friend and literary agent of Pushkin; editor of *The Contemporary* after Pushkin's death. Critic, poet of small talent, professor of Russian literature, member of the Russian Academy.

Letter 21
1. Alexander Andreyevich Ivanov (1806-58)—a Russian artist. He lived in Italy from 1830 until the year of his death. Gogol met him in 1838, and they became close friends.

Letter 22
1. *Dead Souls.*

Letter 23
1. Gogol returned to Russia in October 1841.

Letter 24
1. *Dead Souls.*
2. Gogol had been rewriting "The Portrait." The new version was published in *The Contemporary*, No. 3 (1842).

Letter 25
1. "The Tale of Captain Kopeikin" in chapter 10 of *Dead Souls.* Gogol rewrote it, and the cautious censors authorized the eviscerated version.

Letter 26
1. *Kopeika* means "kopeck"; *pyatka* means "heel." Apparently Gogol supposed the censors might think he was exhibiting insufficient respect for money minted by the government.

Letter 29
1. Shevyryov's interesting essays on *Dead Souls* appeared in *The Muscovite*, No. 7-8 (1842).

Letter 30
1. Maria Vasilievna, Gogol's eldest sister.
2. Maria's son.

Letter 31
1. A comedy—Gogol's poorest—published in his *Collected Works.*

Letter 32

1. Nadezhda Nikolaevna Sheremetieva (1775-1850)—an extremely pious old lady who patronized Gogol.

Letter 33

1. Sergei Aksakov (1791-1859)—the late-blooming author of one of Russia's greatest classics, *A Family Chronicle* (1846-56), a work begun partly at Gogol's urging. His *Story of My Acquaintance with Gogol* is a vital source for Gogol's biography. Gogol was idolized by Aksakov's entire family.

2. Aksakov told Gogol that those who had seen the two plays on the stage preferred *The Marriage*, but later, after private readings, most grew cold to it and considered *The Gamblers* superior.

3. Gogol had originally assigned the role of Kochkaryov (in *The Marriage)* to Shchepkin; he wished to take the role of Podkolyosin.

4. A. N. Verstovsky, a minor dramatist and composer, was director of Imperial Theaters in Moscow.

5. Verstovsky wanted to stage *Leaving the Theater* in Moscow, but the play has few theatrical merits.

6. Gogol's letters of November 28 and December 3, 1842.

7. Konstantin Aksakov, "A Few Words about Gogol's Poem *Dead Souls,"* (M, 1842). Aksakov draws a parallel between Gogol and Homer, calling *Dead Souls* a modern version of the ancient epos. The brochure caused considerable noise—including a pair of snarling articles by the politically-minded Belinsky. Aksakov's piece is translated in *Russian Literature Triquarterly*, No. 23 (1990):253-62.

8. February 28, 1842.

Letter 34

1. Nikolai Mikhailovich Yazykov (1805-46), primarily an elegist, was one of the most important poets of the period. Gogol considered Yazykov a kindred soul, but Yazykov's own letters are full of nasty remarks ridiculing Gogol. His "Earthquake" was Gogol's favorite poem.

2. D. P. Oznobishin—a third-rate poet and translator.

3. The anarchist.

4. Gogol garbles the facts of the story. In the left-Hegelian *Deutsche Jahrbuecher* (1842), Bakunin published an article called "Die Reaktion in Deutschland," attacking German and Russian reactionary policies. He was ordered out of Dresden and moved to Basel.

Letter 35

1. "Stoikovich" (from the verb *stoiat'*, to stand) is a nickname given by Gogol to the act of standing up after dinner—which according to some doctors of the time helped the digestive processes.

Letter 37

1. Alexandra Osipovna Smirnova (née Rosset or Rozetti, 1809-82). Beautiful lady-in-waiting of the Empress. A friend of Zhukovsky, Vyazemsky and Lermontov. Like other poets, Pushkin (who introduced her to Gogol) had written poems to her. Her husband was a rich diplomat to whom she was indifferent. She frequently acted as "notre dame aux bons secours" when her literary friends ran afoul of the censorship. After a rather rowdy youth, her moral development (in the forties) took the same direction as Gogol's. He became her very close spiritual friend.

2. Gustave François de Ravignan (1795-1858) was a fashionable Jesuit priest and writer.

3. Jacques-Benigne Bossuet (1627-1704)—French writer and Catholic preacher.

Letter 38

1. Sofia Mikhailovna Vielgorskaya (Iosif Vielgorsky's sister) married Vladimir Sollogub (1814-82), a writer who enjoyed some popularity at the time. This letter became the basis of "What a Wife Can Be" in *Selected Passages*.

Letter 39

1. A letter in which Gogol attacked Pogodin for printing his picture in *The Muscovite*.
2. Pogodin's wife had just died.

Letter 42

1. A. M. Vielgorskaya.

Letter 43

1. Alexander Petrovich Tolstoy—a rich, super-religious and hypochondriacal friend of Gogol during the last several years of his life.
2. Nikolai I visited Rome in December 1845.
3. Gogol explains this in a letter to Zhukovsky (November 28, 1845). Just before the imperial visit a Polish woman Uniate (a Christian of the Eastern rite who acknowledges the Pope's primacy and agrees with the Latin Church in matters of faith, while differing on matters of liturgy, discipline, etc.) had arrived in Rome with stories about how she had been subjected to torture in Russia for refusing to become an Orthodox Catholic. This angered the already conservative cardinals who suggested Gregory XIV should not see Nikolai I. But the Pope did meet with the Tsar on December 13; an agreement was signed giving the Pope somewhat more power over the Catholic clergy in Russia.

Letter 45

1. It isn't known what poems Gogol received (except for one mentioned in a letter to Aksakov on March 23, 1846).
2. A forty-line poem by Yazykov. The letters Gogol refers to he wrote on December 2 and 29 (New Style), 1844.
3. A veiled description of his next book, *Selected Passages from a Correspondence with Friends* (1847).

Letter 47

1. The essay was "In What, Finally, Is the Essence of Russian Poetry." Gogol does not explain what he means by the "three periods" of his life. One might guess 1809-29 (childhood), 1829-36 (literary and intellectual apprenticeship), 1836-46 (maturity).
2. Alexander Vasilievich Nikitenko (1804-77), literary historian and censor.

Letter 48

1. A dramatic scene in which the characters (Shchepkin was to play the main role) discuss the nature of comedy and satire in general and offer interpretations of *The Inspector General* in particular. In it Gogol suggests the town be seen as "our mental town," the satirized characters as passions which pillage our soul, and that we be aware of the frightening Inspector General who stands at the doors of our tomb. The scene was written in 1846, ten years after the play itself. The allegorical interpretation does seem to have been an afterthought on Gogol's part (though that would be impossible to prove).

Letter 50

1. On December 12, Gogol had written a cruel letter accusing Ivanov of not believing his promise to try to find financial assistance for Ivanov from someone in Petersburg. Apparently Gogol reacted this way when Ivanov asked a few other people to help him. Gogol ordered him to be humble, to stop spitting on his (Gogol's) promises.

Letter 51

1. *Selected Passages from a Correspondence with Friends.*
2. Five essays were not passed by the incredibly dull-witted censors. A number of passages were struck out of the surviving essays.

Letter 53

1. *Selected Passages from a Correspondence with Friends.*
2. Part One of *Dead Souls.*

Letter 55

1. Matvei Alexandrovich Konstantinovsky (1792-1857)—a priest under whose influence Gogol fell during the last five years of his life. It has become customary for biographers (except Mochulsky in his *Dukhovnyi put' Gogolia)* to view him as a fanatical demon who drove Gogol to destruction and death. There is some evidence that he was a fanatic, but there is virtually none that conclusively demonstrates his bad effects on Gogol; and furthermore there is considerable evidence that contradicts the few stories about his fanaticism. As is so often the case in Gogol's biography, it is impossible to reach a certain conclusion on the basis of an evaluation of the evidence.

Letter 56

1. *The Denouement.*
2. This is the epigraph to *The Inspector General.*

Letter 58

1. Nikolai Filippovich Pavlov (1805-64)—a minor prose writer.
2. Baron Yegor Fyodorovich Rozen (1800-60)—a mediocre poet and critic.

Letter 60

1. Sergei Aksakov. The note has not survived.